The Tasks of Chronavon

Ray Filby

==

The Tasks of Chronavon

Publisher : Midhurst

Published by Midhurst

Copyright © Ray Filby 2019

Illustrations by Johanna Holmstedt

Midhurst.
2, Freers Mews,
Warwick,
Warwickshire,
CV34 6DP

ISBN 978-1-9996835-0-4

http://midhurstpublishing.uk

<u>Acknowledgements</u>

The author would like to thank his wife, Sue, for her patience and encouragement during the writing of these stories.

A version of this book was published in 2003 by Pen Press Publishers Ltd.

The illustrations are a mixture of royalty free pictures displayed on the internet and pictures drawn by Johanna Holmstedt.

Apart from obvious historical characters, any resemblance to actual persons, living or dead, is purely coincidental

Contents

Introduction

The Tasks of Chronavon is a trilogy of stories featuring two twelve year olds, Alfred and Alice. While the book is aimed at young people of the same age as the main characters of the story, I think it will appeal to any of a much wider age range who have an interest in English history. The book will be of special interest to those familiar with the Cathedrals of Hereford and Worcester, and the Tower of London, where parts of the stories are set. It also has an underlying Christian theme with subtle examples which illustrate the power of prayer. The idea for writing the book came from a friend who said they really enjoyed stories which involved travelling back into earlier historic contexts. A problem with such stories usually arises from the fact that any such time traveller would be likely to change the course of history. A unique feature of this book is that two young time travellers are set tasks which are required to be fulfilled to prevent a change in the course of history.

Alfred and Alice are taken back through time by an Angel called Chronavon who appears in the guise of a mediaeval monk to the young people as they work in the vestry of their local church.

Their tasks are to thwart the designs of an evil time traveller who is attempting to change the course of history by preventing the accession to the throne of monarchs who had very successful reigns and significantly contributed to the development of the nation. The three stories in the trilogy centre round Edward I, Elizabeth I and Charles II during the dangerous days before they had actually acceded to the throne. Of course the story is a work of fiction, and travelling back through time is supernatural. However, when they are back into the historic contexts to which they have been sent, Alfred and Alice do not have access to magic to fulfil their tasks but have to rely on their own resourcefulness and common sense. Alfred and Alice are excellent role models who have a strong Christian faith and who make use of the power of prayer. However, they realise that in most of the difficult situations they encounter, they themselves must be the agents through which their prayers are answered. Thus, the answers they receive to their prayers, while very helpful in securing their objective, do not involve anything happening which could be regarded as other than completely normal.

The stories are set in real history and the majority of the characters encountered are real historic personages. The book should therefore have an educational value to those interested in history as it reads as if two young people, with whom young readers could readily identify, are actually influencing events which really did take place. Short sections are included in the stories, printed in italics, which may be skipped without detracting from the main narrative. The italicised sections are included to provide additional historical background for readers who are interested in the wider historic context in which the stories are set.

Prince Edward

Can Alfred and Alice secure the Succession of Edward I ?

Henry III

St, Thomas de Cantilupe

Simon de Montfort

<u>Chapter 1</u>

It wasn't the sort of place you'd expect to find an active and energetic twelve year old. The   room was dim and murky. The light which came **through** the stained glass of a gothic window would have been more than ad**equate** to illuminate a room decorated with light reflecting colours, but the anc**ient** oak panelling of this room was dark and dusty. Cobwebs trailed from the ceiling. Black cassocks, the garb of clerics and church choirs, were **stacked u**ntidily across the rush seated chairs and added to the room's general gloominess. Surely, this place must have been the haunt of ghosts and phant**oms.**

Seated at a desk in the corner of the room was an athletic looking twelve year old. He was tall for his age and his intelligent face was crowned with thick, well brushed, brown hair. This was Alfred Jackson. The room in which Alfred sat was the vestry of the parish church of St. Giles in the Cotswold village of Hillington. Alfred was a farmer's son. When not at school, Alfred would spend most of his time helping on the farm or riding **one** of his father's horses across the meadows. However, Alfred was also a server at

St. Giles. One of his tasks was to keep organised the numbers which were slotted into display boards used at each church service, to indicate to the congregation which hymns were to be sung. It was this task which occupied him now as he slid the numbers from the display boards and replaced them in the appropriate sections of their storage box. Alfred was quite oblivious to the spooky ambience of the room in which he now sat.

The vestry door opened and in walked a very pretty girl of about the same age as Alfred. Her long blond hair descended to the waist of her well-tailored blue dress and a wonderful smile illuminated her face. The murky vestry suddenly seemed less gloomy. This girl was Alice Campbell, daughter of the owners of the village hardware store. Alfred hardly looked up from his desk. Alice always came to the vestry at about this time on a Saturday morning to return the church linen which her mother had painstakingly washed, starched and ironed, ready for the Sunday services. Alice would then collect any crumpled surplices and soiled church linen wich had been left out after the services of the preceding week for her mother to launder.

Alice and Alfred were great friends. They attended the same school and shared many interests. They had known each other since they had joined the St. Giles Sunday School as four year olds.

"It's a fab day outside," Alice called over to Alfred. "Let's take the horses out this afternoon. How about a ride along the river Windrush?"

"Great idea!" replied Alfred, looking up with some enthusiasm. "I'll get the horses saddled up by half-past-two. Can you get to the farm by then?" Alice didn't have a horse of her own but Alfred's father had a dozen or so well-bred horses and ponies which were the mainstay of the riding school which operated from Willows Farm. Alice nodded her assent and hurried to gather up any linen which showed the sightest hint of needing to be washed or ironed while Alfred hastily shoved the rest of the hymn numbers into their box. Barely had they finished these tasks when something happened which at first, gave these two young people quite a shock and sent shivers down their spines.

The door opened with a creaing sound. This was unusual in itself, because the hinges were kept well-oiled and the door certainly had not ceaked when

Alice had come in a few moments earlier. It would not have been unusual for the Vicar to enter the vestry when Alfred and Alice were working there, but the figure wich emerged from the dark space beyond the door wich had just opened was not the Vicar. Alfred and Alice had never seen the person who ambled slowly through the door before. Indeed, they had never before seen anyone dressed in the habit of a mediaeval monk. Alfred jumped from his seat by the desk and stood protectively in front of Alice, fearful that this apparition may have been up to no good.

The monk pulled back his brown hood to rveal an amazingly kind and friendly countenance and he smiled at the two young people. As soon as they saw that open and honest face, their anxiety vanished and Alfred and Alice immediately felt relaxed.

"Please don't be afraid," said the person who appeared to be a monk. "Sit down and let me tell you about myself and explain to you why I have come. I am known as Chronavon. I serve the Lord Most High, the Lord of life and light, the one who sends the seasons, and controls the weather, the Lord of time and tide. My Lord can travel through time, forwards and backwards, and this is a gift he has bestowed on some of us who serve him. As humans, you have only been able to travel forwards through time.

One of the rules my Lord made when he created time was that those who were given the gift of travelling back through time should not be able to change anything, for that would cause hopeless confusion. Just think, if someone travelled back through time and killed one of your ancestors before he or she had had children, where would you be now?"

Alfred and Alice thought for a moment on this. Of course, no one could move backwards through time and change something that would affect a future which had already taken place! What monstrous confusion that would bring about.

Chronavon watched the faces of those two young people and was satisfied that they had understood the implication of what he had said. Chronavon continued.

A mysterious monk enters the vestry where
Alfred and Alice are working

"One whom my master regarded as a trusted servant rebelled against him and caused unimaginable harm to everything my master had made. My master has taken steps to remedy much of the damage done and this has angered my master's rebellious servant. He goes by many names. I call him Ahrimanes. Ahrimanes is now trying to violate one of the most fundamental rules of the universe. He is attempting to change things which have already happened in the past so that the course of history will be disrupted in a way which will prevent my master's plans from coming into fruition. However, this evil work is not easy, even for Ahrimanes. My Lord knows what he is up to and he may be thwarted in his evil designs. In order to counter the threat posed by Ahrimanes to the stability of the world, my master needs to enlist the help of two humans. He has sent me to you, Alice and Alfred, - yes, I know your names and indeed, more about each of you than you know yourselves - he has sent me to ask you to be his agents in defeating Ahrimanes!"

Alfred and Alice looked at each other. Similar thoughts were passing through their minds.

Was this person playing some sort of practical joke? Events which had already happened in the past being altered? What a preposterous idea. Whoever was this Chronavon anyway? He seemed to be claiming that he was some sort of angel! How did he come to know their names?

"Yes, you are quite right and very sensible to query my identity and authority. I had expected you to do so. Yes, I am an angel!"

Alfred and Alice looked at one another in even greater surprise. They had said nothing, yet this Chronavon had apparently read their thoughts!

"I am able to prove to you my credentials," continued Chronavon. "Each of you, ask me a question about something which you believe you alone can know the answer and I will show you that the Lord Most High has shared this secret with me."

This sounded like a good game which Alfred and Alice knew they would win. If Chronavon came up with the right answers to the questions they could pose, then he really would be who he claimed. However, they were not fanciful young people. They could recognise where reality ended and fiction began. No one in their right mind would believe Chronavon's far-fetched tale. They pondered for a moment to come up with good questions. Alice spoke first.

"When I got up this morning, I didn't put on the dress I'm wearing now," she said. "What did I put on?"

"You put on jeans and a T-shirt as you usually do on a Saturday morning, but then, you remembered that you had to call in and see your grandmother on your way to church and that it would be nice to let her see you wearing the dress she had bought you for your birthday. So you changed before anyone had seen you and came down to breakfast."

An incredulous expression passed over Alice's face. Perhaps somebody who knew her intimately well might have guessed that jeans and a T-shirt would be the clothes she would first select on a Saturday morning if she had momentarily forgotten that there was a reason for wearing something different, but this was a complete stranger. Chronavon's next statement provided conclusive proof that he was someone with very special insight and knowledge.

"The jeans you put on were the maroon coloured ones which you very seldom wear and the T-shirt was navy blue." Alice's jaw dropped and her eyes opened wide with surprise. She had a choice of three colours for jeans and about a dozen different clean T-shirts. Chronavon was right first time without having to probe with the further questions he would need to ask if he was just guessing about the colours she had chosen.

Now it was Alfred's turn. Sometimes, Alfred had a very convoluted way of thinking. He could see from Alice's reaction that Chronavon had been right and Alfred was impressed. But if he was going to trust this strange monk/angel, whatever his real identity, and embark on some course of action, he would need to test whether or not he was benevolent, and whether or not Chronavon really trusted them.

"While I was sitting here this morning," started Alfred, "I was wondering how I could best help someone. Who was I thinking of and what idea had come to mind and was it a good idea?"

"Chronavon will refuse to answer this if he doesn't trust me," thought Alfred, "because I can always claim to have been thinking of something different to prove him wrong and there's no way that he can provide concrete evidence to the contrary. But if he can accurately read my thoughts, well, this would be rather frightening. It would mean that he must really be what he claims."

"You were pondering how you could help Mr. Jefferson, your Vicar, who you know has a bad cough. You were thinking of taking him round a bag of cough sweets. This was a very commendable thing to do, but no, it would not be the best course of action. Far better to call on Mr. Jefferson and ask first if you can help him and how. Mr. Jefferson has received a prescription which will deal with his cough far better than cough sweets, but he needs someone to collect it for him from the chemists. This is what he would ask you to do."

There was now absolutely no doubt. Chronavon was some sort of angel, indeed, a good angel, for his last words to Alfred had been sound common sense.

"If he had come from the Lord Most High, which surely was not in doubt now," thought Alfred, "then what a privilege to help him in the task of defeating Ahrimanes. Ahrimanes must surely be another name for the devil himself."

"You're quite right in what you've said," replied Alfred. "Yes, I'm game m help you in any way I can. How about you, Alice?"

Alice had already decided and she vigorously nodded her head.

Chronavon gave the two young people a most charming and grateful smile "I was sure that you would be ready to help. Indeed, you have been identified as the two people who are most likely to succeed in this venture. However, one thing over which I have no control is how humans choose to use their gift of free will. It was not until you spoke your words of assent to that I could be certain that you two really were the right ones."

Chronavon then lowered his voice and continued in a very serious tone.

"I must warn you both that there's considerable danger in what you're about to do. If even a small thing goes seriously wrong, it will change the whole history of England, indeed, of the world, and could well mean that you could not actually be born at all in the twenty-first century! Do you still want to go through with this?"

Chronavon paused to allow them to take that in. At that moment they could have changed their minds, but Chronavon did not expect them to do so. He knew that they had been well chosen. Alfred and Alice nodded, intently listening to learn about the task ahead. Chronavon continued.

"In order to fulfil the task that faces us, you are

going to have to travel **backwards** through time to where Ahrimanes is working with his agents to drastically change the outcome of an important situation and set history on a different course. In a moment, we will pass through that door and you will be in the year, A.D. 1265. It may take many days to fulfil your task. You could therefore be worried that your parents are concerned about you, not knowing where you are. However, rest assured. When you have hopefully finished your task, you will return to this room and the time will be exactly the same as the time you left it. My Lord, the Lord of time and tide, will ensure this.

With these reassuring words, Chronavon opened the now creaking door of the vestry and led the young people through. They fully expected to find themselves back in St. Giles church, but no, they were in a very different place indeed.

Chapter 2

Alfred and Alice surveyed the very large and beautiful room which they had entered. It was decagonal. A fluted pillar at the centre of this room supported a lofty ribbed vault. Illumination came through ten tall gothic windows filling most of the upper space on each of the walls of the room. The lower part of the wall had a stone seating bench around the full circumference of the room, except for the large doorway through which they had just entered. This was the sole entrance to this magnificent room.

Alfred recognised this room as a typical chapter house, the meeting room of senior clerics and monks in cathedrals and abbeys. He had visited **Salisbury** Cathedral and Westminster Abbey which had chapter houses, very similar to the one in which he now stood, but which were octagonal rather than ten sided.

 Once the door was closed behind them, Chronavon's first words confirmed Alfred's realisation.

"You are now in the chapter house of the great
Cathedral of Hereford. No one will be using
this room today so that gives me time to put
you in the picture but first of all we had better get
you dressed for the parts you will be playing."

Hereford Cathedral

Chronavon pointed to a chest by the wall.

"Have a look through that," he suggested. "I think
you will find something suitable to wear that
will fit"

Alfred and Alice ran excitedly over to the chest. Although reinforced by iron bands it was not locked and they easily lifted the lid. The clothes inside were quite different to anything they had worn before. It wasn't difficult to sort out boys' from girls' clothes and they had a lot of fun trying on the various alternatives available. Most of the garments fitted them surprisingly well and after about half an hour, they decided they were satisfactorily attired. They presented themselves to Chronavon, Alice in a very plain, full length, green dress and Alfred in a brown tunic, fastened round the waist with a stout leather belt, and fawn coloured hose. Chronavon nodded approvingly.

"You'll pass off very well as young people of the thirteenth century," he said. "Now carefully fold up your twenty-first century clothes and put them back in the chest. You'll need them when you return to your own time.

Let us now talk about the task in hand. 1265 A.D, what do you think was happening in the country then?"

Alfred and Alice loved history and this was surely one of the reasons they had been identified as suitable for the great task ahead. However, they had difficulty in remembering the exact dates of many of the key events of history. In this respect, they were no different from all their school friends. Nonetheless, they had an astonishingly good sense of the way the nation's life and character had been moulded by its history. "King John was a thirteenth century king," ventured Alfred. "Was the Magna Carta being signed?"

Alice realised that this couldn't be quite right.

"No." interjected Alice, "Magna Carta was signed very early on in the thirteenth century. I reckon King John's son must have been on the throne. Wasn't that Henry III? I know that he had a very long reign."

"Yes, of course," added Alfred. "He was only a boy when he became king and I think he rather messed things up. Didn't some nobleman, Simon de Montfort I think, start a rebellion and defeat him at the Battle of Lewes?"

"But in the end, wasn't Simon de Montfort finally defeated at the Battle of Evesham?" Alice added triumphantly.

Chronavon clapped. "Well done, well done, " he applauded, "but you have come here to make sure that history does indeed run that way. You have come back to a moment in time before the battle of Evesham has taken place. Ahrimanes is working to change things so that the Battle of Evesham may not even happen. If Ahrimanes' plan fails, he will try to change the outcome of the battle and this will completely change the course of English history!

*Let me fill you in with more background. Much of this you will know already, but it will pay to go over the details now. Yes, as you say, Henry III did make a bit of a mess of things. When **Henry** was just a boy king, England was wisely ruled by a regent, **William Marshall.** William died three years into Henry's reign and much of the responsibility of running the country fell to Hubert de Burgh, who held efface as a Justiciar, that is, a legal officer who could act with full royal authority. However, when Henry reached his majority, he fell out with Hubert de Burgh and took all authority into his own bands.*

*Henry married a French wife, Eleanor of Provence, and started to grant her friends from **Poitou and** Provence high positions at court and in the church. It appeared to the English that they were being effectively ruled by the King's French friends because of the influential positions they held at court. Henry further alienated he English people by a number of unwise and naive **actions. He taxed the people** very **heavily and the money raised** appeared **to be wasted by** extravagant living at court. He was unduly subservient to the Pope who tricked Henry into giving him money in return for the gift of the Kingdom of **Sicily for Edmund,** his second son. This was an empty gesture, for a large army would, have been needed to secure that gift. Resources were wasted in futile wars on the Continent and Henry made no secret of the fact that he wanted to rescind the provisions of Magna Carta!*

One of the foreigners, special(y favoured by the King, was Simon de Montfort who had inherited the Earldom of Leicester from his grandmother. Simon became the king's brother-in-law when he married Henry's youngest sister, Eleanor. He even became godfather to Henry's eldest son, Edward.

However, with his usual lack of tact, Henry fell out with de Montfort. Although a Frenchman, this Earl of Leicester had become in some ways, more English than the English lords. He led a rebellion against the King and as you have rightly remembered, he defeated him at the Battle of Lewes.

Simon's victory was partly *achieved by providing a decoy which made it appear as if he stood among* ***the*** *troops he had raised from London. In reality, Simon was directing the battle from elsewhere on the field. As the* **king's eldest son, Prince Edward, a** *great* **and able soldier, harried** *these troops in an attempt to get to Simon. These troops fell back, luring Edward from* ***the*** *main battlefield.*

By the time that Prince Edward returned to the point where hostilities had commenced, the battle had been lost and the King had to accede to Simon's demands. Simon set up an institution which has evolved over the centuries and become a force by which the best possible national government has been established, the institution of parliament by which the government of the country would no longer be solely in the hands of an autocratic

monarch but influential nobles and men of stature,
elected by the people, would have their say."

The Battle of Lewes

The King was not deposed but to ensure that he was
kept in check, King Henry's eldest son, Prince
Edward was held by Simon as a hostage."

Alfred and Alice listened intently as Chronavon
described a situation of which these young people
had only hazy recollections from their school
history lessons.

"How awful for a prince to be locked in prison because he had a stupid father," Alice interjected.

"Things weren't quite as bad as that," continued Chronavon. "Although in the early days after the Battle of Lewes, Edward's movements were quite severely restricted, Simon was not a monster. He had a great admiration for his nephew and godson but he just couldn't trust King Henry. Edward came to be given quite a bit if freedom. After all, he was rightful heir to the throne of England and would one day be king. Prince Edward was able to move much as he chose around the various castles where he was confined as hostage, but always in the company of trusted members of Simon de Montfort's party who would see to it that he didn't escape."

Simon's own position became increasingly difficult. In spite of his success in getting Henry's hated French courtiers removed from their positions of influence and establishing a parliamentary system of government, he began to lose popularity. Some would not forget that in spite of the way he championed the cause of the English people and nobility against their king, he too was not truly

English but came from aristocratic French stock. Many of the English nobles on both the royalist and de Montfort's side refused to release prisoners they had taken in battles which had been fought in this civil war. From the safety of their castles, they held on to any prisoners whose relatives could afford to pay a rich ransom.

Although powerful, Simon de Montfort, Earl of Leicester, did not quite have royal authority. In his battles against the King, Simon had to rely heavily on two other noble Lords, the Earl of Gloucester and the Duke of Norfolk. These three were the most powerful lords in England, and although supporting Simon in his battle against King Henry, Gloucester and Norfolk were unwilling to regard themselves as subservient to Simon. Simon de Montfort, Earl of Leicester, and Gilbert of Clare, Earl of Gloucester, fell out, reducing the reliable military support which Simon would need in the event of future fighting. "

Alfred had been waiting patiently to hear just what Ahrimanes was going to do to try to change the course of history and what part he and Alice could play in making sure that things did not go wrong. At last Alfred could contain his curiosity no longer.

"What might happen to change the course of history?" he demanded at last.

Chronavon paused and smiled at Alfred and Alice in a way which reassured them that the key to situation was about to be revealed.

"Forgive my expounding such a long history lesson," he continued, "but the more you know of the situation, the better you will be able to play your parts. Ahrimanes does not want Edward to become king, and his plan is to get him assassinated while still held as a hostage at Earl Simon's court. He has managed to get an evil knight, Gregory de Grossmont, established in Earl Simon's circle. Gregory's plan is to persuade Earl Simon to find an excuse to do away with Prince Edward, but if his persuasion is unsuccessful, then he will attempt to murder Edward himself!"

"However can we stop him?" demanded Alice, her eyes wide open with apprehension as she began to consider the enormity of the task ahead.

"I am hoping that you will be able to do a great deal," continued Chronavon. "Ahrimanes has chosen to work through a loud mouthed and vulgar knight who will be very conspicuous. He will quickly make himself unpopular. Others will not happily cooperate with him. These factors will make it difficult for him to do things which are clearly contrary to Earl Simon's wishes. Ahrimanes has made a bad choice of servant.

On the other hand, you are both sensible and well-presented young people. Although I am aware of how mature and sensible you are, an ignorant person like Sir Gregory will regard you as no more than children and will not realise that you may have the ability to thwart his evil designs!

You have not been selected at random for this task. Besides being sensible and mature for your age, you both have a great grasp and understanding of the history of your country, you have high moral integrity, you are both excellent at riding horses, an important accomplishment in mediaeval England, and most important of all, you are both very prayerful young people."

Chronavon paused again at this point, interested to observe the young people's reactions. Alfred and Alice looked at each other. They were beginning to tingle with excitement at the prospect of the adventure which lay ahead, but they were surprised that their being prayerful should come up at this point.

"My master and your master, the Lord Most High, has heard your many prayers and has been able to answer them so easily because for the most part, they are not prayers, asking for things for yourselves. They've been unselfish prayers in which you've thought carefully about situations and asked for things which would meet the needs of others around you who've found themselves in difficulty. Because your prayers have been private matters, you will not have known until this very moment that there are great similarities in the way you both pray. You're great friends, but young people, even those who are great friends, don't often talk to one another about their prayers.

Your task will be to ensure that Prince Edward does not fall foul of the evil designs of Sir

Gregory. You'll face emergencies and problems which are difficult to overcome. If you rely on your own ingenuity and cleverness, you'll surely fail. However, if you avail yourself of the power of prayer, you'll surprise yourselves in discovering how effective you will be in this enterprise to which you've been entrusted.

But we've spent long enough in this room. Let's proceed to the Cathedral. How better can we start this work than by spending time in prayer, and what better place to make our prayers than in this great house of God."

Chronavon stood up and led Alfred and Alice through the great doors of the Chapter House.

Chapter 3

Alfred and Alice followed Chronavon through the door by which they had entered the Chapter House, but they did not find themselves in the gloomy vestry from whence they had started out. Instead, they were in a vaulted walkway whose unglazed windows looked out on to a square garden. This was the ambulatory of the Cathedral cloister. A short walk along this passage took them to another door which opened into the main building of the Cathedral.

Alfred and Alice looked around themselves, awe struck at the scale and splendour of the building in which they now found themselves. It was obviously quite a busy place. Men, women and children were coming in and out of the great doors at the end of the Cathedral and meeting in groups or talking to the clergy. The clerics could be readily identified by their long white robes and brightly coloured cloaks. Albert and Alice realised that they themselves were dressed in a similar style to the peasant folk who were so actively involved in whatever business brought them to the Cathedral and there was no reason why anyone should pay special attention to Alfred and Alice as they followed Chronavon who walked ahead of them at a good pace.

Chronavon turned into a deserted side chapel and knelt on a rug placed in front of the altar. Alfred and Alice followed and knelt at each side of their mentor who would have passed off as a monk, for whom it would have been natural to be found in that setting. After a moments silence, Chronavon prayed aloud.

"Heavenly Lord and Father, thank you that Alfred and Alice are willing to serve you in the great task that is before them. They realise that it is dangerous, and failure would have disastrous consequences. Keep them ever under your protection Lord, and guide them in all the situations in which they will find themselves. Keep them vigilant against all the attacks that the enemy will launch against them and grant them success in their mission. Amen."

Chronavon remained kneeling for quite a few minutes after uttering this prayer. Although they had earlier felt very apprehensive about the task in which they were to be involved, Chronavon's prayer brought Alfred and Alice a great sense of peace and reassurance. After a time, Chronavon rose to his feet, and the children stood up with him.

"God doesn't require much speaking before he hears a prayer he can readily answer, but prefers words which are concise and to the point."

Chronavon now began to give these young people more information about their new environment.

"I must now take you to the home where the adventure which has been entrusted to you will start. As we go, I'll tell you more about the people and places which will play a part in the events.in which you'll be involved. You'll find that a great deal of preparation has been done to help you in this enterprise. First of all, something which may surprise you. You can both see me and I expect you think I am some sort of monk. In fact, I am not a human being at all but a spirit being and the only people who can see or hear me are those whom I specially choose. I am a messenger of the Lord Most High and I appear to you like this because men and women find it far easier to receive messages from someone who looks like a human than a messenger in any other guise."

This divine messenger led the children out of the chapel and made his way towards the great west door of the Cathedral. They stepped out into the city of Hereford. To the south of the Cathedral they could see a beautiful river meandering between the lime trees and willows which grew along its banks. They realised that this river was the Wye, carrying the clean water it had gathered from its catchment area in the Welsh mountains. Small boats plied up and down the river and fishermen on the banks were casting their nets into the clear waters.

The City of Hereford itself was totally different to any town or city that Alfred and Alice, from their twenty-first century environment, had ever been in before. There were no big shops, no busy pavements and no roads congested with cars. In the large open space in front of the cathedral, a busy market had been set up. Traders were vociferously selling vegetables, presenting meat in a way which would not satisfy our modern hygiene laws, and displaying loaves of bread baked into many different shapes, all sold from crude wooden tables. Livestock had been herded into makeshift pens. Alice was particularly interested in one of the vegetable stalls where an enthusiastic trader was verbally advertising his wares and vigorously bartering with those who came to buy. Piles of cabbages, carrots, turnips, peas and beans were displayed in a somewhat haphazard manner, but there was not a potato in sight.

A few carts of varying sizes, drawn by oxen, lumbered along the road which led to this market and some of them stopped to replenish stalls. The houses beyond this market square were barely more than wooden shacks. A very small number of single storey stone built houses could be seen. The houses were not neatly arranged in rows, but clear thoroughfares passed between the clusters of buildings. A well-built city wall could be seen beyond the houses and a very impressive castle. There were no buildings beyond the city walls, only open countryside.

Chronavon, Alfred and Alice
leave Hereford Cathedral to enter the
mediaeval city of Hereford

48

Alfred looked to left and right to assess the size of the city in which they were stood and came to the conclusion that it was barely more than a large village.

As they made their way from the Cathedral through one of the main thoroughfares, Chronavon continued with his briefing.

"You are going to stay tonight at the home of Ralph and Margaret. They know me and I have prepared them for your arrival. Ralph is the chief ostler at the castle stables. No doubt, at some time during your stay here, he will be able to make excellent horses available to you so that you can continue to enjoy your much loved past-time of horse riding.

Ralph and Margaret are very discreet and they won't ask you about where you have come from. It's sufficient for them to know that I have selected you to play important parts in this great design. I must stress that it is essential that you tell no-one that you come from a future time. They wouldn't understand what you were talking about, and in any case, that future is not ensured unless you succeed in your mission!"

Chronavon raised his voice to impart this last statement as a way of emphasising the crucial nature of the challenge they now faced.

Chronavon continued. "You'll need to spend a few days with Ralph and Margaret to acclimatise yourselves to the very different environment in which you now find yourselves. Simon de Montfort is currently holding court at Hereford Castle.

The plan will be for you, Alfred, to infiltrate the castle as a page, and you, Alice, to become a maid to Lady Maud Mortimer, wife of Roger Mortimer, and a friend of Prince Edward. Lady Mortimer is residing in Wigmore Castle, which is a few miles from here, and she can provide help and support from outside Hereford in the task of rescuing Edward.

However, unless Edward and Lady Maud can communicate, no rescue can be effected. This is where you are both going to be so important. Because you are young, no one in Earl Simon's party will suspect that you're in anyway significant in great affairs of state. However, by riding out to meet each other and keeping Edward and Maud in touch with events within and without the castle, you'll enable an otherwise impossible venture to come to a satisfactory conclusion."

Alfred and Alice were now beginning to see clearly how they might be of use in this enterprise, and they realised that considerable planning had already taken place.

Chronavon directed his attention towards Alfred. "In order for you to fulfil your part of the mission, you must obviously find a method of communicating with Edward in a way that doesn't arouse suspicion. Also, it will help you if l also tell you just a little about some of the key characters whom you'll observe at the court. Simon de Montfort, Prince Edward and Gregory de Grossmont you already know about. King Henry of course is there but apart from his title, he's really unimportant. He can have little influence on what happens. He's an impotent hostage to Simon and merely a pawn in the great game that's being played.

Some of the more important nobles on Simon's side are Hugh, the Dispenser, Ralph Basset of Drayton, William of Valence, John FitzJohn and Humphrey

51

de Bohun. Two of Simon's sons, Henry and Peter are also there in-the castle.

Henry Ill's brother, Richard, Earl of Cornwall, may be there but he is always moving to and fro as he seeks to reconcile the antagonists in this affair. He is very much a neutral party in the power struggle which has been taking place. Richard is one of those genuinely nice and well-meaning people, a rare breed of person. Would that he had been king rather than Henry, but he was a younger son. Richard has tried to mediate and bring about a peaceful solution to the crises which have racked the nation but alas to no avail.

There are three clerics who need to be mentioned, Peter of Aigueblanche, Bishop of Hereford, Walter de Cantilupe, Bishop of Worcester, and Walter's nephew, Thomas. Pay great attention to this Thomas. He's a very wise and saintly man. His uncle, Walter, recognised his ability and promoted his education. Thomas became Chancellor of Oxford University at a very young age. Although still only a young man, Thomas de Cantilupe has a very powerful and important position. He's now Chancellor of England, no less!"

Chronavon saw a puzzled expression come over the faces of Alfred and Alice, and he read the source of their bewilderment. They'd heard of chancellors of universities but Chancellor of England was a title they'd not previously encountered.

"There's no exact equivalent to Chancellor of England in the twenty-first century from which you come," Chronavon continued. "I suppose he is the nearest thing to Prime Minister in mediaeval England. No new law becomes effective until the Chancellor of England has set his seal to it.

Let me now tell you something about the castle which has been kept so secret that no-one today is aware of its existence. There is a secret passage which threads the walls of the castle. Apart from enabling you to get from one place in the castle to another in a very short time, it passes many of the main rooms and enables someone in the secret passage to listen in to conversations taking place in rooms next to this secret passage. This is not the sort of thing I should be encouraging you to do, but it may be necessary to eavesdrop in the interests of successfully fulfilling your task.

The location of this hidden passageway is so secret that even I, messenger of the Lord Most High, can't tell you exactly where it is. However, I can give you a cryptic clue which I hope you'll be able to solve, once you have had a chance to look round the castle.

If you do succeed in finding this place, and I'm sure that you will, you'll find that you can use it to discover still more secrets!"

They'd now reached a well-constructed wooden house, right at the edge of the city, no more than twenty yards from the city walls. A man and woman, who must have heard Chronavon's voice as he continued his briefing to the young people as they walked through Hereford, came out to meet them.

Chronavon ceased speaking about Hereford Castle and introduced the couple who had just emerged from the doorway opposite them.

"This is Ralph and Margaret who'll be looking after you."

Margaret, a homely looking woman in her mid-forties rushed forward and hugged the children. "And you must be Alfred and Alice. Welcome to our home. Chronavon has told us of the great task that you have to perform. Come in and rest awhile. If you have spent the best part of the day with Chronavon, you both must be tired out. Once Chronavon gets going, he has so much to say, but I will say this for him. He never wastes his words. Everything he says turns out to be important."

Ralph warmly shook the hands of all three of them. He was a well-built stocky man with a friendly face. Alfred sensed that he was a much quieter character than his gushing wife.

"Come on in and have some food," he said. "Chronavon is always so perfect in his timing. You've arrived at just the moment he said you would."

The three of them followed Ralph and Margaret into their cosy looking home.

<u>Chapter 4</u>

The room into which they entered was sparsely furnished but looked comfortable. In the centre of the room was a largish table, surrounded by half a dozen crudely made chairs. There were a number of chests around the walls of the room. Smoke rose from a circle of large stones in one corner of the room and issued through a hole in the roof Alfred and Alice guessed that this was the safest way to contain a fire in a building, made largely of wood. A large bucket of water stood by the fire which was no doubt there as a safety precaution.

Ralph motioned them to sit on the chairs while Margaret went through to a back room and returned with a steaming bowl of stew and some loaves of bread. Ralph put out some square pieces of wood in front of each of his guests. These had been scrubbed clean and Alfred and Alice realised that these were to function as plates. Ralph then brought round some wooden spoons and knives which resembled daggers. There was no sign of any forks.

"You'll find eating here very different from the way you ate in the place from which you've come," observed Chronavon. Alice and Alfred noticed that he didn't say 'time from which you've come' while in the presence of Ralph and Margaret. "Your main eating implements are your hands, and the daggers are to cut up anything that you can't easily bite off with your teeth. It may sound very unhygienic to young people who've come from your particular lifestyle, but I can assure you that while you're on this mission, you've been given immunity from any sort of illness or infection.

There will be a number of other things you'll find very different and my best advice to you both is to carefully observe the behaviour of those around you. This will enable you to find out how you need to act to fit in with this new environment. Ralph and Margaret know that you have been specially chosen and come from a place totally unlike this, but as I explained on the way here, they too have been specially chosen as the ones to look after you as you settle in. They will help you in many ways. One further thing. When you proceed to the other places where you'll be needed to carry out this venture, it would be wise not to advertise the fact that you have a connection with Ralph and

Margaret. This is a precaution to protect them should something go seriously wrong this mission and those, who become your enemies, seek out any known to be your accomplices. If you need a cover story, just say that you had to leave your home village of Hillington when it was burnt down during the fighting. That story will suffice. No one in Hereford will know the whereabouts of Hillington, and the country is full of refugees and orphans who have had to flee the ravages of the civil war which King Henry's foolishness has brought upon the country.

And now the time has come for me to leave you. Although you'll not now see me for some time, I won't be far away. I can be summoned to provide help if an emergency arises, but I'm hoping that all will go well and I'll not need to reappear to you until your mission is successfully accomplished."

Chronavon now turned to Ralph and Margaret.

"Thank you both for your hospitality to my two young friends here and the help you will provide them with to engage with the task to which they've been entrusted. The food you have prepared looks lovely but you know that it is one of the rules of my order to strictly observe the fasts which are all part of my high calling, so, I'll now bid you adieu."

With that, Chronavon stood, gave a little bow and went out through the-door by which they'd entered.

"What a shame he can never stay and share our hospitality," sighed Margaret. "Chronavon is so interesting and has many tales to tell. I've never met anyone as learned and knowledgeable as he is. Alas, he never seems to eat anything, but you two now, don't let your food get cold. Let's eat up."

Alfred and Alice had by now built up a healthy appetite and could hardly wait to start eating. They followed Chronavon's advice and watched the way Ralph and Margaret dealt with the food. They soon got the hang of using the dagger and their hands to eat with, and they found the stew absolutely delicious. It was beginning to get quite dark as they finished their meal. Ralph and Margaret showed them to their sleeping quarters.

This was a room behind the one where they'd just eaten. It was a communal bedroom for the whole household. There were five or six low trestles which obviously served as beds. Three of the beds were furnished with straw filled sacks which functioned as mattresses. These were covered with roughly woven woollen blankets.

The larger bed was obviously Ralph and Margaret's. Alfred and Alice were shown two smaller beds on which they were to sleep. There was no changing into night dresses and pyjamas. Alfred and Alice discovered that you just took off the outer layer of clothing and slept in your underclothes. Once they'd laid down and covered themselves with their blankets, Alfred and Alice found that they were far more comfortable than they'd anticipated when they first saw their sleeping quarters. They soon fell into deep slumbers, as thoughts of the mission that Chronavon had imparted to them filled their dreams.

They woke the following morning to bright sunlight, streaming in through the window of the room where they'd slept. Ralph and Margaret were already up and about. Alfred and Alice hastily put on their outer clothes and made their way to the main room of the house where Margaret was bustling about. She beamed as she saw them and enquired after how well they'd slept. She motioned them to the table and shortly brought them porridge, bread, eggs, butter and black currant jam. The young people made a good breakfast. When they'd finished she told them that the task Chronavon had set Ralph for the day was to familiarise them with the important places in Hereford. She looked out of the front door and called to Ralph who was busy putting old horseshoes in a sack.

Ralph returned into the house and expressed a hope that Alfred and Alice had slept well and satisfactorily breakfasted. He then took them out into the town. The traders were just beginning to set up their market stalls. Many were going to sell their wares straight from the ground of open areas they'd commandeered as their patch. The cathedral, castle and city walls dominated the town, even more than they do our modem cities where many new buildings vie with these ancient edifices for size and importance.

They made their way towards the castle.

"That's where the King and Prince Edward reside," Ralph explained, "but everyone knows that they're really no more than prisoners of the Earl of Leicester. Since the court moved from Northampton to Hereford, they've been short of pages and cooks at the castle. Chronavon has indicated to me that you, Alfred, will be able to secure entry to the castle by enlisting as a page. From there, you'll be able to discover better than any of us outside what is the true state of affairs and what steps may be necessary to restore England to normality."

By now, they had reached the castle. Traders carrying provisions were wandering across the drawbridge to the castle but were carefully checked by the guards at the gate before they were allowed to pass under the portcullis into the bailey beyond. Every now and then, a knight would ride up, clad in armour and bearing a shield with a brightly emblazoned coat of arms. Traders and townsfolk scattered as these haughty war lords galloped by with scant regard for persons or property which impeded their path. They didn't have to be checked as they crossed the drawbridge. The men at arms recognised them by their armorial bearings and waved them through. Ralph, as a senior worker in the castle, was also recognised and ushered through. Alfred and Alice followed, unchallenged. Two children could pose no threat to the fortresses security.

"Let me show you my stables," said Ralph. "I'm very proud of the steeds in my charge"

Alfred and Alice knew horses well and eagerly accompanied Ralph as he strode to the stables on the far side of the bailey to inspect the animals on view. Their eyes soon adjusted to the lower light level inside and they were both highly impressed with the creatures in the stalls.

They were for the most part, Old English War Horses, a breed which became extinct well before the twenty-first century when horses were bred either for strength or speed, shire horses being an example of the former and race horses of the latter.

Ralph shows Alfred and Alice round
The stables of Hereford Castle

These horses in the stables of Hereford Castle

combined both the strength to carry an armoured knight with the speed to launch a momentous charge against hostile opposition.

One particular stallion particularly caught their attention. This was a huge, coal black war horse who stood pawing the ground with his hooves as if ever anxious to be on the go and in the action. Ralph saw where their attention was directed.

"That horse is called Conqueror," he told them. "He really is a great horse and he needs to be. He belongs to a knight called Sir Gregory de Grossmont. Very few horses could comfortably carry that knight when in full armour but Conqueror bears him well."

Alfred and Alice looked at each other at the mention of that knight's name. He was the one identified to them by Chronavon as Ahrimanes' servant, bent on evil.

Not all the horses in the stable were war horses. A number of palfreys occupied stalls at the far end.

"This is Duchess, Prince Edward's horse," said Ralph indicating a frail looking palfrey. "Earl Simon cannot keep someone of Prince Edward's standing in close confinement, but he harbours a fear that the Prince will try to escape. He has therefore allocated a horse to Prince Edward that he knows cannot outrun the war horses of the Lords who have the task of guarding the Prince. However, don't be deceived by appearances. Duchess is a horse of great mettle and would give some of those war horses a good run for their money if it ever came to a chase."

Alfred and Alice were absolutely enthralled by what they were learning and plied Ralph with questions about the horses they were seeing. Ralph knew his horses well by temperament and performance.

"This horse goes by the name of Confessor," said Ralph, pointing out a very docile looking war horse. "He has a wonderful temperament and that may be why he was given that name but again, don't be deceived by appearances. He is battle tried and tested and has never once disappointed his rider. Also, he is by far the fastest horse in the stable. Conqueror, carrying Sir Gregory, would be no match for Confessor in a race. The only horse who could come near Confessor is this one," Ralph continued, pointing out a war horse rather less heavily built than the others in the stable. "This is Hannibal. Not only is he fast but he has great endurance and can keep running all day provided he's not bearing too much weight. However, he wouldn't get far if he had the likes of Sir Gregory on his back."

And so they spent the best part of the morning, admiring the horses and learning about their relative strengths and weaknesses. The time went by quickly. As they came out of the stable, the sun was high in the sky.

"I hadn't realised it was so late," said Ralph. "We must be getting back for some lunch!"

As they returned, Ralph pointed out other details of the castle, the keep with its various entrances, the fortifications, the well house and the storage sheds. His mind turned to other matters as they left the castle and made their way back home. Ralph started to tell them more about how he and Margaret had come to be involved in this adventure.

"Chronavon appeared at our house one day and told Margaret and myself that two young people were coming to Hereford to perform some very special task which would safeguard the future of England.

Pembridge Castle near Hereford

You are those young people. He told us that this

task would require you to keep Prince Edward in touch with Lady Maud Mortimer. He's given us no more details of what the venture involves but has asked us to help you in any way we can.

Although we have only known Chronavon for just over a month, since he came to visit us and tell us that he wished you to stay with us, Chronavon has impressed us as being a very special sort of person. He seems to know things that humanly speaking, it is impossible to know! We have therefore, every faith in him, and we've been making plans which we think will help you."

Ralph continued.

"On Friday, the new pages will assemble at the castle. It'll be quite easy with my help for you, Alfred, to infiltrate that group. There'll then be no suspicious circumstances associated with your entry into the castle.

The following day, Elaine, one of Margaret's friends who serves Lady Maud Mortimer, will be coming to Hereford to recruit a maid for her mistress. Margaret has already let her know that she has found someone who'll be very suitable and who can give her news of Prince Edward. That's you, Alice. Lady Mortimer is a great friend of Prince Edward and wife of one of his noblest supporters, Sir Roger Mortimer. They'd do anything to help the Prince, should he experience danger. However, he never leaves the castle but in the company of those who are responsible to see that he doesn't escape. That means that Prince Edward and Lady Maud can't communicate with each other.

Alice, you'll return with Elaine to the Mortimers' castle at Wigmore and there, you can tell Lady Maud that you've a friend in Hereford Castle who can bring her news of the Prince. I'm sure that'll mean that she'll want you to come back to Hereford so that you can return to her with news of what is happening. That news can be provided by Alfred. We'll need to identify a secret rendezvous out of sight of the city walls for you both to meet and keep in touch.

This leaves you with some quite difficult tasks, Alfred. You must find some way of speaking privately to Prince Edward in the castle. This will be no easy matter, for a lowly page won't easily be able to arrange a private audience with the King's son.

You'll also need to find a way of leaving the castle to meet up with Alice at prearranged times in a way that does not arouse suspicion. This could be very difficult if you are set tasks to perform at times which will severely limit your freedom to move in and out of the castle.

I don't know how I would fare if I were in your position, Alfred. However, I know that Chronavon has selected both of you because of your abilities and resourcefulness, and Chronavon doesn't seem the sort of person who makes mistakes. The fact that you're both young will be very useful to you, because we live in an age where adults underestimate the ability of children. There are many things that you'll be able to do, which no grown up possibly could without arousing suspicion."

Alfred and Alice were feeling increasingly

excited. Ralph had put them more fully into the picture and they were now beginning to see how they could fulfil the task for which Chronavon had commissioned them. What an adventure!

The next couple of days were spent in getting further acclimatised to mediaeval Hereford. As chief ostler at the stables, Ralph obviously had no difficulty in borrowing horses from the castle. On the Wednesday, Ralph rode out of the city with Alfred and Alice and they found a thicket, a couple of miles or so, north of the city which seemed to satisfy the conditions required for a suitable rendezvous where Alfred and Alice could exchange news and intelligence. Alfred and Alice decided that they would provisionally set midday, the following Monday for their first meeting. Should they find that their new work situations made this impossible, they would try to get word to Ralph and Margaret so that their fears could be allayed if they were unable to meet. However, they realised from what Chronavon had said the previous day, that contacting Ralph and Margaret should be a last resort. They were obviously going to be involved in an affair which some in power may have regarded as treasonable and Alfred and Alice had no wish to put Ralph and Margaret in danger by virtue of their known association with them.

Thursday was the last day that Alfred and Alice were together before the start of the adventure proper. Nothing had yet happened which could jeopardise Ralph and Margaret through being found to be connected with young people who'd displeased the powerful lords, currently residing in Hereford Castle. It was Ascension Day and the four of them attended a service at Hereford Cathedral. A most impressive sermon was preached by a red headed young priest. This was none other than Thomas de Cantilupe, Chancellor of England. Chronavon had specially directed Alfred and Alice to pay attention to this scholarly person.

Chapter 5

Friday dawned. Although excited about what lay ahead, Alfred felt some trepidation. Although Margaret had laid a good breakfast, Alfred's appetite had left him and he found it difficult to tuck in as he normally would. Alfred could sense that Alice too was somewhat apprehensive but she did justice to the food before her.

Breakfast ended.
"We must be making our way to the castle now," said Ralph. "You two had better say goodbye because the next time you've arranged to meet is a few days away."

Alfred and Alice hugged each other and then Alfred set out with Ralph for the castle. They went through the main gate and Ralph pointed out a group of half a dozen boys of about Alfred's age, give or take a couple of years.

"Those are the boys who've been recruited to become pages," Ralph explained. "Go and stand among them and in due course, someone will come to organise something for you. Good luck," smiled Ralph as he held out his hand. "It would be best that you don't advertise your connection with me but I'm around the stables if an extreme emergency arises."

They shook hands and Alfred made his way down to the group of apprentice pages. Nothing seemed to be happening. Two or three more boys joined the group during the next half hour. Alfred started up a conversation with another boy with a cheerful looking face. He was shorter than Alfred but stockily built with a mop of fair curly hair. Alfred discovered that this boy was called William and that he'd been living with his uncle for the past few weeks. His mother had died some years earlier and his father had been killed when fighting on the Welsh border a few weeks earlier. His uncle had decided that he would be safer in the castle than living in a village located in the Welsh Marches and had volunteered his services as a page.

Alfred decided that William was a very likeable boy and was amazed that he could remain so cheerful after the tragic loss of both his parents.

Just then, an imposing figure in a red tunic and black hose descended the steps which led out of the castle keep and strode over to the group of boys.

"You're the boys who have come to learn to be pages at the King's court, right?'

The boys all nodded apprehensively. None of them knew exactly what life was going to be like in the castle. Alfred knew that in reality, it was Earl Simon's court, but the King was held there and his name gave everything the mark of importance and respectability.

"You're very fortunate, for pages are usually chosen from great and noble families. However, we now live in difficult times and there are more knights being called to court than there are regular pages to serve them. That's why boys like yourselves have been recruited to serve in this most honourable role. My name is Sir Geoffery Beauchamp. I'm Seneschal of this great castle and it's my responsibility to see that you're well-trained to serve the noblest in the land. Behave well and do what I say, and we shall get on very well together.

Behave badly and disobey me, and your fate will be too terrible to contemplate. Now follow me."

The boys hurried after this tall figure as he re-climbed the steps to the keep and entered the great hall of Hereford Castle. The hall was fairly dark, some light coming through the arrow slits, high on the walls and the rest coming from giant candles strategically placed on stands around the hall. Alfred's eyes soon adjusted to the lower light level. Colourful banners hung from the ceiling. Swords and shields were arranged in neat patterns on the walls. One wall of the chamber was lined with large statues of heraldic beasts. Three very long tables were arranged at one end of the hall in an open square. There were benches on the outside of this open square so that any sitting there had an unimpeded view of anyone else who might be sitting at table. The inner part of the open square was clear so that the tables could be easily approached by anyone serving or clearing the tables. The floor was carpeted with rushes.

The Seneschal stopped in the middle of this chamber and waited for the boys to gather round.

"You are now in the great hall of Hereford Castle," he told the boys, declaring the obvious. "This is where the Lords and Ladies come to eat. You'll not be involved in preparing the food but one of your jobs will be to serve at table. This afternoon, each of you will be allocated to a particular lord or knight to whom you will act as a personal servant. However, when serving food, you're not to favour your particular master but see to it that the wants of all at table are satisfied."

Sir Geoffery then led the boys into the kitchen where the food was being prepared. Scullions and cooks were toiling over tables crowded with vegetables, poultry and partially dismembered animal carcasses. The atmosphere in the kitchen was made unpleasantly hot and humid by the steam which rose from huge cauldrons, boiling away on fires located in alcoves around the walls of the kitchen. It was from this kitchen that the boys were to serve food at meal times.

The tour of the castle next took in the armouries, stocked with pikes, swords, shields, many quivers of arrows and rows of neatly stacked long bows.

Suits of armour were neatly arranged along one side of the armoury. The boys' attention was taken by an absolutely huge suit of black armour. Whatever giant could have worn that? Sir Geoffery noticed where their attention was fixed.

"The knights keep most of their armour in their rooms and these are the spare suits," explained the Seneschal. "Very often, a knight will want to change some of his armour for something down here if it seems to be in better condition or a better fit. No one has ever needed to borrow any pieces from that suit," he said, pointing to the large suit which had attracted the boys' interest. "That belonged to Sir Peter of Thirsk, the largest knight I ever saw. He was six foot six inches tall and must have weighed all of twenty stone. Sadly, he was killed when unhorsed at the Battle of Lewes."

The Seneschal next showed the boys round the stables. This was 'déjà vu' for Alfred. Sir Geoffery then took them to the chapel, a small chamber, sparsely furnished with about a dozen seats and a rugged altar. It was clearly in regular use. A clean linen cloth was spread over the altar whose only other furnishings were a simple cross and two candles which had both been lit. After this, they were then taken to the dormitory which was to be their sleeping quarters and finally to a room off the main hall where food had been laid out for them.

After they had eaten, they were lined up in the main hall so that the knights who had only recently arrived at the castle could choose their pages. A group of a dozen or so knights swaggered in. Conspicuous in this company was a grossly overweight, loudmouthed warrior with thick black hair and an even blacker beard. He either had some precedence over the others, or was one of those personalities who would push to the front anyway. He walked up and down the line, weighing up the merits of boys available as pages. He quickly made his decision.

"I'll have that one," he said, cuffing the ear of William, Alfred's new found friend. "Follow me!" and the pair left the hall.

Alfred was to discover that this was Sir Gregory de Grossmont of whom he had been warned by Chronavon.

Alfred was selected by another knight, Sir Stephen of Selby. Alfred was lucky. Stephen proved to be a truly chivalrous knight. Alfred returned with Stephen to his quarters. He had an interesting lesson on how to assemble and care for armour and he spent an enjoyable afternoon, cleaning and oiling Sir Stephen's accoutrements, the breastplates, helmets and gauntlets he would wear into battle. Sir Stephen had recently changed some of his armour and he sent Alfred back to the armoury with the unwanted pieces. Pages carrying heavy pieces of armour to and from the armoury was a very common sight in the castle.

The final task of the day was to serve at evening meal. Alfred listened carefully to all that was said so that he could discover the identity of each of the assembled nobility. The really important personages sat along the end table. King Henry III sat at the centre of this table by virtue of his office but he no longer wielded any real power. That rested in the hands of Simon de Montfort, Earl of Leicester, who sat a few places down from the King. Alfred readily recognised the red headed cleric, Thomas de Cantilupe, whose sermon in the Cathedral the previous day had created made a great impression on Alfred, as it had indeed on all who had been present at that act of worship. Next to the King on his right sat a very tall young man who seemed to be bursting with vigour and energy. This was King Henry's son, Prince Edward. The King's brother, Richard, Duke of Cornwall sat to his left. Two older men in clerical garb were the bishops of Hereford and Worcester.

Alfred's new master, Sir Stephen of Selby, sat at one of the side tables and Sir Gregory de Grossmont sat at the other. Even in this gathering, Gregory was conspicuous. He quaffed vast quantities of the mead and beer which freely flowed among the knights as they dined. The presence of eminent clerics in no way inhibited the foul language which Gregory used to colour his conversation, and he spoke so loudly, rudely interrupting and contradicting anything which was not to his way of thinking. Although the Seneschal had told .the pages that they were to serve the Lords and Ladies of the castle, there were no ladies present. This was just as well, if only to spare the blushes which would have come to the cheeks of any high born lady listening to the foul mouthed utterings of Sir Gregory.

When two of the pages accidentally collided, spilling hot soup all over themselves, this was very much to Sir Gregory's delight, and he guffawed with uncontrollable laughter as he banged the haft of his dagger on the table shouting "encore". His mood quickly changed when he found himself served with a piece of bad meat.

"**********,   *************,
**************, *************." he swore.

(I dare not print even the initial letters of the words he used, lest my reader should incorrectly assume them to be the rather less offensive swear words with the same initial of which he or she may be aware through coming within earshot of coarse company in our modem day and age)

At last it was time to retire to bed. Before falling to sleep, Alfred focused his thoughts on the task ahead. How was he going to create the opportunity to communicate privately with Prince Edward? How was he going to make the rendezvous with Alice the following Monday? Alfred did what he always did when confronted with a challenge which he didn't know how to meet. He prayed for the wisdom, skill and opportunity to meet that challenge in the way that his Lord and God would want him to, and he prayed through the Lord Jesus Christ, knowing that anything asked in his name would be granted.

Even after praying, something still nagged Alfred's mind. What was the special feature of the castle which Chronavon had told him would be especially useful to him in this task? Why, yes, it was a secret passage, but how did one enter that concealed space? Chronavon had only left a clue. Alfred struggled to remember the cryptic words Chronavon had spoken.

'When the sun's beam shines twixt the Griffin and the Lion, Press hard on the hand that the shaft lights upon'

What did it mean? Alfred prayed once again that
God would reveal this secret to him. He then fell
into a deep and tranquil sleep.

<u>**Chapter 6**</u>

The next morning, the boys rose to the shrill cock crow of a bird who ruled the roost of a hen coop located within the castle walls. They went down for their breakfast and Alfred sat next to his new friend, William. Alfred was disturbed to see that William's face was quite red and he had a swollen ear. They started to talk about the experiences of the previous day and the conversation soon focused on the respective knights in whose service they had been placed.

Alfred had nothing adverse to report about Sir Stephen but William had a catalogue of complaints to make against Sir Gregory.

"However hard I try, he's never satisfied," moaned William. "He blames me for every little thing, even his own mistakes, and he's pretty free with his corporal punishment," added William, pointing to his swollen ear which had ended up on the end of Gregory's fist during one of his violent outbursts.

Alfred felt outraged. What could be done about this bully? Alfred and William agreed that it might not be wise to report this to the Seneschal just yet. Sir Geoffery seemed to be unduly in awe of the knights and nobles whose comfort was his responsibility while they resided in the castle, and they didn't expect him to stand up for them against the formidable figure of Sir Gregory. However, with an experience of twenty-first century fair play, quite unknown in mediaeval England, Alfred didn't want to let Sir Gregory get away with this totally unacceptable behaviour towards his friend.

Breakfast ended. The boys all made their ways to their respective knight's quarters, William with rather more trepidation than the others. Alfred found Sir Stephen the same amiable person whose armour he had been trained to care for the previous day.

"Today we must exercise my horses," Sir Stephen declared. "What sort of a rider are you? Do you think you can manage a war horse? I have two fine steeds. They are fast but quite docile if rightly handled. Come, let us take them out for a gallop."

They made their way to the stable and Alfred discovered that the horses belonging to Stephen were two of the horses whose abilities and temperaments had been described by Ralph during his earlier visit to the stable, Confessor and Hannibal. Sir Stephen was fortunate in having two of the fastest horses in the stable.

"This one's called Hannibal," said Sir Stephen, unaware that the chief ostler had already taken Alfred on a conducted tour of the stable and introduced him to some of the horses. "You can ride Hannibal and I'll take my favourite steed, Confessor. Get them saddled up for me and I'll be back in a quarter of an hour."

Half an hour later saw Alfred following Sir Stephen through the city gates, each mounted on a mettlesome stallion and making their way into the open country beyond the city. Alfred was a good rider and could control his mount but this war horse took some handling. Hannibal was strong and ever eager to go. Sir Stephen ahead of him on Confessor was obviously a very able rider and frequently let go of the reigns, controlling his mount entirely by the pressure imposed by his knees. He could wheel and turn and even send Confessor **walking** backwards.

A mediaeval knight could not survive in battle without these skills, for one hand would be bearing a shield and the other wielding a weapon. Alfred could not match these manoeuvres but the object of the exercise wasn't to train Alfred to become a knight. It was to exercise the horses. After some good gallops up and down the heath land, they returned to the city. Sir Stephen was gracious in his praise of Alfred's horsemanship.

"Not many pages of your age could handle Hannibal as you've done. I can see that I can safely entrust you to take my horses on exercise. I have other things to see to over the next few days so every morning, I want you to take them out. They like being exercised together so you'll need to ride one and lead the other. So long as they both have a good gallop, they'll keep fit and ready for action."

They returned to the stable where Alfred was left to unsaddle the horses and rub them down. Alfred then returned to the castle, ready to serve up the midday meal. He was relieved to hear that William had had a rather better day with Sir Gilbert.

Alfred had no special duties to perform that afternoon and began to take stock of his situation. One of his prayers was being wonderfully answered. His responsibility to exercise Sir Richard's horses would give him the opportunity to rendezvous with Alice on the Monday. Alfred decided that he could use his free time now to seek out the secret passage that Chronavon had told him about, but wherever should he start looking for this? The words of the clue passed through his mind.

> **'When the sun's beam shines twixt the Griffin and the Lion, Press hard on the hand that the shaft lights upon.'**

Where would he find a griffin and a lion? A griffin wasn't a real animal anyway. Alfred wandered around the passageways of the castle, up and down the steps of the turrets and towers from which the castle could be defended by archers. Alfred returned always to the great hall, the words of the clue echoing through his mind. He looked out of the arrow slits, gazed up among the knights' banners suspended from the ceiling, peered along the row of statues of heraldic beasts ------- **Yes!** , here might be something worth investigating. There was more than one lion there, a stag, a unicorn, a wild boar, some animals Alfred could not identify and three which must have been some sort of dragon or wyvern. There was only one point in the row where a griffin and lion stood adjacent to each other. It was mid-afternoon and the light from an arrow slit behind Alfred fell on one of the statues, a proud unicorn.

"As the sun moves round, this light will pass across all the statues, yes, and in time it will be directed between the lion and the griffin," mused Alfred. His heart started to beat with excitement at the thought of being on the edge of deciphering the clue. Alfred estimated that the sun would reach the lion in about half an hour. There was no point in just waiting there. This would look suspicious and the sight of an idle page might lead to some unwanted work being put his way. Alfred wandered off, intent on returning at the crucial time. He had no watch. This was one of the items he had left in the chest in the cathedral chapter house when he changed into mediaeval clothes. Alfred just had to judge the time. As is usually the case when one is anxiously awaiting the fulfilment of an event with no time piece to moderate one's impatience, Alfred underestimated the time.

He must have walked past those statues two or three times before the sun's rays actually shone on the lion. A few minutes later, the beam passed between the statues of the griffin and the lion to fall on the wall of what would otherwise have been a very dark comer of that great hall.

Alfred made his way to the wall where the suns beams were now shining. The light revealed that there was a painting of a figure on the wall, some ancient king, which would normally have been almost invisible in the subdued light of that poorly illuminated chamber. Alfred began to tingle with excitement as he noticed that the main part of the beam of sunlight was directed on to the hand of this figure. Alfred looked around him.

Alfred regards the statues of heraldic beasts,
standing in the great hall of Hereford Castle,
one of which is illuminated by a sunbeam
from an arrow slit.

There was no one nearby who could have seen into that normally dark comer. Alfred pushed hard on the hand and he felt it give. It was not so much stiff but very heavy to move, but as Alfred continued to apply pressure, the large stone on which the figure had been painted began to swivel and a space opened up, large enough for Alfred to squeeze through.

Alfred found himself in the secret passage that Chronavon had told him existed in the castle. It was dark but not completely dark. Enough light entered that passageway through cracks in the wall and holes in the ceiling above for one to be able to navigate one's way along that passage. Alfred noted that the stone he had just rotated had a handle inside which would enable it to be pulled rather than pushed open by someone trying to get out of the passage from within. Alfred pushed the stone back into place behind him and started to explore this new discovery he had made.

As he walked along the passage, his eyes became adapted to the low light level. He found that the cracks in the walls were sufficient to enable him to see different parts of the main hall. Then he began to climb some steps, many, many steps which led him to a new level. As he peered through the cracks at this level, he realised that he was looking into the knights' rooms and into council chambers of varying sizes. Most of the rooms were empty. In one room, a knight was talking to his page. Albert stopped outside what must have been a council chamber where some sort of meeting was in progress. He looked and listened intently to see if he could identify those present.

Earl Simon of Leicester was there. Sitting opposite him was Richard, Earl of Cornwall. On one side of the room sat the Bishops of Worcester and Hereford, and next to them, Thomas Cantilupe, Chancellor of England. Two knights were there also, Sir William of Valence and one of Simon's younger sons, Henry de Montfort.

The Earl of Cornwall was speaking.

"Yes, England is indeed in a perilous state. You're in danger Simon of the barons rising against you. You've done a good job in establishing parliament, Simon. This will temper the power of any future king. There's no point in your jeopardising the rest of your life. Restore the monarchy now that parliament has set a limit to the power any king may wield."

Sir William of Valence spoke next. "We know that you're a man of good council and peace, my Lord Cornwall, but none of us want King Henry to have another opportunity of reneging on solemn and binding promises. He made no secret of the fact that he wanted to rescind Magna Carta! There is no guarantee, even now, that he'll listen to parliament."

Thomas de Cantilupe stood to speak. "Earl Simon, I agree with Richard of Cornwall that you have done well in establishing the institution of parliament. Hitherto, too much power has been wielded by those who can maintain their influence, solely by force of arms, but the strength to wield a broadsword or brandish a battle-axe provides no measure of a person's wisdom and integrity in the matter of ruling and governing people. There are out there now, peasants ploughing the fields who would have the wit and wisdom to govern well should such an opportunity present itself to them. I foresee a time when this will indeed become possible, but the feudal system hasn't yet run its course. The government of this country by men selected purely on their wisdom and integrity is a vision for the distant future.

I agree too with de Valence that King Henry is not to be entrusted again with power to rule, or to put it more appropriately in his case, to misrule. Prince Edward is a different sort of person altogether from his father. Yes, he has all the prowess of being a great knight, but he also has intelligence and wisdom. Earl Simon, do you think that the time is approaching when we should negotiate with Prince Edward to take over the reins of government with the provision that we, whom he may regard as his captors and enemies, are given full indemnity?"

Simon sat pensively nodding as Thomas spoke, but before he could reply, there was a knock at the door, and without being asked to come in, the door burst open, and in walked Sir Gregory de Grossmont, his portly figure barely able to force itself through the portal.

Simon looked distinctly angry. "I was not aware that you had been invited to join the Great Council, Sir Gregory," he said with a distinct tone of annoyance.

Anyone else would have slunk out of that room in shame, but not one of Sir Gregory's ebullience.

"Forgive my intrusion," Gregory said with uncharacteristic contrition, "but we knights think you should listen to us and not just to these stuffy clerics or royal brats," he said looking first towards the bishops and then at Earl Richard of Cornwall. "You're the greatest lord in the land, Earl Simon. Make yourself king and do away with this Henry."

Gregory expressed his own view as if it was a general consensus among the knights, but in reality, no soundings had been taken. Gregory was one of those overbearing people who consider that they may automatically speak for the crowd. Gregory reckoned he could always see both sides to every question, his own view and the wrong one.

Thomas de Cantilupe stood again. "Gregory de Grossmont, you forget that Prince Edward is rightful heir to the throne. The hereditary principle is there to prevent powerful men fighting and squabbling over succession when the leader dies, so weakening a nation's cohesion and reducing its manpower. The man who wins a throne by power of the sword is no more likely to be good ruler than he who inherits the crown. Those who take up the sword to achieve power usually fall by the sword. This is in line with the Bible's teaching where we also read, 'He who exalts himself shall be abased.' "

Gregory de Grossmont was not used to that sort of language but even he had wit enough to know that these words had been spoken by a wise and intelligent man and couldn't be safely ignored.

" 'He who exalts himself shall be abased' just sounds like empty priest talk. What does it mean in normal language, anyway?" Gregory asked.

"It means that he who seeks to make himself great can end up by becoming very, very small," replied Thomas.

"Well," said Sir Gregory, returning to another point at issue, "if heredity is important, and Prince Edward had an accident, you my Lord have as good a claim to the throne as William, Duke of Normandy had in 1066 because you, Lord Simon, are the King's brother-in-law!"

"We do not wish to hear such counsel, my over bold knight. Will you now leave us." snapped Earl Simon.

With the exception of the totally insensitive Sir Gregory, everyone in that chamber was aware of how angry and irritated. Earl Simon was becoming. Irritation and annoyance were in fact, emotions welling up in everyone else present in that council chamber except Sir Gregory.

Sir Gregory always interpreted what he heard as being his preconceived idea of the answer he wanted to hear. Sir Gregory bowed and left the chamber.

"Earl Simon doesn't want to be counselled to arrange an accident for Prince Edward," thought Gregory. "He wants to hear that it's happened. He's sent me out to arrange it."

With Sir Gregory gone, tempers calmed down and the discussion continued a short while longer. Thomas de Cantilupe undertook to spend some time with Edward to ascertain what his priorities might be if he became king, and what his attitude would be to those who had opposed his father and defeated them at the Battle of Lewes. The session closed and the members of the council left the chamber.

Alfred had been fascinated by what he had heard. He carefully descended the steps in that passage and returned to ground level. He cautiously pulled open the secret entrance stone. No one was about in that dark corner of the hall. Alfred was able to emerge from the secret passageway and reclose the stone without being seen.

<u>Chapter 7</u>

Alfred was not in a position to be able to eavesdrop on the conversation which took place when Thomas de Cantilupe visited Prince Edward. However, it is important to record this discourse because it throws much light on the characters of the two men who may be regarded as key characters of English history, every bit as much as Simon de Montfort.

After the council meeting, Thomas made his way to Prince Edward's chamber in one of the turrets of the castle keep. Two knights were seated at a table at the base of the stairs which led up to the Prince's chamber. Edward had reasonable freedom within the castle, but Earl Simon was not unnaturally apprehensive that if not kept under surveillance, Prince Edward might one day escape with calamitous consequences for himself.

Thomas knocked on the door of the Prince's chamber, entered when he heard the Prince's "Come in!", and courteously bowed to the King's son.

Edward motioned Thomas to take a seat. The two often met for discussion, and although on opposing sides of the civil divide which split the country, enjoyed each other's company.

"One day, when this wretched affair is resolved, you will become King," started Thomas. "What are the qualities for which you would like to be remembered."

Edward knew that Thomas would be able to come up with a better set of qualities than he could think of, off the cuff. However, Edward was wise and teachable. He realised that by playing along with Thomas, he might learn from him things which would indeed be useful, should he in fact succeed to the throne. Edward inwardly wondered if he would ever come into his inheritance. He was in the power of his father's enemy, Simon de Montfort. In spite of the strength and leadership qualities of Earl Simon, he had inevitably grown unpopular with the other barons. His father, Henry Ill had been rejected as ruler. The country might be descending into the anarchy which characterised the reign of King Stephen. The ultimate outcome of the situation could be a completely new form of government for the country.

Edward thought for a moment. "It cannot be denied that the kings which are highly esteemed by posterity are the great warlords like Alexander the Great and Charlemagne. I cannot pretend that I wouldn't have some ambitions in that direction. However, beyond that, I would like to be a king who ruled his country so wisely that the people were all prepared to work harmoniously together under the king to secure those good things which were common to the national interest, prosperity, security, a just society and influence with other nations."

"Yes," said Thomas, nodding, that's a good answer, "and that's the sort of country which would exist if men worked for the common good. However, men are not like that. Each man is basically selfish and will therefore be motivated by self-interest. That's why the country is littered with strong castles, occupied by barons with their own private armies. Now that the king is no longer recognised as the overlord who has a right to receive feudal dues of tax and service, each man holds on to his own and only co-operates with his neighbours if a common interest is threatened, such as an invasion from a foreign power."

"A strong king could re-establish the feudal system as it was in the days of the first King William." replied Edward.

"That would be turning the clock back in a way people wouldn't accept. Now that there's a parliament, the people will demand some say in national government. To try to suppress this now would result in many more years of civil war. Future kings must be prepared to accept that to a certain extent, they will have to rule by consent." said Thomas.

Edward nodded. "Yes, I agree. Parliament working with the king can lighten the burden of responsibility the king has to bear and make it much more likely that the people will readily accept the laws and taxes which are needed to run the country. However, we have a parliament now, and the country is still in disarray. Why do you think that might be? Surely, a king is needed to be recognised as the focus of administration, and Earl Simon has removed the king from that rightful position."

Thomas partially agreed with Edward. "Power sharing to ensure fair taxation and good laws is certainly the sensible way ahead. Magna Carta, imposed on John, your grandfather, and the Provisions of Oxford, established by Earl Simon, have provided the basis for power sharing, but the country lacks good laws. Moses stands out as one of the greatest heroes of history because he was a great law giver. Your Plantagenet ancestors have been happy to tax the people, but this has caused discontent because they have not developed a legal system which provides a manifestly fair framework, within which men and women can live their lives. "

"I am well aware that many laws need to be created to provide the framework of which you speak, and also, an acceptable means of ensuring that those

laws are enforced," replied Edward. "For example, a law is required to define the barons' rights to the property they occupy. Otherwise the country will continue to run under the principle that 'might is right' and the barons with the strongest private armies will continue to plunder their neighbours lands. Further, the country will only be weakened if the large estates which define this realm continue to be broken into small units which are hardly self-sufficient.

Also, the wealth of the nation is very much dependent on the trade generated by its merchants but the tunnage and poundage system by which they are taxed is not properly codified so that terrible anomalies exist. Legislation can regularise all this so that England will become a country whose merchants know where they stand with regard to taxation, and who will not be inhibited in expanding the trade and commerce which will build up the nation's wealth.

While you nod in agreement to what I have said so far, Thomas, a prominent churchman like yourself would not approve of laws to limit and reduce the wealth of the church. However, what I see of the church is not so much a holy body, concerned with promoting the Kingdom of God, but rather, a political faction, largely preoccupied with increasing its own wealth. The Pope regards himself as some supra national overlord, and he is able to suck in so much of the nation's wealth into the coffers of Rome because the church in England is all too ready to be subservient to him."

Thomas replied, "You may be surprised that churchman as I am, I do not totally disagree with your attitude to the church. As you know, Pope Clement was papal legate to England before he became supreme pontiff, and in the role of legate, he indeed behaved as if he had supranational authority for directing the affairs of the realm. I am amazed that countries across Europe are prepared to ascribe such enormous authority to the Bishop of Rome. Popes have used excommunication as a political instrument to wield power, rather than a means of curbing sinful excesses. In this way, they have succeeded in creating a clerical feudal system which transcends national boundaries. That became possible because missionaries from Rome continued to pay allegiance to their mother church in Italy and hence, to the Pope, long after the churches they had founded became independent. This should not have been the case in England where a thriving church existed, long before Augustine established his mission centre at Canterbury.

In France, Earl Simon's father, another Simon de Montfort, was commissioned by the Pope to commit acts of extreme barbarism against a sect known as the Albigenses. While it is true that the Albigenses were not completely sound in their doctrines, the quality of their lives was far more Christian than what passes now for Christianity in churches paying homage to Rome.

The persecution they suffered was totally repugnant to all who know the Lord Jesus and the love he has for all men and women, regardless of the faith they hold. His wish is that all should be won to him by love and not by force and brutality. No, the Pope was not motivated by a wish to gently correct any distortions in the doctrine of the Albigenses but by his concern that this sect should not become a threat to the influence of the Roman Church in that part of

France. I know that Earl Simon is not proud of the part played by his father in this, and the affair has made myself and many other churchmen aware that the Church of Rome is motivated to achieve political power rather than genuine spirituality.

No, Edward, I do not totally disagree with your suggestion that the church's wealth may need to be reduced as so much of it finds its way to Rome. I have no doubt that at some time during my career, I shall have a serious fall out with that Church, and perhaps face excommunication!"

The two young men continued their discussion, respecting each other's view points and agreeing on so many matters of church and state. However, while Thomas de Cantilupe remained committed to the cause of Simon de Montfort, an alliance could not be struck between them.

Chapter 8

A task which involved the pages was that of helping their knights put on their armour for weaponry practice. This took place in the tilt yard, just outside the keep. The knights would lumber into the courtyard bearing their shields and armed with broadsword, axe or mace. They would aim token blows at one another as they sought to improve their techniques of warfare and their ability to use their shields as an effective defence.

Sir Gregory was always a spectacle on these occasions as he staggered around in the huge suit of black armour needed to fit his portly frame. Large and powerful though he was, the other knights usually got the better of him because they were more nimble and Gregory was usually suffering from the after effects of heavy drinking.

The pages would be at hand to assist their masters if any adjustment was found to be needed to their armour, or should a knight decide to change the weapon with which he wished to develop his skill.

Sir Gregory invariably brandished a mace. As Alfred watched this knight during one of these sessions, he couldn't help but be reminded of the huge armour of Sir Peter of Thirsk that he'd seen in the armoury on his first day in the castle. It was the same colour and design as Sir Gregory's armour but even larger.

Now, because Alfred has been selected as a very special young person to fulfil a very important mission, my reader may assume that Alfred was a paragon of virtue without an ounce of mischief in him. This was not the case. Since the time that he had discovered the way Gregory mistreated his friend, William, Alfred had been racking his brains to devise some way of avenging the wrongs William had suffered. A mischievous idea came to Alfred's mind.

On the next opportunity that Alfred had to chat with William, he made the suggestion that they could replace the breast and back plates of Sir Gregory's armour with the even larger pieces of Sir Peter and see what Gregory's reaction might be. This would be an easy but risky thing for

William to do for there was no knowing what might befall the page who messed with Sir Gregory. However, William was game for playing this practical joke.

"Sir Gregory is so often in a semi-drunken stupor that he hardly ever thinks or behaves rationally," said William. "When he puts on his armour, he's unlikely to suspect that I have tampered with it. I could very easily go to the armoury when he's sleeping off one of his drinking bouts and arrange to swap round parts of the suit without his realising what I've **done!**

The next day, those present in the tilt yard beheld the bizarre sight of Sir Gregory with the upper half of his body apparently grossly inflated. The visors must have hidden many a smiling face as the other knights worsted Sir Gregory more easily than usual in the mock duels which weapon training involved, as Sir Gregory's outsize armour severely restricted his flexibility of movement. Alfred was puzzled as to how he was able to wear the armour anyway.

Alfred could not wait to hear from William how his knight had reacted when he tried on the armour. They both rocked with laughter as William described how Gregory bewailed the fact that he seemed to shrinking. William told Alfred that Sir Gregory had declared that it was that pestilent priest (Thomas de Cantilupe) saying that anyone who tries to become big can end up by becoming very, very small. Alfred remembered the words he had heard Thomas say to Gregory when Alfred was hiding in the secret passage outside the Council Chamber where Simon de Montfort was meeting with his senior advisers. William tried to recall some of the colourful language that Gregory had used as he rattled within the oversized suit.

"But however did he make the armour fit at all?" asked Alfred.

."Gregory sent me to fill some sacks with straw which could be used to pad out the voids which existed between Gregory's body and the breast and back plates." laughed William. "When we had got the right amount of straw in the sacks, I had to sow them to the webbing and straps inside the armour."

Another wicked idea flashed through Alfred's mind.

"Next time Gregory is slumbering off his intake of ale, cut the sacks free from Sir Peter's armour, return it to its rightful place in the armoury, and sow the sacks back into Sir Gregory's real armour."

William thought that this was a capital idea and both boys laughed until the tears ran down their faces at the prospect of what Gregory's reaction might be when he tried on his own armour which would seem far too small while padded out with sacks of straw. I will leave my readers to surmise themselves the hilarity which William had to disguise as Sir Gregory gradually came to the realisation that he had grown back to his right size and that he could make the armour fit again by getting William to cut out the sacks of straw. Sir Gregory never did find the true explanation for his apparent shrinkage and re-inflation.

Alfred encountered Sir Gregory again a little later that week in a most unexpected situation. Alfred was again exploring the secret passage which he was able to enter in the comer of the great hall. The entrance was partially hidden by the giant statues of heraldic beasts. As he went by the knights' chambers, he peered through the crack in the wall behind Sir Gregory's room. He could see his friend William, busy cleaning Sir Gregory's armour, but there was no sign of the obese knight.

Some way further down the passage, Alfred was conscious of a voice which he recognised as Sir Gregory's but sounding more muffled and quiet than usual. He peered through one of the many cracks which allowed sufficient light into that passage to enable a person to walk safely, provided he stepped carefully. There, in a small room, he could see Sir Gregory plotting something with three of the most evil looking varlets that Alfred had ever seen. The words were indistinct but Sir Gregory seemed to be implying that Simon de Montfort wanted Prince Edward to encounter some sort of fatal accident and that they would be richly rewarded if they co-operated with Sir Gregory to bring about this event. Alfred was unable to ascertain from the hushed discussion, the means which was to be used to bring about this calamity but the time this nefarious deed was to take place was repeated several times - nightfall on the following Thursday.

Then there followed an argument which seemed to be about money. These villains were not prepared to do anything without some payment in advance. After several moments of hushed but heated discussion, Sir Gregory reluctantly handed over three bags which Alfred realised must have contained the payment on account.

Alfred's mind raced as he returned down the passageway. Today was Sunday. He was meeting Alice at the thicket outside Hereford at midday on the morrow. Three days later, Prince Edward would come to an untimely end unless some means could be found of getting him out of the castle. There was no chance of this being achieved unless Alfred could, at the very least, communicate privately with Prince Edward. It appeared to be quite impossible for one of the most menial servants in the castle to be able to approach, let alone have a secret conversation with, a closely guarded royal prisoner.

<u>Chapter 9</u>

The day after Alfred had gone into service at the castle, Alice woke with a similar feeling of excitement to that which Alfred had experienced the previous day. Margaret had looked up some dresses which had fitted her when she was younger and which were considerably more attractive than the one which Alice had chosen from the chest in Hereford Cathedral Chapter House. Alice selected the one she liked best and Margaret made the few alterations necessary for it to be a really good fit. Margaret's friend, Elaine, arrived at midday, complete with an extra horse for Alice and a soldier from Lady Mortimer's garrison to escort them safely back to Wigmore.

After a meal, Alice bade her farewells to Ralph and Margaret and mounted the palfrey which was to bear her on the journey. Although an experienced horsewoman, Alice had never before ridden side saddle but she soon got used to this mode of riding. The soldier who accompanied them was very taciturn but it was reassuring to have an escort on a journey at a period in history where there was very little disincentive to crime. There was hardly any prospect of a highway robber being apprehended and brought to justice.

Elaine was a very pleasant travelling companion. She was an attractive woman in her mid-thirties who was very protective of her young charge. Elaine asked Alice about herself and Alice used the cover story advised by Chronavon, that she had come from a village called Hillington, many miles from there, but had had to leave when it was burnt down during fighting. Elaine expressed her sympathy and spoke of how often she had heard similar stories from young people who had been displaced as a result of the violence and warfare which characterised the time in which they lived. Realising that Alice was a stranger to those parts, Elaine took great trouble to point out landmarks on the route to Wigmore, should she ever find herself isolated and away from the castle and need to navigate her way to safety.

After a pleasant ride of eleven miles or so, Wigmore Castle came into sight. Alice heard the shrill blast of a trumpet sounding from the battlements. They were expected, and this was a sentry signalling that they had been sighted. They rode up the slope to the castle, through the gate which could be secured by lowering the portcullis in times of danger, and out into the courtyard.

An elegantly dressed lady in a long sleeved gown and a wimple came out to meet them from a tower opposite the main castle gate. Alice and Elaine dismounted and the lady hugged Elaine, her lady in waiting. Alice guessed that this was the Lady Maud Mortimer, a truly lovely and gracious lady. Elaine introduced her charge to Lady Maud who beamed at Alice and held out her hand for her to kiss.

"And how is my Lord, Prince Edward?" enquired Lady Maud.

Alice had to explain that they had no reason to believe that he was anything but well, but that Alice herself had not been able to see the Prince. She explained to Lady Maud that her friend was actually in Hereford Castle and that she had arranged to meet him just outside Hereford on Monday to gain first hand news of the Prince's welfare.

Wigmore Castle c 1270

"That is well," nodded Lady Maud and she led the way back into the tower from which she had emerged a short time earlier. She directed Elaine to show Alice her room.

Alice and Elaine rode into the courtyard of
Wigmore Castle to be greeted by Lady Maud
Mortimer

"As we know that you're going to be a royal messenger, Lady Maud wants you to have very special accommodation," explained Elaine, leading Alice up a flight of steps to a small but lovely looking room with a small window overlooking the countryside. The bed was a considerable improvement on the one she had slept in at the home of Ralph and Margaret. It had a proper mattress and delicately embroidered blankets. A table by the wall supported an earthenware bowl and a ewer of cold water.

"I'm sure you'll want to freshen up after our long ride," said Elaine, gesturing towards the table with the bowl and ewer. "I'll shortly send up a maid to conduct you to the refectory were food is being prepared for us."

Alice sprinkled water over her face and dried her hands and face with a linen towel which had been draped over a chair standing next to the wash table. After a few minutes, a serving maid of about twenty years of age came to the room and escorted Alice to the refectory. Here, a long table was laid with bowls of steaming vegetables and meat which had been sliced and placed on large wooden platters in the centre of the table. Lady Maud was already seated at the end of the table and motioned Alice to sit next to her. Soon, all the places around the table were filled and the meal commenced. Alice looked around the table and realised that there were only a few men. These must have been knights who garrisoned the castle. There were a number of elegant looking ladies and several young girls whom Alice judged to be about the same age as herself. A minstrels' gallery was located high on the wall above where they were eating and music was provided by a trio, two female singers accompanied by a lutenist.

Lady Maud explained to Alice that the ladies were her entourage and the girls of Alice's age were their maids in waiting. She explained that there were very few men available to defend the castle because most of the soldiers were away with her husband, Sir Roger, fighting on the Welsh Marches. She introduced Alice to the assembled company as one who would be able to bring them news of Prince Edward.

Alice spent a very pleasant three days at Wigmore. Life seemed to move at a very leisurely pace. Her duties as maid in waiting to Lady Maud were very light and the other maids were a very happy and lively bunch. They made Alice feel very welcome as a new friend. She discovered that most of the girls were local and had been recruited for service from the local villages. A lot of time was spent playing ball games or hopscotch in the castle yard. There was a rotation of serving maids as some left the castle to spend a few days with their parents while replacements came to the castle from other local villages. Alice found herself to be an object of sympathy among others in the castle as a young lady who had been left orphaned when her village had been burnt in the fighting, and everybody was sensitive enough not to probe further into Alice's background.

As Monday approached, thought had to be given to Alice's return to Hereford to meet up with Alfred. Lady Maud considered that it would be dangerous for Alice to travel alone, but she was desperate to know how to provide an escort. Several soldiers had been taken sick over the past couple of days, and this had left the garrison well below the level to which Sir Roger would allow Lady Maud to let it fall when he was away.

Alice had seen no source of danger when she had ridden to Wigmore from Hereford and she considered that she would not be a target for highway robbers if she appeared to be no more than a farm girl, riding an unpretentious horse. Lady Maud was reluctant to allow Alice to ride out alone, but so anxious was she for news of Prince Edward that Alice prevailed. Alice was given some hempen homespun garments of the type worn by girls from the poor villages. The skirt was short enough for Alice to be able to ride astride her horse. Alice insisted that this was important, because she would have been at a great disadvantage riding side saddle, should the need arise for her to ride fast to escape danger. Alice was provided with an unpretentious looking palfrey equipped solely with saddle and reigns. There were no lordly accoutrements to divulge the secret that this horse came from a noble household. Although Minerva, the name of her palfrey, was not much to look at, appearances can be deceptive. Alice was assured that Minerva was both fast and strong and, when carrying a girl of Alice's weight, she could out ride many a stronger horse, carrying a fully grown man.

Lady Maud and Alice's new friends stood at the castle gate to wave her goodbye as she set out early on Monday morning to make the return trip to Hereford. The journey was uneventful. Alice had taken good note of the landmarks which Elaine had pointed out on the outward journey and arrived at the thicket where the rendezvous had been arranged, well before midday. Alfred was already there. Nearby, he had tethered two impressive war steeds, Hannibal and Confessor, whom he was taking for their daily exercise.

Alfred and Alice had so much they wanted to tell each other about their recent experiences, but the business in hand had to take priority. Alfred reported that Edward was currently well, but that an attempt was to be made on his life, Thursday night. This meant that they had to formulate a plan for Edward to escape. He told Alice that he would meet her there with Edward at midday on Thursday, and together they could return to

Wigmore before they realised in Hereford Castle that the Prince had gone. Alfred spoke confidently of this plan to Alice, but inwardly he was in a turmoil. At that point in time, he had not even worked out how he was going to communicate with Prince Edward, let alone, get this closely guarded prisoner away from the castle and his guards to the thicket at the appointed time. Alice left to return to Wigmore in high elation. Alfred returned to the castle in a state of despair.

Chapter 10

Alfred rode Hannibal back to Hereford Castle, leading Confessor by the reigns. As he settled these war horses back in their stalls, anxious thoughts churned over in Alfred's mind. He had the means for Edward to escape at his disposal and a safe house was ready to receive him once he had been able to leave the confines of Hereford, but however was Alfred going to communicate with the Prince and devise a way of his leaving the castle? Whatever would he say to Alice when he met her at the thicket on Thursday if he was without the Prince? If he failed in his part of the task that he had accepted from Chronavon, the whole history of England would be changed! He and Alice may never come to be born at a later period in time!

Alfred was a young person with an optimistic frame of mind and he had not completely given up hope that something would turn up before Thursday to resolve this dilemma. What should he do now? Alfred decided he would do what he always did when confronted with life's problems. He would turn to prayer. The answers Alfred had received to his prayers were not always what Alfred had expected, but as he looked back to the times in his young life when he had resorted to prayer in crisis situations, he realised that things had happened in relation to those crises which could only be real answers to the prayers he had offered. He then thought back to the words Chronavon had spoken on that morning when he had first appeared to Alfred and Alice,

"You have not been selected at
random for this task. The most
important thing of all is that you are
both very prayerful young people."

Alfred entered the castle keep and made his way to the chapel. It was empty. It usually was. Alfred knelt in front of the crude altar and closed his eyes. He remembered how God had already answered some of his prayers.

"Thank you God for the thrill of being able to experience this exciting time in history." he prayed silently, the thoughts passing through Alfred's mind but no words issuing from his lips. "Thank you God for showing me the entrance to the secret passageway in the castle. Thank you that Prince Edward has friends outside the castle who want to help him. Thank you that you have made it easy for me to have the horses that Prince Edward will need to escape. But God, all this will mean nothing if I cannot speak to Prince Edward in private. You've put me in this place God, and I'm only a page with no influence over anybody else. I'm too lowly a person to be allowed to speak to a prince, and anyway, there are always guards around the Prince who would keep me from speaking to him. Unless you help me God, I'm going to fail you in the task you've given me. The whole history of the world is going to change from your plan and it will all be my fault. Please help me God."

Tears started to roll down Alfred's cheeks as he continued to offer silent prayers. He opened his eyes. There standing by the altar was none other than the Chancellor of England, Thomas de Cantilupe, watching Alfred.

"You seem to be upset young man," said Thomas kindly. "Can you talk to me about your problem? Can I help?"

What was Alfred to say? Here was one of the most important men in England, a trusted advisor of Simon de Montfort who was holding the Prince in captivity. What could Alfred say?

"Prince Edward has many friends in England who are concerned for his welfare," began Alfred. Alfred was speaking the truth but he was not saying anything that Thomas did not already know. "Because I work in the castle," continued Alfred, "they think that I can take messages to him and he can send messages back through me, but I'm only a page boy. I can't speak privately with Prince Edward. He's always so well guarded, and in any case, a page boy has no place in the company of a Prince."

"That's only a man-made convention," answered Thomas. "We're all equal in human dignity in the sight of God."

Thomas continued, "Did you know that I saw you, even before you became a page boy at the castle?"

Alfred looked puzzled.

"You were there in the Cathedral when I preached on Sunday."

Alfred was amazed that someone of Thomas's standing should have noticed him among all those people.

"I must admit that I first noticed the very attractive girl who was sitting next to you then." Thomas smiled. "Yes, even a priest like me who has taken vows of celibacy, is allowed to appreciate the beauty God has created in women. That young lady will certainly grow up to become a very beautiful woman. Is she one of your friends who is concerned for the Prince's welfare?"

Alfred nodded.

"It's so unusual to meet a young person who knows and uses the power of prayer. I'm so glad to be able to meet with you and speak with a prayerful young person, here in the chapel. What's your name?"

"I'm called Alfred."

"Alfred, I think God has sent me to be a means of answering your prayer. Come with me and we'll see if Prince Edward is about."

With that, Thomas made his way to the door of the chapel while Alfred hastily rose from his knees and followed him. They went down the stairs that led to the main hall and up another spiral stairway which led to the turret where Prince Edward was accommodated. Two knights were lounging on chairs on the landing outside Prince Edward's room. They stood when they realised that the Chancellor of England was approaching.

"This young man would like an audience with the Prince." stated Thomas, speaking in the confident way of those used to exercising authority. "He won't be there long. When he comes out, direct him to the main hall."

Thomas knocked at the door and entered when he heard the Prince's voice, inviting him in.

"This young page is called Alfred," said Thomas as he introduced him to the Prince. "Your friends in England are anxious to hear of your wellbeing and this young man can bring them word. I will depart now and leave you both to have a chat."

Thomas left the room and closed the door behind him. Alfred had never been in the company of a prince before, let alone the heir to the throne of England. Edward motioned him to take a seat. Alfred bowed awkwardly and sat down on the chair opposite the Prince.

"I am getting out of touch with what's going on in the world outside," started Edward, "so I welcome someone like you who can bring me up to date. Is Earl Simon really doing the wonderful job in running the country which he obviously thinks he is? Are all the people happily paying their taxes and the nobles all behaving themselves? I very much doubt it."

"I cannot tell you much about all that," replied Alfred, speaking quietly so that his voice could not be heard by those sitting outside, "but I can tell you something about what is happening inside the castle which you really have to know about. I overheard Sir Gregory de Grossmont making plans to involve you in an accident which he hopes will kill you!"

Prince Edward raised his eyebrows and lowered his voice as he replied, for the same reason that Alfred had spoken softly.

"An assassination attempt no less, but Gregory is never very subtle in anything he does. I doubt that he would succeed, especially now that I've been given advance notice and will be on my guard whenever he's about."

Alfred was amazed at how calmly the Prince had taken the news that his life was in danger. "Thank you, indeed, for warning me, young man. Pray, when is this accident supposed to happen?" asked Edward.

"As I was in hiding, I could only just hear what Sir Gregory was saying to his accomplices, but Thursday nightfall was mentioned several times," replied Alfred.

The Prince nodded his head, thoughtfully.
 "Three days' time," he mused

"Your friend, Lady Maud Mortimer, wants you to escape to the safety of her castle," continued Alfred. "I can get the horse you would need to get there, but however can we get you out of this place?"

"Lady Maud?" enquired the Prince at the mention of a familiar name, "and Sir Roger, is he all right?"

The welfare of his friends seemed at that moment more important to the Prince than his urgent need to plan an escape.

"Roger Mortimer is on the Marches, fighting the Welsh who are stealing his cattle," Alfred informed the Prince.

"Ah, it is ever the same with the Welsh," said the Prince. "Before the disaster at Lewes put me in Simon de Montfort's power, I spent more time organising the forces in my border castles to chase the Welsh back where they belonged than almost anything else I did. Those Welsh marauders need to be taught a lesson. But that's something for another day. You say you can provide me with a horse, a fast horse?"

"Among the best in the castle stables," replied Alfred. "As a page, I regularly exercise my master, Sir Stephen of Selby's horses, and they are both fast, but how can it be arranged for you to have one of these and a clear run from Hereford?"

"Let me think," said the Prince, and he leaned back in his chair gazing at the roof of his turret room for a few minutes. Then suddenly he sat up and continued the conversation.

"My captivity here is not as irksome as you may think," the Prince explained to Alfred. "Everybody from Earl Simon down is aware that it is not unlikely that I shall become King myself one day, and no one wants to treat the heir to the throne so badly that he becomes an implacable enemy. Provided that I'm in the company of a few trusted knights to guard me from escaping, I can go pretty well anywhere I please. When I ride out with these knights, I am mounted on a jade, while they have fast war horses. If I could arrange things so the knights I'm with tire their horses and then switch to one of your master's fine horses, I could out ride them and make the safety of the Mortimers' castle. Where could you be with Sir Stephen's horse during the next few days?"

"I'm meeting my friend Alice at midday on Thursday morning at the large thicket, about a mile or so to the north of Hereford."

"I know it well," interrupted the Prince.

"Alice is a girl, the same age as myself," continued Alfred. "She will be riding from Wigmore Castle on one of Lady Mortimer's horses and will be able to guide us to Wigmore if you can throw off the knights who guard you."

Prince Edward laughed.

"That's great," he said. "You have planned things well. As someone who has spent so much of his time in the Marches, I know the way to Wigmore well, but your young friend will be good company for us on our escape from here. I can arrange to be in the meadows with my knight companions soon after the midday meal," continued the Prince, using a euphemism to describe his guards. "Stay hidden under the cover provided by the thicket until you see us arrive. Then arrange for your friend, Alice, to come into view and then return to you in the thicket.

A girl on a horse won't arouse suspicion among the knights who are with me but it will be a sign to me that all is ready as planned. I'll then devise a stratagem to tire my friend's horses while keeping mine fresh. When I'm confident that I can out ride them, I'll race to the thicket. When you see me approaching at speed, come into view with the horse you have procured for me. I'll change horses and we'll be away."

The Prince sounded so confident and the plan seemed so simple. Surely, nothing could go wrong.

"And now my good page," said the Prince, raising his voice to a level at which it might be heard outside, "I'm sure you have duties to attend to. Thank you for bringing me news of the friends of whom I have heard so little since being in Hereford."

The Prince opened the door so that Alfred could leave. The two knights were still lounging on the chairs outside.

"Do visit me again at the end of next week if there is any more news of my poor sick cousin. I hope he'll recover soon."

The knights registered that Alfred must have spent his time with Prince in small talk touching family matters. Alfred made his way down to the great hall, his mood, now one of elation in stark contrast to the way he had felt earlier that day.

Chapter 11

Alfred felt on tenterhooks right through the Wednesday. He could hardly conceal his anxiety as he impatiently awaited the Thursday. His friend William sensed that Alfred was anticipating some momentous event, but Alfred couldn't even share the cause of his trepidation with his special friend and this added to the stress experienced by Alfred that Wednesday.

Thursday dawned at last and after clearing away the remains of breakfast the knights and lords had devoured that morning, Alfred proceeded with his regular task of exercising Sir Richard's horses. They were in fine fettle. Alfred saddled them both and proceeded to the thicket which rendezvous was to be the focal point of the escape planned for the day. Alfred moved the horses at a leisurely pace, a trot rather than a gallop or canter. It was essential that he conserved their energy for the mission they would have to fulfil in the early afternoon.

Alfred reached the thicket well before midday and tethered the horses to graze in the pasture behind the thicket, well out of sight of the rolling grasslands which stretched back to the city. It was from these meadows that Prince Edward would have to outwit or outmanoeuvre his guards if he was to outride them on an inferior horse and gain the thicket sufficiently ahead of his pursuers to change his mount and further his escape. This was going to be the crucial event in ensuring the success of the venture.

Alice arrived sometime later but just before midday. She had ridden hard from Wigmore to make the deadline and her slight palfrey was in a lather. The palfrey was set to graze with the war horses and recover from her morning's exertions. Alfred and Alice took up positions in the thicket where they would be well concealed from the meadow land which swept towards them from the city walls. Half an hour went by, then an hour. Alfred and Alice became increasingly anxious that the Prince had not been able to make the arrangements which were essential to the plan. Then they saw the sight for which they bad been waiting. In the distance, four horsemen could be seen leaving the city. Alice went to the back of the thicket, untethered her palfrey and rode into the open so that she was in full view of the horsemen coming in her direction. A distant young girl on a horse was of no significance to Prince Edward's guards, but the Prince saw the signal and knew that it was time to test his own ingenuity.

The knights who had been charged with guarding the Prince that afternoon were one of Earl Simon's younger sons, Sir Henry de Montfort, Sir Peter of Falconbridge and Sir Gregory de Grossmont no less, mounted on Conqueror. Henry de Montfort and Peter of Falconbridge also bad fine mounts, but Edward was riding his frail looking palfrey, Duchess.

"You have a fine mount," Prince Edward said to the young de Montfort. "I would say that he looks the finest horse I have seen in the stables here at Hereford."

Edward knew that that remark would provoke Sir Gregory who was justifiably proud of Conqueror and wasted no opportunity for extolling his horse's virtues.

"There's no finer steed in the land than my Conqueror here," declared Sir Gregory, patting his raven black horse's flowing mane.

"How are you going to prove that," challenged the Prince. "I would wager fifty crowns that both Peter and Henry's horses could beat yours by fifty yards in a race over half a mile."

Sir Gregory was never one to duck a wager he was confident of winning.

"You're on," he declared "but we're not going to be fooled by all riding off and leaving you alone. I will first race Sir Peter and then Sir Henry. You're going to be fifty crowns poorer tonight my young prince. Where's the course going to be?"

Edward pointed to a distant tree in the direction of the thicket. "There and back," he said.

The race between Sir Gregory and Sir Peter was duly started and the two horses charged off. Although he carried the bulky frame of Sir Gregory and hence, very much more weight than Sir Peter's mount, Sir Gregory's pride in Conqueror was fully justified. He reached the distant tree only just ahead of Sir Peter, but he had great stamina and increased his lead all the way back to Sir Henry and Prince Edward at the starting point. Sir Gregory exhibited childlike glee at the ease of his victory.

"Now let's see you race Sir Henry," challenged the Prince.

"Conqueror needs just a few minutes to recover," declared Sir Gregory. "He's been ridden hard and Sir Henry's horse is completely fresh."

"If your horse were anything like as great as you claim him to be, he should still be fresh as a daisy," said the Prince. "A horse that is clapped out after just one fast gallop is no good to anyone."

"All right," said Sir Gregory. "Just two minutes
and I'll take on Sir Henry."

The second race was started, and this was a much
greater challenge for Conqueror as he raced
against a fresh steed. However, Conqueror was
a really game horse, and he kept neck and neck
with Sir Henry's mount for most of the race and
just managed to pull ahead at the end, arriving
back fractionally ahead of his rival.

Sir Gregory was flushed with his success.
"There's not a horse in the land could beat my
Conqueror," boasted Sir Gregory "You owe me
fifty crowns, my young Prince," he gloated, "and
I want to be paid tonight."

Sir Gregory was wanting his payment before the
Prince had his 'accident'"

"All right," said the Prince, "You won your bet
fair and square, but I wasn't really impressed
with the way any of your horses ran. With a
twenty yard start, even my Duchess would have
beaten you all."

Sir Gregory looked scornfully at the Prince's frail looking palfrey. "I could give that old hack a fifty yard start and Conqueror would overhaul her before she had gone another fifty."

"All right," said the Prince, "I'll take you on. Double or quits."

"Agreed," said Sir Gregory. So confident was he of victory that he did not demand recovery time for Conqueror. The Prince took up a starting position which was agreed to be near enough fifty yards ahead of Sir Gregory and the race was off. Sir Gregory had underestimated the spirit of Duchess. Duchess began to gain on the tiring Conqueror. Alfred and Alice had been observing what was happening. They had got their horses ready and brought them out into the open. Duchess did not turn at the tree but the Prince urged her on .towards the thicket. When he reached the point where Alfred and Alice were waiting, he nimbly jumped from Duchess and mounted Confessor. The three of them set off at a good gallop. The chase was on. Sir Gregory was barely twenty yards behind them and they could hear him swearing as he realised what was happening and how he had been tricked.

Gregory's tired horse could not keep up with fresh mounts, and the foul expletives of Sir Gregory became fainter as they accelerated away and he was soon not only out of earshot but out of sight. The three of them rode fast, but Prince Edward and Alfred were careful to see that they kept abreast of Alice's slower mount. Although Alice's horse had had a rest, she had had a hard ride in the morning and after just a few miles, she began to noticeably slow up. They reached a shallow stream and stopped to decide how to proceed.

Alice knew that her horse was holding them back and she told the men folk to take their horses down the stream for a couple of hundred yards, and then emerge from the stream to continue their journey to Wigmore.

(Alfred had explained to Alice that the Prince was not in need of a guide to reach the Mortimers' castle.)

In this way, their pursuers would lose their tracks and would have no way of knowing to which of the many border castles which belonged to the Prince or his friends, they would be heading. Alice on the other hand would cross the stream and hide up in the first village she came to.

The riders looked back at the wide swathe of trampled grass which had been left by three hard driven horses and realised that if their pursuers saw only a single track on the side of the stream which was directly opposite, they would guess

Prince Edward, Alfred and Alice are
pursued by Sir Gregory

that they had separated and would look for tracks emerging from another part of the stream. Alice had already anticipated that problem.

"When I reach the village." she said, "I will return to the stream to leave a second track of trampled grass and leave a third track as I return to the village."

The plan was a good one but the men were unwilling for Alice to expose herself to the risk of being caught by the pursuing soldiers who by now would have been mobilised to chase after the Prince. Alfred suggested that he and she should exchange horses and he would leave the false trail. Alice was adamant that she should do this.

"Sir Gregory already knows what you look like," she advised "and I wouldn't fancy your chances if he gets hold of you, Alfred. However no one from Hereford Castle knows me except Ralph so I should be safe."

Time was of the essence and further argument would have only wasted this valuable commodity. Alice's plan was accepted. The Prince on

Confessor and Alfred on Hannibal waded down the stream while Alice crossed the stream directly and rode on to the next village about a mile further on. She returned to the stream and back again to the village to leave a three horse width, false trail. This took a little while as her horse was now very tired.

Alice looked back and could see a distant troop of horsemen coming in her direction. There was no obvious hiding place in the village. Her horse was exhausted and could go no further. Soon, the soldiers would be upon her. It was now Alice's turn to recourse to prayer. She prayed first and foremost that Prince Edward and Alfred would make the safety of Wigmore Castle. She then declared her own predicament and prayed for some means of deliverance from the jeopardy in which she now found herself as the soldiers got ever closer to the village.

A shrill voice called,
"Hallo Alice, fancy seeing you here."

It was Philippa, one of the maids from Wigmore Castle. She lived in this village and had a few days leave to spend at home. Alice explained the situation in which she now found herself. Everybody at Wigmore had known about the errand which had been entrusted to Alice, and Philippa was glad that she was now in a position to help.

"We can hide the horse in the shed at the back of our house," she said. "It's quite big and has been used to stabling horses before. You come home and have a wash and change into one of my dresses so that you won't look as if you have just been riding. I will rub down the horse and get him some food."

They went into Philippa's house and her mum readily co-operated in providing Alice with the clothes which would change her appearance. No sooner had Philippa returned from seeing to the horse and had Alice slipped on her dress when the troop of soldiers, led by Sir Gregory, reached the village. There was no clear trail to follow through the hard ground of the village, and they proceeded through, expecting to be able to pick up the trail on the other side. On failing to find any trail, they returned several minutes later, suspecting that their quarry may have been hiding in the village. The two girls, perhaps rather foolishly, came out from the house to see what was going on. Although now in different clothes which were not suitable for riding, Alice's long fair hair was very distinctive, and this feature of the girl who had ridden out of the thicket was remembered by Sir Gregory.

"Has anybody ridden through this village this afternoon," he asked looking suspiciously at Alice.

"Two men and a girl rode through about an hour ago, but I didn't see which way they went," volunteered Philippa. "They may have gone on to Marlbrook, or Aulden or Wharton," she added, giving the names of three nearby villages.

Sir Gregory ordered the soldiers to see if there were any horses around which showed signs of recently being hard ridden. The soldiers reported a number of horses, but none of them were war horses and none looked as if they'd been ridden recently. They'd noticed the palfrey in the shed behind Philippa's house but Philippa had done a good job in rubbing her down and there were no obvious signs of her day's exertions.

Sir Gregory looked once again suspiciously at Alice. The fact that she had long fair hair like the girl who had ridden off with the Prince was not conclusive evidence that she was indeed the same person. Anyway, it was the Prince and not some peasant girl they wanted. There were any number of castles in the area where the Prince could find a safe refuge. Sir Gregory had no alternative but to forlornly return to Hereford, empty handed.

Later that evening, Alice safely reached Wigmore Castle, much to the relief of Alfred and the Prince who had arrived there earlier in the afternoon amid great rejoicing. The castle was more strongly garrisoned than when Alice had left, for some of Sir Roger's men at arms had returned to bring news of the situation on the Welsh border.

Chapter 12

The following morning, the Prince held his first council of war. He first took stock of the intelligence provided by Sir Roger Mortimer's soldiers who had returned to Wigmore to reinforce its over stretched garrison.

The Prince had discovered that the Earl of Gloucester who had previously been a great supporter of Simon de Montfort had fallen out with the Earl of Leicester. Gilbert de Clare, Earl of Gloucester, had taken offence at, among other things, the high handed way Simon de Montfort had cancelled for no good reason, the grand tournament which Gilbert had carefully organised at Dunstable. The Earl of Gloucester was now with Sir Roger Mortimer in the Welsh border region at Ludlow Castle.

The Prince was very much the young general.
"We will join up with Gloucester and Mortimer at Ludlow," he declared, "and then march on de Montfort at Hereford. We must prevent the reinforcements which de Montfort's son, Simon

the younger, is raising in the south of England from joining this Earl of Leicester. Much of Simon's backing comes from London and Bristol. If we can hold the Severn crossings and keep him in the west, we'll cut him off from this support."

Meanwhile, Simon de Montfort was in a state of some disarray in Hereford. He had no idea where his son, the younger Simon de Montfort, might be or when the reinforcements would arrive. These were desperately needed, now that Prince Edward was on the loose and organising a campaign against him. Not only were Simon's intelligence services unable to inform him of his son's movements, but they could give him no idea as to the whereabouts of Prince Edward. De Montfort moved from Hereford to the border country where he attempted to gain help from Llewellyn, Prince of Wales, but the best he received was no more than a few hundred foot soldiers. They were good border guerrillas but they were lightly armed and not familiar with the way warfare was waged on English soil. De Montfort returned to Hereford where he realised that he must at all costs cross the Severn to regain a foothold in the main part of

England. Prince Edward had already deployed troops at most of the bridges and fords to prevent Simon from crossing the Severn, but he managed to cross the river at Kempsey, a manor held by one of his supporters, the Bishop of Worcester.

Having crossed the Severn, he made his way to Evesham where he took up a defensive position and awaited the reinforcements he hoped that his son, Simon the younger, would have raised. Throughout this manoeuvring, King Henry was moved about with Simon's army, enabling Simon to pretend that the forces he deployed were fighting in the name of the King rather than himself, and they therefore marched under the royal standard to add weight to this false claim.

Meanwhile, Prince Edward's larger army closed in on Evesham. He sent Roger Mortimer to hold the bridge over the Avon in the south to prevent Simon's force escaping in that direction while Edward with the Earl of Gloucester continued their advance. A mediaeval army on the march, led by its mounted knights bearing their brightly coloured banners and escutcheons, was a wondrous sight to behold.

From the tower of Evesham Abbey, de Montfort saw this force approaching and as the standard bearer in the van was carrying the royal coat of arms, three leopards or, passant et regardant, on a field gules, he believed at first that these were the desperately needed reinforcements being brought to him by his son. He was to be disappointed in this hope, for Prince Edward marched under the royal standard.

Simon now realised that his cause was hopeless. He urged his son, Henry de Montfort, and the noble, Hugh Despenser, to escape while they still had the chance but they refused, declaring their loyalty to Simon.

Prince Edward's army continued its march in impressive marshal array, the armoured knights in the van. When they came within a longbow's range, the archers came forward between the knights' horses leading the advance, and fired a flight of arrows at de Montfort's army. They then retreated a few paces to be behind the knights, so gaining the protection afforded by the armour worn by the knights ahead of them from the answering salvo.

De Montfort, with a smaller number of knights, had deployed most of these around the aged King Henry, and they therefore provided little protection to the lightly armed foot soldiers ahead of them who suffered terrible casualties from the lethal flights of arrows which steadily descended on them as Edward's army advanced. When no more than two hundred yards from de Montfort's force, the knights of Edward's army charged and the smaller number of knights in the vanguard of de Montfort's force moved forward to counter this charge.

Among these was Sir Gregory de Grossmont who rode at the Prince to engage him in single combat. This time, it was not a knight suffering from the effects of the previous night's heavy drinking who charged the Prince, but a completely sober, powerful and experienced man at arms, eager to expiate his shame in allowing the Prince to escape from his charge. Edward, alert as ever, saw him coming and parried Grossmont's crashing mace with his shield, striking back with a well-aimed blow of his broadsword. The two knights continued their duel, displaying expert horsemanship as Sir Gregory wheeled and turned Conqueror while the Prince similarly manoeuvred his mount to avoid losing any advantage that the greater range of a broadsword might have over the close range superiority of the mace. The Prince had much the better of their early exchange of blows. Then disaster struck. A spike on Sir Gregory's mace somehow caught in the handle of the Prince's sword, wresting it from his hand. The sword was flung several yards away from the sparring knights. With his hand free to use the reigns and all his attention concentrated on using his shield to parry the frenzied blows that Gregory aimed at him, Prince Edward was able retain his posture and avoid a fatal blow. However, without an offensive weapon, Edward could not have maintained his defence indefinitely.

Prince Edward encounters Sir Gregory
de Grossmont

Alfred and Alice had followed the Prince's army with the Lady Maud, some other noble ladies, pages and squires, and other non-combatants, and were observing the battle at a safe distance on a nearby hill. Alfred had made his way forward until he was just behind the line of engagement. He was still in a state of some euphoria, for in aiding the Prince to escape, he believed that he had completely fulfilled his part of the mission. His attention was naturally drawn to the Prince in whose ability to winthis battle, Alfred had complete confidence.

Alfred saw with total dismay, the sword fly from the Prince's hand. A terrifying thought passed through Alfred's mind.

"Gregory de Grossmont may yet prevail and so change the course of history."

Alfred then did something extremely courageous. He made his way forward through the melee of soldiers and horsemen engaged in conflict, to the point where he had seen the Prince's sword fall. He picked up the sword and held it aloft. As the Prince and de Grossmont whirled around in their conflict as they manoeuvred their horses, Sir Gregory trying to get in a position where he could deliver a telling blow and Prince Edward maintaining the best defensive position. The Prince suddenly came into a position where he could see Alfred, several yards behind Sir Gregory, holding Edward's sword above his head. The Prince parried yet another heavy blow from de Grossmont's mace. He spurred his horse past Sir Gregory to Alfred. The Prince firmly grasped the hilt of the sword which Alfred proffered. Sir Gregory turned Conqueror to follow the Prince. As he reached Alfred, Sir Gregory swung his mace at him. Alfred ducked to evade the blow. A spike on the mace caught Alfred's shoulder. Prince Edward had by now turned his horse to face Sir Gregory. The knight's rode at each other. Turning his horse at the last moment to be out of range of Sir Gregory's mace, Prince Edward aimed a blow at Sir Gregory with the sword he had just recovered. He struck Sir Gregory on the breastplate. He followed this with another blow which unsettled Sir Gregory from his saddle. A third blow was struck and Sir Gregory fell from his horse. Three foot soldiers rushed forward to finish off Sir Gregory but he was already dead, his neck broken as he fell awkwardly, his helmet striking the ground first before his heavily armoured body slithered from saddle on which he had so skilfully ridden Conqueror during that epic encounter. Alfred made his way from the field of battle, pressing his tunic tightly on to his shoulder in an attempt to stench the bleeding.

From among the ring of knights around King Henry, Simon de Montfort watched the battle being waged below. He observed with pride young Henry de Montfort acquit himself well, slaying several of the knights who fought in the Earl of Gloucester's part of the field. Then, from de Montfort's viewpoint, disaster struck, young Henry was unhorsed. As he got to his feet his armour was pierced by the lance of a knight who charged him. Henry was dead.

"Come, let us to the fray," Simon urged the knights around him, and they charged down the hill. Simon wielded his sword with the might of some latter day Hercules until his horse was slain from under him. Still Simon continued on foot, laying low assailants which came within range of his flailing sword, striking mighty blows until he himself was struck from behind and slain. .

The battle was then soon over, but not before King Henry himself, although hardly a belligerent in this battle, was wounded. He was saved by the valour of those around him and de Montfort's defeated troops fled from the field.

Alfred had his wound dressed and managed to find his way back to Alice who was attending Lady Maud Mortimer, waiting with the other ladies who had followed Prince Edward's army as they rode into battle. A message reached them from the Prince.
"He wishes to see you both now," Lady Maud excitedly told the young people.

A knight took them to the marquee which had been hastily erected to accommodate the leaders of the victorious army. He led them to where they were to have an audience with the Prince. He was sitting on a chair in high spirits, the Earl of Gloucester, Sir Roger Mortimer and other nobles with him, enjoying the euphoria of victory. They came before the Prince, Alfred bowing and Alice curtseying when they reached the spot to which the knight directed them. The Prince was concerned to see that Alfred's shoulder was heavily bandaged.

"It's only a scratch, Sir," said Alfred as he uttered this cliche. He was really quite proud to have been bloodied in the battle.

"You have both served me well," said the Prince, "Better than it is in my power to make adequate repayment now, but I will not forget your services. One day you will make a fine knight," he said to Alfred.

"And you young lady will break many a nobleman's heart before you choose the one with whom you wish to share your life," he added as he spoke to Alice. "Who knows? Perhaps someday, my young brother Edmund will seek a worthy damsel to share with him the throne of Sicily."

The Prince smiled, knowing that these were merely pleasant words, for the Pope's bestowal of the Kingdom of Sicily to Henry Ill's son was a hollow gift.

"See that these young people are well dined." he commanded.

They turned, expecting to be led to some banqueting area by the knight who had brought them into the Prince's presence, but there was a monk, beckoning them to follow him. It was Chronavon.

"We must now make our way to the Abbey," he told them. They followed him to the beautiful church where the monks of Evesham Abbey were waiting by the north-west porch to welcome them.

Evesham Abbey c. 1270

Chronavon led them through the nave of the church and up the three steps which led to the choir. They made their way between the choir stalls to the steps before the high altar where Chronavon motioned them to kneel. Chronavon prayed aloud,

"Thank You, Lord, for all the protection that You have given Alfred and Alice as they have sought to serve You during this dangerous time. Thank You, Lord, that they have followed the guidance of Your Holy Spirit and have served You faithfully and effectively. Thank You Lord that Your purpose has been accomplished and the history will unfold, according to Your great design.

We pray now that as they return to their own time, Alfred and Alice will continue as Your faithful soldiers and servants and continue to be channels through which Your will and purpose may be accomplished. Amen."

They remained a little longer on their knees. Then Chronavon led them to a chamber just off the main building of the Abbey.

"You have both done well," Chronavon said as he smiled at the young people, "Really well, as I knew you both would. It's now the moment when you must return to your own time. You'll find your clothes in there."

Chronavon pointed to an oak chest, reinforced with iron bands, which looked identical to the one where they had deposited their twenty-first century clothes in the Chapter House of Hereford Cathedral. They opened the box, and sure enough, there were their clothes, neatly folded. They changed back and put their mediaeval clothes in the chest. Chronavon then motioned them to follow him through the door they had just entered. They expected to find themselves back in the Abbey, but no, they were in the familiar vestry of Saint Giles' Church, Hillington.

"Goodbye," said Chronavon, "and thank you once again. Who knows, I may need your services again. In which case, this will not be 'adieu' but merely 'au revoir'."

With that, Chronavon went back out of the door. What time or space he entered then we may not know for when Alfred and Alice rushed to the door and opened it, there was no sign of Chronavon, just St. Giles' Church which they both knew so well but not a person in sight. Alice noticed that she had pinned to her dress a small brooch that Lady Maud Mortimer had given her when she was at Wigmore Castle. Alfred rolled up his sleeve to examine the wound he had received at the battle of

Evesham, but it had healed, leaving just a faint, but none the less, definite scar."

Alfred and Alice looked at each other. What a wonderful adventure they had just enjoyed. Now they were back in their own time and had to pick up the threads from where they had left off so many days ago it seemed, but here they were, back at the same time as they had left!

"Is the ride by the Windrush this afternoon still on?" asked Alice, remembering the arrangement they had made, just before Chronavon had come on to the scene.

"Certainly, but I must first see if Mr. Jefferson wants me to collect his prescription," said Alfred, remembering Chronavon's words before they had stepped back to a former time.

<u>**Family Tree of descendants of King John, showing Edward I's near relatives
and his relationship by marriage to Simon de Montfort**</u>

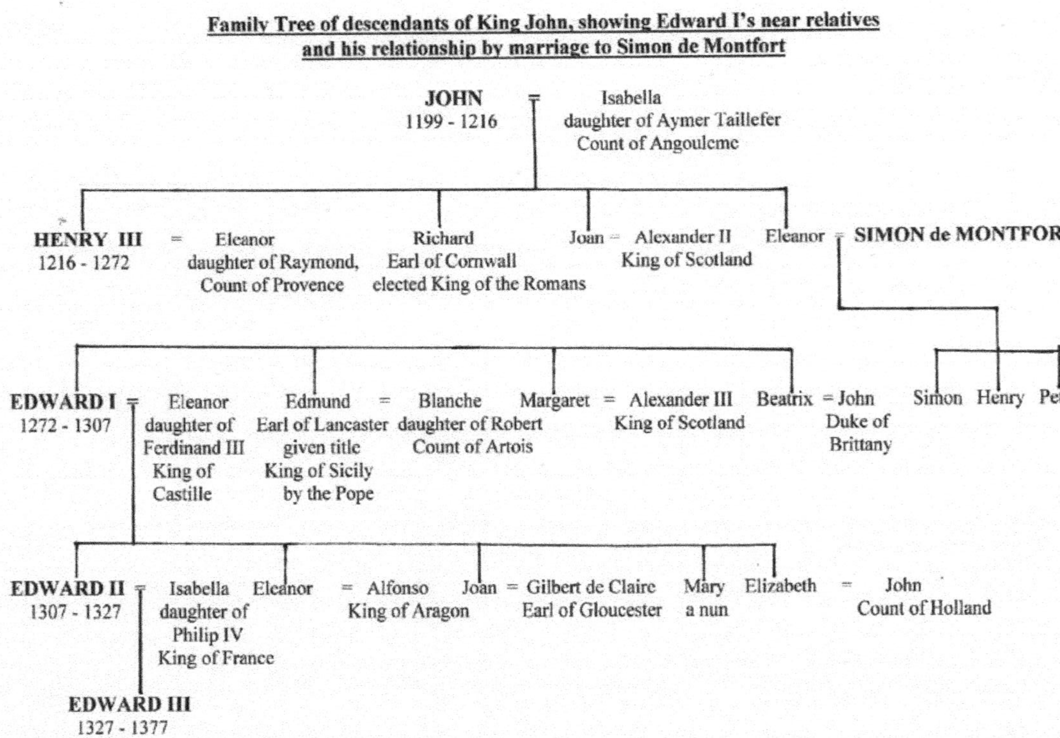

Family Tree of showing Thomas de Cantilupe's near relatives

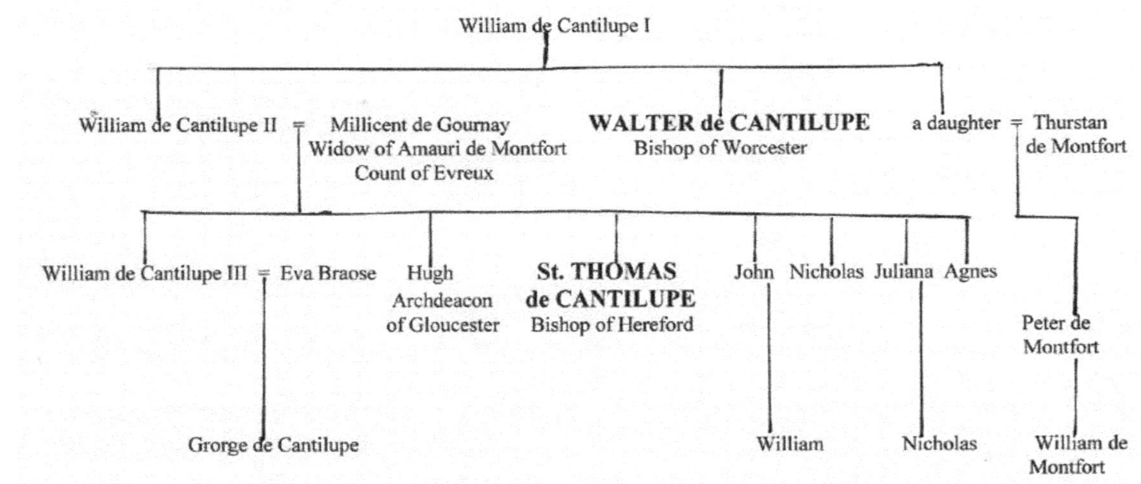

Princess Elizabeth

Can Alfred and Alice secure the Succession of Elizabeth I ?

Queen Mary I

Stephen Gardiner

<u>Chapter 1</u>

It was early April. Alfred and Alice were hard at work in the room where they were so often to be found on Saturday mornings. They were in the dingy vestry of St. Giles Church, Hillington. The following day would be Mothering Sunday. On Mothering Sunday, the Vicar distributes posies during morning service for the young children to give to their mothers. Thus, the task which Alfred and Alice had in hand was the preparation of these bouquets. The flowers, mainly golden narcissi, but with a number of red tulips and mauve irises, had been brought to the vestry earlier that morning by the ladies of the Mothers' Union who had generously contributed from the spring flowers growing in their gardens. Alfred and Alice were selecting flowers to make up well balanced mixed bunches for the thirty or so children who were expected to be in church the following morning. The bouquets, which were being neatly arranged on a dysfunctional pew, caught the sun streaming through the lofty window and for once, that normally dull and dingy vestry looked bright and cheerful.

Alice and Alfred were seated with their backs to the door, but they immediately turned round as it creaked open. The door swung on well-oiled hinges and normally opened noiselessly, but a few weeks earlier it had creaked uncharacteristically as it opened. The adventure which that sound heralded was still fresh in the memories of Alfred and Alice.

"Chronavon!" they cried in unison as they turned to see the hooded figure of a monk enter the vestry. What excitement stirred in the young people's hearts as they anticipated the challenge of a new adventure which Chronavon might bring.

Chronavon drew back his hood and his wise but kind and friendly face could be more clearly seen.

"Greetings to you both," said Chronavon as he beamed warmly at the expectant young people. "You both served me well when last I visited you. You were able to thwart the evil designs of Ahrirnanes to change the history of this country and hence, that of the whole world."

"We've never had so much excitement in all our lives as we had then," replied Alice with some enthusiasm. Her lovely face brightened as she tossed back the long golden hair which glorified her appearance.

"Indeed," answered Chronavon, "things worked out well and you may remember with some satisfaction the way you were able to counter the influence of Ahrimanes' agent, Gregory de Grossmont. I don't know if you realised what great dangers you both faced. I hate to contemplate what the consequences would have been, both for yourselves and for young Prince Edward had things gone wrong! My Lord and Master was delighted with the way you both used your horsemanship, your intelligence and your integrity to -perform some very difficult tasks in his service. He was especially pleased with the way you used the power of prayer to enable you to fulfil your mission."
A frown clouded Chronavon's face and he suddenly looked grave.

"Ahrimanes is up to his mischief again. Once more, he has misused the power he was given which enabled him to travel through time. Even now, he has chosen another agent to interfere with my Master's plans at another crucial point of history."

Alfred and Alice were all ears, hopeful that Chronavon had come to recruit them once again to counter Ahrimanes' evil plans. They were not to be disappointed.

"Are you willing to help my Master maintain the course of history on his ordained plan?" asked Chronavon, his eyebrows raised imploringly as he made this request. "I must warn you that the task will be as difficult and as dangerous as before. You will not have the opportunities you had in your last adventure to exploit your equestrian skills but many of your other abilities will be needed if you are to be successful. Of course, the power of prayer is available. It's largely because you were seen to use this power so well that you have again been identified as young people suitable for this service, but my Master insists that you should only agree to accept this task if you're fully prepared to face the risks and dangers involved."

"You bet we are!" "We can't wait to get going!" Alfred and Alice responded enthusiastically to Chronavon's request, both speaking at once and saying slightly different things to express how keen they were to embark on yet another momentous adventure.

"Come with me then," said Chronavon "and I will give you a full briefing."

Alfred and Alice followed Chronavon through the creaking vestry door. They were not surprised to find that it did not lead back into St. Giles Church because they already knew from their last adventure that when opened by Chronavon, this door was the entry to a new place and a different time.

Chapter 2

As had happened in their last adventure, they found that Chronavon had led them into the Chapter House of some great cathedral or abbey. This chapter house was larger than the one they had entered at Hereford.

"Larger too than the chapter houses at Salisbury Cathedral and Westminster Abbey," thought Alfred as he mentally compared the building in which he now stood with other great mediaeval chapter houses he had visited when on holiday with his parents.

"You are now in the Chapter House of St. Paul's Cathedral, London," explained Chronavon.

Alfred and Alice looked at the pointed windows and the lofty gothic vault soaring above them. They were puzzled. They had both visited St. Paul's Cathedral and they knew that it was not constructed in the gothic style of architecture. Indeed, they had explored London's great cathedral very thoroughly and they could not remember there being a separate Chapter House.

Chronavon smiled as he observed the quizzical expression which passed over the faces of both these young people. His next remark began to resolve the mental discrepancy which was perplexing the minds of Alfred and Alice.

"The year you have now entered is 1554. That is just over one hundred years before the Great Fire of London destroyed much of the City including its cathedral which in the twenty-first century is referred to as Old St. Paul's. After the Great Fire of London, Sir Christopher Wren built his masterpiece which we must refer to as New St. Paul's. This is the cathedral which both you have visited. It's built in a style called 'Classical' or 'Romanesque'. You are now standing in the glorious gothic Chapter House of Old St. Paul's Cathedral!

Can you think back to your history lessons and remember what things are happening in England in 1554 A.D.? What royal dynasty rules the country? Who sits on the throne?"

Alice could not specify precisely which monarch was sitting on the throne of England but her reasonably good knowledge of dates enabled her to identify the dynasty.

"The Wars of the Roses ended in 1485, " she stated "when the Earl of Richmond defeated Richard III to become Henry VIL the first king of the Tudor dynasty. As none of Henry VIIl's children had offspring, the dynasty came to an end in 1603 with the death of Elizabeth I. 1554 would therefore come in the reign of one of the later Tudors, Edward VI or Mary I?" ventured Alice.

"Well done, well done," re-joined Chronavon, clapping as he congratulated Alice. "You are very close. 1554 is just into the reign of Mary Tudor as Edward VI tragically died last year at the tender age of only sixteen."

"Mary Tudor!" snorted Alfred. Was he displaying disappointment or disgust? "Hers was just about the most dismal reign in English history. Have you really taken us back there, Chronavon?"

Alfred knew that wherever Chronavon had taken them, there would be a very good reason, but he was anxious to display that he had some knowledge of this period of history.

"Indeed I have," admitted Chronavon, "and yes, Mary Tudor did have a pretty dismal reign."

"But Mary's reign was followed by the most glorious reign in English history," interjected Alice with a triumphant tone of voice, "that of Elizabeth I"

"That's the way my master ordained things to happen," added Chronavon, "but even now, Ahrimanes is working through one of his agents to change the course of events so that Elizabeth never comes to the throne. Your task will be to thwart Ahrimanes' evil design."

Alfred was anxious to learn more about a historical situation of which he'd only superficial knowledge.

"Who's this agent of Ahrimanes? Is he a well-known historical character?" asked Alfred. "I must confess that I'm rather hazy about the situation which existed at the beginning of Mary's reign. I know that she went a bit over the top. She sent a lot of people to their death because they weren't Catholics. So they called her, Bloody Mary."

"Let's not be too hard on Mary," said Chronavon. " Yes, it's true that many Protestants were martyred during her reign, not just men of prominence like the bishops, Ridley, Latimer and Cranmer who became known as the Oxford martyrs. Many ordinary men and women were executed too because they adhered so firmly to their faith. Mary has some very good qualities, she is honest, loyal, pious and very resolute. Unfortunately, she lacks two qualities, highly esteemed by men and women. She has neither great beauty nor high intelligence. Sadly, in her desire to do what is right in God's sight, Mary has allowed herself to be unduly influenced by one she believes to be a good and holy man, namely Stephen Gardiner, the Bishop of Winchester. She has appointed him, Lord

Chancellor of England. Bishop he may be, but unlike Thomas de Cantilupe, the Chancellor of England you met in your last adventure, Stephen Gardiner is not a saintly man. It's through his influence that so many Protestants have been martyred. Stephen Gardiner is very much afraid that Elizabeth, who was brought up as a Protestant, will one day become queen and he's urging Mary to have her executed."

Alice was horrified to hear this.
"If she's done no wrong," she exclaimed, "how can she be executed?"

"No, indeed," replied Chronavon, "although Mary regards her very intelligent and passably beautiful half-sister, Elizabeth, as dangerous, she will not execute Elizabeth unless it is proved that she's committed an act of treachery. If clear evidence can be produced which proves that Elizabeth has plotted against the Queen, she will be executed. Evil man though he is, there are limits to the lengths that Gardiner is prepared to go to get Elizabeth executed. Hard as he has tried, he's failed to persuade Parliament to vote for Elizabeth to .be condemned and Gardiner wouldn't go so far as to fabricate false evidence himself to secure her execution. However, Ahrimanes has prepared a villain, the Reverend Tobias Maltravers, to do this very thing and provide such evidence for Bishop Gardiner!"

"The Reverend Tobias Maltravers?" queried Alfred. "If he is up to such mischief, why do you refer to him as Reverend?"

"Aha!" replied Chronavon, "Do not suppose that because a person is in holy orders, he's necessarily good or saintly! Bishop Gardiner certainly isn't! Tobias Maltravers is vicar of a small parish in Hampshire, but he's anxious to advance his career. He sees that this may be achieved by currying favour with his Bishop, Stephen Gardiner. The challenge before you both now is to thwart Tobias Maltravers' scheming. I'll arrange for you have positions which will give you a very good chance of influencing what happens but the outcome is far from certain. It will be up to you both to keep your wits about you and to act when you see anything happening which could endanger Elizabeth."

Chronavon continued.

"I need to give you a bit more information to fully explain the situation you will find yourselves in when I have to leave you to work on your own initiative.

Elizabeth has realised that she is doomed if she makes no attempt to accommodate her sister's wishes and she is therefore prepared to learn about the teaching of the Catholic Church. This in itself does not mean that she's a professing catholic or is prepared to become one, but she's indicating that she has an open mind. Queen Mary is pleased that Elizabeth is seeking to remedy the fact that she was prevented from learning about Catholicism as a child and is now prepared to study the catholic faith. She further believes that if she can marry off Elizabeth to a devout catholic, catholic succession to the English throne will be ensured in the event of her not producing an heir herself She has arranged for Elizabeth to come to know a really splendid young man called Edward Courtenay.

Besides being a wonderful young man, this Edward is a devout catholic and should succeed to the title,

Earl of Devonshire. Because they held so firmly to their faith, Edward and his parents were imprisoned in the Tower of London during the previous reign. Edward's father, Henry, Earl of Devonshire, was actually beheaded but on Mary's accession to the throne, Edward and his mother were released. Edward's mother has become lady-in-waiting to Queen Mary and Edward has been courting the Princess Elizabeth. Now this Edward Courtenay is the great grandson of the Yorkist king, Edward IV. So you see, Edward Courtenay has himself a claim to the throne of England! The Princess Elizabeth really is in love with Edward. Should Edward and Elizabeth marry each other, and Mary Tudor die without producing an heir, they could become joint sovereigns."

Chronavon paused. Alice knew full well that English history did not follow this course and she enquired of Chronavon what had happened to prevent this marriage.

Chronavon went on to explain.

"Mary was aware that Edward and Elizabeth's strong claims to the throne of England posed a threat to her own security. However, she knew that her lady-in-waiting, Edward's mother, would keep her informed if any outside pressures were brought to bear on Elizabeth and Edward to encourage them to seize the crown for themselves."

"Surely a dutiful princess like Elizabeth wouldn't consider doing such a thing!" said Alice, sounding a little outraged.

"No, indeed not," continued Chronavon, "but unfortunately, a rebellion with the objective of placing Edward and Elizabeth on the throne did take place without their knowledge!"

"Who led this rebellion?" asked Alfred.

"The rebellion was led by one, Sir Thomas Wyatt," answered Chronavon. "Thomas was the son of another Thomas Wyatt, a poet who held Princess Elizabeth's mother, Anne Boleyn, in high esteem. Indeed, had not the King, Henry VIII, made it clear that he wanted Anne Boleyn above all other women at the court, Thomas

Wyatt would have sought to marry Anne himself. Partly, because of the resentment felt concerning the injustice which led to Anne Boleyn's execution, and partly to end the persecution of Protestants, the younger Thomas Wyatt took up arms against Mary Tudor with the objective of making Anne Boleyn's daughter, queen. Thomas Wyatt wrote to Elizabeth and Edward, informing them of his rebellion and the intention to put them on the throne, but the letters were intercepted. Although ignorant of this letter, Elizabeth and Edward came under suspicion of being party to the rebellion and action has been taken against them

Edward Courtenay has been sent into exile.

Princess Elizabeth will soon be escorted to the Tower of London where she'll be imprisoned. She'll be in great danger, for Ahrimanes' creature, Tobias Maltravers, will use all his cunning to help Stephen Gardiner, Bishop of Winchester and Lord Chancellor of England, to have her executed.

Now this is where you will both have roles to play to counter Tobias' plotting. I'm going to take you to the Tower of London before the Princess Elizabeth herself arrives. The Lieutenant of the Tower is called Sir John Brydges. I'm a great friend of this Sir John. Sir John is a devout Roman Catholic. He's a very pious and most kindly man. Above all, he's entirely honourable. I've asked him to arrange for you to be admitted into rather special service.

Alice, you are to become serving maid to Princess Elizabeth while she's incarcerated in the Tower.

Alfred, you are to become a serving boy to Stephen Gardiner, Bishop of Winchester and Lord Chancellor of England.

Alfred, as Stephen Gardiner's servant, you'll have the opportunity to observe what goes on and you'll hopefully be able to take action if the opportunity arises to foil Tobias Maltravers' evil plans. Listen careful to all that goes on in Bishop Gardiner's house. Yes, although I shouldn't be the one to suggest this, do a bit of eavesdropping.

Unfortunately, you won't find a convenient secret passage in Bishop Gardiner's house as there was in Hereford Castle for you to hide in. You'll have to be rather more ingenious in the way you listen in on conversations which are thought to be being held in private!

The pair of you must also find ways of communicating with each other. This will be more dangerous and difficult than you might imagine. Any news of the outside world to be imparted to the Princess Elizabeth will be strictly censored. Elizabeth's adult maids won't be able to converse freely outside Elizabeth's prison. However, you two have youth on your side. Children won't be suspected of discussing matters concerning state and national security. Alfred, it's likely that the Lord Chancellor will want you dressed in his livery. You will therefore be recognised as the Lord Chancellor's servant and no-one will suspect you of doing anything which could be helpful to the Princess Elizabeth.

However, we must lose no more time. We must hasten to the Tower of London or the Princess

Elizabeth will be there ahead of us. You obviously cannot go dressed in your twenty-first century clothes. See if you can find anything more suitable in there."

Chronavon pointed to a chest by the wall of the Chapter House.

Alfred and Alice eagerly rushed across to open it up. They remembered the fun they had had in dressing up in clothes appropriate to the age in which they found themselves when in Hereford Cathedral Chapter House. The clothes in this chest were rather more splendid garments, attire suitable for young people commended to enter the service of the most exalted in the realm.

Princess Elizabeth, in spite of her current predicament, was heir to the throne of England. Stephen Gardiner, in spite of his unsavoury reputation, was Lord Chancellor of England.

They soon found clothes which met with their approval. Alice selected a really lovely, full length mauve dress, delicately embroidered with

Tudor roses. The dress had a white ruff and lace trimmings to the sleeves. Although Alice deemed the dress good enough for best, she also put on a white apron as she was mindful that her role would be that of a serving maid. Alfred sported a maroon tabard and matching hose and cap, the latter audaciously adorned with a long feather. Chronavon approved their new garb. The twentieth century clothes were stowed back in the chest along with the alternative Tudor clothes they'd looked at but rejected. They were now ready for action.

"Follow me," Chronavon commanded as he led them through the Chapter House door.

Chapter 3

Alice and Alfred found themselves in the one of the four passageways which made up the square cloisters. Alfred was surprised at the layout of the cloister walks. Most chapter houses are located to the east of their associated cloister. This Chapter House of Old St. Paul's Cathedral was in the centre of a cloister court, much smaller in area than the squares enclosed by the cloister walks of Westminster Abbey or Salisbury Cathedral. Also, these cloisters were two tiered. Alfred recognised this as another exceptional feature.

Chronavon led them along the short cloister passageway into the main building of St. Paul's Cathedral. The young people were truly impressed at the scale of the huge edifice they'd just entered.

"Let's get our priorities right at the beginning of this adventure," said Chronavon.

Chronavon leads Alfred and Alice away from the
bustling nave of St. Paul's Cathedral towards the
east end of this huge church

He briskly led them away from the bustling nave where merchants and clerics met in little discussion groups and a party of scarlet robed city dignitaries was following a small procession of choristers and priests, directing their steps towards the east end of the cathedral where it seemed likely that a civic service was going to be conducted. Chronavon entered a small side chapel where the clamour from the excited voices of those meeting and talking in the main church could hardly be heard. In this quiet setting, Chronavon knelt before the altar and Alfred and Alice followed suit.

"Thank you Lord that your servants, Alfred and Alice, are again prepared to face the dangers associated with the task they have been asked to carry out," prayed Chronavon, speaking in a soft and reverend voice. "They know that the destiny of the world depends on their being successful. May they have the knowledge and assurance of your unseen presence to support them during this hazardous mission. Help them to bring this venture to a successful conclusion, Amen."

Alfred and Alice firmly repeated the 'Amen' and they remained kneeling for a while, contemplating their need for the divine support which would they knew would be available in response to the prayer they had just made.

After a few moments, Chronavon rose from his kneeling position and the young people followed. He led them back into the bustling nave, through the great cathedral portal and out into the even more bustling streets of London. In spite of the clamour which now surrounded them, Alfred and Alice found that a sensation of peace and confidence was added to the excitement they had experienced from the moment that Chronavon had entered the vestry of their little church in Hillington. They passed between the timber framed buildings which lined the narrow streets. The upper storeys of these shops and houses jutted out, restricting the light that could reach street level. Young men pushed barrows which clattered as the wheels bumped over the cobbled streets. Dogs ran after the barrows, barking and snapping, occasionally finding that some tasty morsel would fall from a barrow for them to hungrily devour as they competed for this prize. Children chased one another up the narrow alley ways which led from the main thoroughfares.

Chronavon warned them to avoid the gutters running down the centre of the street where all sorts of unmentionable, unhygienic mess oozed its slimy way to join with gutters from other streets and issue into some open sewer on its route to join the Thames.

Alfred and Alice noticed a number of largish birds they hadn't seen before, gorging themselves on rubbish that littered the streets through which they walked, Chronavon noticed their interest.

"They are red kites," he told them. "There will not be many around in the time you come from, but they are very numerous in England now. They are scavengers and do more than most to remove muck and waste food from the filthy streets of London."

They reached a wider street which they discovered was called Cheapside. Alfred turned to look towards the Cathedral they had just left and which could now be seen, rising above the shops and houses through which they'd just passed. Alfred caught his breath at the immensity of the structure which had come into view and he nudged Alice to look round too.

St. Paul's Cathedral c.1555 showing
Chapter house in centre of cloisters.

Alfred had been impressed by the beautiful spire of Salisbury Cathedral which he had visited with his parents the previous summer, but the spire they now beheld must have been half as high again. Chronavon noticed that this had caught the young people's attention and stopped so that they could take in this breath-taking sight. Chronavon had the unnerving ability to accurately read the thoughts of those around him.

"Yes," he said, "the spire of Salisbury Cathedral is magnificent but it is a mere four hundred feet high. The spire of St. Paul's is nearly five hundred feet tall!"

After they had spent a short while admiring this impressive London landmark, they continued on their way to the Tower of London. Suddenly, as they came round a corner, the White Tower, the keep of London's grim fortress prison, came into view beyond the end of the street. This was the central part of the Tower of London which had been built nearly five hundred years earlier by William the Conqueror.

Tower of London with entrance to
Traitors' Gate in foreground

As Chronavon and his companions emerged from the street, they were able to take in a view of the whole Tower of London, the bailey walls punctuated by crenelated round towers, surrounding the central White Tower, and in turn, surrounded by a wide moat of green stagnant water. Alice and Alfred suddenly felt awe-struck and not a little frightened. They knew that during the period of history into which they'd now been taken, many who entered the Tower went there to meet their doom!

Chronavon led them to the land entrance to the Tower, a gate in a fortified building known as the Middle Tower. Their way was barred by two yeoman warders in their spectacularly bright red, yellow and black uniforms. They were armed with halberds. M. R. was emblazoned in large letters across the front of their uniforms. M. R. stood for Maria Regina and left one in no doubt that Mary Tudor was now queen. Chronavon pulled a document from under his habit and thrust it at the guard. The guard scrutinised the papers and then called to a more senior yeoman warder who came down from a room within this Middle Tower. After a quick glance at the papers, the senior warder nodded and called to yet another warder who must have been towards the interior of the Tower of London, beyond the Middle Tower where they now stood. When this warder responded to the call by coming to the entrance of the Tower, a brief discussion ensued with the senior warder.

The warder who had just been summoned beckoned Chronavon, and Chronavon, accompanied by Alfred and Alice, followed this warder, through the gate, across the drawbridge, and through a gate in another fortified building which they found was called the Byward Tower. They were now within the bailey walls of the Tower. A little further into the Tower, they reached an attractive timber framed building.

The warder knocked at the door with his halberd. The door was shortly opened by a maid and the warder told her that some important guests had arrived. The maid went back into the building and returned a moment later, followed by a gentleman, resplendent in elegant clothes. The royal coat of arms was prominently embroidered on to his velvet tunic. This was Sir John Brydges, Lieutenant of the Tower. As soon as he saw Chronavon, Sir John came straight out of the building and enthusiastically shook his hand. The two obviously knew each other well.

"How good to see you again after so long," said Sir John as he greeted Chronavon.

"The pleasure's mine," responded Chronavon. "Let me introduce the two young people I've recruited to be of service to the Princess Elizabeth and the Lord Chancellor of England. This is

Alfred and this young lady is Alice."

Sir John beamed benevolently at the young people.

"Welcome to royal service," he said. "The Princess Elizabeth is expected at the Tower later today and tomorrow, the Lord Chancellor is coming. They'll be able to explain to you better than I the duties they'll need performed.

Have you had anything to eat?" Sir John enquired of Chronavon.

"Not for some time," replied Chronavon "but I'm currently fasting. However, I know that these young people would welcome a morsel."

"Well, Chronavon, I hope that at least, you'll join us in a drink," said Sir John as he led them into a pleasant, well lit room whose dark oak beams contrasted starkly with the freshly whitewashed walls.

Sir John motioned them to sit at a large polished oak table and tinkled a hand bell which stood among other highly polished brass bric-a-brac on a fairly ornate dresser.

The maid who'd answered the door when they'd arrived, responded to the summons. She bustled through the door, wiping her hands on the white apron which protected her neat grey dress. Her hair was concealed under a white mob cap.

"Philippa, please would you serve up lunch for myself and my two young friends," requested Sir John, "and a mug of ale all round, including our esteemed Chronavon who always seems to be fasting when he pays us a visit."

The food had obviously been cooking, even as Sir John spoke to Philippa, for the maid soon reappeared with plates furnished with seasoned venison, boiled cabbage, carrots and turnips. Potatoes were conspicuous to Alfred and Alice by their absence, for although this vegetable had by now been discovered in the New World, it hadn't yet found its way to England.

They settled down to eat. As in Hereford, Alfred and Alice discovered that the eating utensils were a dagger and their hands. Bowls of water were placed on the table for the diners to rinse their hands. Alice and Alfred were glad to see that Chronavon at least enjoyed his ale, even if he declined to eat.

"Can you bring us up to date with the latest news," Chronavon asked Sir John. "I've heard the gossip but my young friends here are just up from Gloucestershire and news takes a long time to reach those country parts.

Alfred and Alice had time to study Sir John Brydges as he recounted the current situation. A rosy faced man with shoulder length hair and a short beard, Sir John indeed seemed the amiable gentleman that Chronavon had described. He always seemed to have a twinkle in his eye and was ever attentive to the needs of his guests.

"Come on you young people, help yourselves to more meat. Chronavon, your tankard needs replenishing. Philippa, bring in the fruit."

However, Sir John Brydges face became grave when he answered Chronavon's question and he brought the small group up to date on the news.

Sir John's brow furrowed and his eyes momentarily lost their twinkle.

"Ah, it's a bad business," he sighed. "Sir Thomas Wyatt led a rebellion to dethrone Queen Mary but the Queen's troops routed the rebels and Sir Thomas Wyatt surrendered at Temple Bar a few days ago. He's now here, a prisoner in the dungeons. My Lord Bishop Gardiner is convinced that the Princess Elizabeth put him up to this rebellion and he's closely 'interrogated' Sir Thomas for the past few days."

Sir John inclined his head and gave Chronavon a knowing look as he said 'interrogated'. Alfred and Alice guessed that this meant that torture had been used they each experienced a shudder of fear.

"However," Sir John continued, "Sir Thomas cannot be shaken on his insistence that he acted entirely on his own initiative and that neither Elizabeth nor Edward Courtenay, the Earl of Devon, were in any way involved. As a precaution, Edward Courtenay has been exiled and the Princess Elizabeth has been arrested. She is being brought to the Tower and should be arriving at any moment now."

The discussion then turned to the roles Alfred and Alice would be fulfilling.

"Your quarters will be in the Bell Tower where the Princess Elizabeth will be confined," said Sir John to Alice. "I am afraid that being a maid to a prisoner in the Tower involves sharing the prisoner's loss of freedom. The powers that be are always afraid that the prisoners will communicate with dangerous enemies of the state and even servants of important prisoners, no, especially the servants of important prisoners, are regarded as potential messengers, receiving and returning information from and to the outside world."

Alfred and Alice shared an anxious glance. They knew that they would need to communicate with each other to protect Princess Elizabeth should they need to initiate action if danger threatened her. Sir John had set alarm bells ringing in their minds.

Chronavon came to the rescue.
"Alice and Alfred are such great friends," he said.

"Will they not be able to meet up while Elizabeth is confined to the Tower?"

Sir John was reassuring.

"Elizabeth and her ladies will spend a short time each day in the exercise area. As Alfred will be working for my Lord Bishop of Winchester, he'll be a regular visitor to the Tower and he'll be recognised as a servant of the Chancellor of England. The guards will place few restrictions on his movements. Provided you're discreet about it, Alfred, there should be no difficulty in your exchanging a few words with Alice during exercise time, but I must warn you most strongly that if you start having lengthy conversations, the guards will become suspicious, even though I know that two lovely young people like yourselves pose no threat to our security."

Just then, a sharp knocking was heard at the door.

"Enter," called John in his deep sonorous voice. A yeoman warder entered to inform Sir John Brydges that the barge conducting the Princess Elizabeth to the Tower had just entered Traitor's Gate.

"Come with me," said Sir John as he stood and reached for his cloak and hat which were hanging nearby on the wall. Chronavon, Alice and Alfred followed Sir John Brydges as they left the comfortable dining room and made their way to the dreaded Traitor's Gate.

Traitors' Gate,
The Tower of London

Chapter 4

Few who entered the Tower as water borne prisoners through the Traitor's Gate left the Tower alive. Most ended their stay in that fortress prison with a short walk to the block on Tower Green or to nearby Tower Hill to have their head severed from their body by a masked executioner, wielding his tool of the trade, a long handled axe. The Princess Elizabeth's mother, the ill-fated Anne Boleyn, had made this sombre journey some eighteen years earlier where she had been granted her request to be executed by a swordsman rather than an axeman.

As Sir John and his party of guests left the Lieutenant of the Tower's residence to make their way to the nearby Traitor's Gate, Alice and Alfred were conscious that the weather had significantly deteriorated from the bright sunlight they had enjoyed during their walk from St. Paul's Cathedral to the Tower, earlier that day. It had started to drizzle. A cold wind blew in from the Thames, wafting in the faint but unpleasant odour of the decaying rubbish and sewage of the City of London which had been directed to the City's main waterway, first via the open drains which polluted the centre of most of London's streets, and then the River Fleet which, besides being a tributary to the Thames, was a disgusting open sewer.

On the landing stage, just inside the stark black bars of Traitor's Gate and beneath St. Thomas's Tower which formed an arch over the gate, the party following Sir John from his house could see a young woman sitting on a stone. This was the newly arrived Princess Elizabeth. She was tastefully but not extravagantly dressed. Her jewellery consisted of no more than a double rope of pearls. Beautiful clothes were not necessary to enhance the beauty of this high born young lady in her late teens. She looked every bit a royal princess. Princess Elizabeth sat surrounded by a dozen or so guards and officers, the latter being young aristocrats, trusted by Queen Mary to safely conduct her half-sister to the confines of the Tower. Two nervous looking ladies in waiting stood anxiously in attendance.

The Princess Elizabeth was resolutely refusing to move in spite of the drizzle from which St. Thomas's Tower above her gave only partial protection. The drizzle was gradually turning to an unpleasant shower of rain.

"What an insult to bring a truly loyal subject and daughter of a king no less to this place through an entrance whose shameful name proclaims her to be a traitor," said Elizabeth as she spat out the words. "My sister, Mary, never had a truer subject and I trust you will convey this message to her. Well, I'm now within the Tower. You gentlemen have discharged your duty. I choose to remain here. You may now depart!"

The officers and guards looked despairingly at one another, not wishing to lay restraining hands on their royal prisoner, but knowing that she must be conducted to secure accommodation within the Tower.

Sir John Brydges stepped forward to resolve the situation. He took off his hat with a flourish as he bowed before the Princess.

"I'm Sir John Brydges, Lieutenant of the Tower," began Sir John by way of introduction.

"I know very well who you are!" snapped the Princess.

"I consider myself most privileged to be your host in this noble castle." continued Sir John, unperturbed by Elizabeth's curt reply to his introduction. "There's no other building in this realm of England that could offer you greater protection from any who might seek to do you harm during these troublous times than this royal bastion. I've had the best room in the castle prepared for you. It's in the Bell Tower, the noblest of all the towers, fit to accommodate an honoured guest. To see to your comfort and to help you settle in, I have arranged for a young lady to be a maid for you."

Sir John Brydges identified Alice with a demonstrative gesture while the anxious ladies in waiting shot a surprised glance at each other. Alice had the presence of mind to curtsey.

"Her name is Alice. She has been recommended for this service by a friend of mine who is always to be trusted in his judgement. She'll be able to perform for you so many duties with which you would not wish your high born ladies-in-waiting to demean themselves."

Elizabeth looked somewhat mollified by Sir John Brydges eloquence and courtesy. She also realised that there was no point in sitting indefinitely in discomfort in the chilling rain. She rose imperiously to her feet.

"Lead on then, Sir John. Let us see if the quarters you have provided for me live up to your boast!"

Sir John Brydges turned and, followed by the Princess, led the party to Elizabeth's quarters in the Bell Tower. Alfred and Alice sensed the relief of Sir John when his tact had made it possible to conduct Elizabeth to her internment in a dignified manner. Sir John ascended the steps to Elizabeth's apartment, followed by Elizabeth, her two ladies-in-waiting and Alice. Alice exchanged an apprehensive glance with Alfred. They'd no idea how this venture was going to work out. When would they see each other again? The door closed behind Sir John and the ladies.

Alfred was now beginning to get quite wet as the rain fell more heavily. After a short period, perhaps only five minutes, but augmented in Alfred's mind through the discomfort of standing in wet and cold clothes, Sir John emerged from the door which secured the Bell Tower. He posted two guards at the door and thanked the escort which had conducted Elizabeth to the Tower. He gave them leave to dismiss. He then motioned Chronavon and Alfred to follow him back to his quarters.

"I think we could all do with drying out and a change of clothes," he said, giving a shiver, once they had returned to the comfort of his quarters. "However, I think the ladies' needs are greater than ours."

He called Philippa and told her to go to the Bell Tower to show the ladies where he had arranged for spare clothes to be stored.

"I know that my Lady Elizabeth has a very refined taste in clothes so I have arranged for a number of suitable dresses to be available for her in the Bell Tower," said Sir John with the air of satisfaction of a man who thinks of everything and plans well ahead. "There are also clothes suitable for her ladies-in-waiting, and Chronavon, as you had given me a good description of the young lady who was coming to be an extra maid, there are clothes there which willfit Alice."

"You think of everything, Sir John," said Chronavon, "I'm most impressed."

Sir John beckoned them to follow him and Chronavon and Alfred entered another room. Sir Alfred opened the doors of a large wardrobe which contained all manner and sizes of clothes, including some which would fit Alfred, and even a few monk's habits which might have been suitable for Chronavon.

Alfred set about finding replacement clothes for himself but Chronavon declined the invitation to select a different set of clothes.

"I'm all right," he said. "It takes more than a shower of rain to soak these clothes."

Sir John Brydges and Alfred both felt Chronavon's clothes. They were absolutely amazed to find that Chronavon's habit was bone dry, even though he had just spent some time, standing in the rain. Sir John chuckled and his whole body seemed to vibrate as he laughed.

"You really are an incredible fellow, Chronavon. I never cease to marvel at the tricks you come up with."

Sir John then adopted a more serious tone.

"Chronavon, I'm most grateful for the help and guidance you have given me over the years. I would never have been offered this position without your advice. You put me wise to the politics which would affect the attitudes of those who were responsible for making the appointment. You've also kept me up to date with the nasty bits of court intrigue which have helped me avoid saying the wrong things to those who have influence in high places. I've heard recently that I'm being considered for elevation to the peerage! I really owe you an incalculable debt of gratitude for all the help you've given me over the years, Chronavon."

Chronavon waived these plaudits with a shake of the head and a gesture.

"I only wish that there were more men of your calibre and integrity whom I might consider worth helping as you believe I have helped you, Sir John. The world would then be a much better place. Sadly, most of those who advance to high office are self-seeking adventurers whose ambition is their god and who would betray their own mothers if by so doing, they could advance half a step up the career ladder. There are all too few like you, Sir John, who are genuinely concerned to seek the common good."

Chronavon spoke with some warmth as he commended Sir John for the public spirit in which he conducted his office at the Tower.

"But soon," added Chronavon, "I must be on my way for I have other business to attend to. I know that you'll see that Alfred is well accommodated tonight."

Chronavon then turned to Alfred, now attired in dry clothes.

"Tomorrow, Alfred, you will meet with your new master, Stephen Gardiner, Bishop of Winchester and Lord Chancellor of England. Bear in mind all the advice I've given you. Don't lose sight of the real task ahead. I shall know if you're in real need or danger and I'll endeavour to help you, but I have every confidence that you and Alice will succeed in the commission I've given you without any intervention from myself. However, the outcome is not guaranteed. If you rely on the power of prayer you'll have no need to fear."

"You've taught me so much about the power of prayer, Chronavon," said Sir John Brydges, picking up Chronavon's words to Alfred. "Please don't leave us before we spend some time in prayer together. As you know, there's a very special chapel in the White Tower. Let's go to that holy place to bring before our God, the dangers which our realm now faces and to pray for men and women who are being persecuted for holding dear to their faith."

"What a splendid suggestion," said Chronavon, responding warmly to Sir John's request. "I've prayed with you in the chapel of St. John before. It is indeed an oasis of light within this castle where so much misery and suffering is inflicted on those unfortunate enough to be imprisoned here. I know too that Alfred would appreciate an opportunity to spend time in a place of prayer for he's likely to be apprehensive about serving a new master, especially one with the standing and reputation of Bishop Gardiner."

The three of them left the Lieutenant's house. It was no longer raining and the sky was a faint grey with the brighter stars beginning to appear in the falling dusk. There were very few people around. Two Yeoman Warders could be seen at different positions by the outer walls of the bailey, visible in the gloaming, only because they bore torches with which they were lighting small beacons to provide limited illumination to the courtyard of the Tower. The threesome made their way across the courtyard of the Tower to its central keep, William the Conqueror's White Tower, but now it looked anything but white. It appeared as a black silhouette against the faint grey of the sky. They climbed the outer steps to the main door, situated well up the wall and hence, fairly inaccessible to any who might try to breach that door with a conventional battering ram in time of siege. However, the White Tower had never had to withstand such an assault. There was no threat to the Tower now. The door was not locked and Sir John raised the heavy latch to admit Alfred and Chronavon into this bastion. A few torches supported in wall brackets provided sufficient illumination for them to find their way to a spiral stairway which led to the upper storeys of this tower.

They emerged on to a landing and made their way to St. John's Chapel. This was well lit with candles on the altar and on two large candelabra. A priest was adjusting a missal on the altar. This was the first person they had seen since entering the White Tower. He was the senior chaplain to the Tower. He turned as he heard the sound of footsteps, gave a small bow when he saw it was Sir John Brydges in the company of his guests, and walked silently to the edge of the chapel, disappearing into the darkness as he passed through one of the arches which defined the perimeter of the area, consecrated for prayer and divine worship.

Sir John went forward and knelt on the runner which extended across the space in front of the altar. He was joined by Chronavon and Alfred. They knelt for some moments in silence. Alfred took in the ambience of this place, very plain, very simple, the massive Norman architecture lending an overwhelming sense of peace and stability. Although the round Norman arches surrounding the place where they knelt were the sole feature which gave any definition to the shape of this chapel Alfred appreciated the simplicity of the design which lent the chapel a certain beauty.

Sir John was first to break the silence as he prayed aloud for the comfort and well-being of Princess Elizabeth, her ladies in waiting and for Alice. Alfred extended this prayer, making special mention of the help that Alice would need to adjust to living in close confinement with three people who knew each other very well but who did not know Alice.

Chronavon prayed for Sir Thomas Wyatt, that he might have the fortitude to bear the ordeal through which he was passing as he faced the prospect of certain execution. They prayed for the security of the realm, for affairs of state, the planned marriage of Queen Mary with King Philip of Spain, and for those who were being persecuted and even martyred for their faith.

They prayed that a time would soon come when people in England would feel free to worship according to their conscience without fear of persecution.

They prayed for God's guidance for the ministers of state and for the bishops of England, very especially for Cardinal Pole, Archbishop of Canterbury, and Stephen Gardiner, Bishop of Winchester and Lord Chancellor of England. It was felt appropriate to pray that God should overrule, should the bishops lead the people into adopting practices which were not in line with His will.

Chronavon finished the prayer session with an impassioned plea that God should protect the Princess Elizabeth in all things, and very specially from any attempt to dishonestly incriminate her of committing acts of treachery against her sister.

After about half an hour, the three of them left St. John's Chapel and the White Tower. Although it was now quite dark, Chronavon was insistent that he now had to leave the Tower because he had other urgent business to attend to in London before the end of the night. Sir John was reluctant to see Chronavon leave but he acceded to his request and they made their way to the Byward Tower. They passed the inner sentries who stood to attention as they recognised that Sir John Brydges approached. They crossed the drawbridge, went through the archway of the Middle Tower and passed the sentries posted outside this entry to the Tower of London. Here, Chronavon bade Sir John and Alfred adieu.

Alfred returned with Sir John to his house. They walked together in silence. They both had much to ponder. When they reached the house, they found Philippa was still busy in the now candlelit dining room. Sir John told her that he was sure that Alfred would be very tired by now. Philippa conducted Alfred to a small but cosy bedroom. The bed was made up with blankets, sheets and pillows. It was a great improvement on the beds he had slept in during his Hereford adventure. Alfred was soon fast asleep.

<u>Chapter 5</u>

The next day, Alfred woke as the sun streamed in through the window of his room. He dressed himself in the clothes he had carelessly thrown on the floor in his tiredness the previous night. There was a knock on the door.

"Come in!" called Alfred.

The door opened and Philippa put her head round.

"I thought I heard movement," she said. "I'll bring you some water."

Philippa reappeared a short while later with an earthenware jug of warm water which she poured into a bowl on a table in the comer of the room. There was no soap and Alfred washed himself as best he could. This was certainly better than his experience at Hereford when he had had very few opportunities of washing, and then, only in tepid water. Alfred then went into the room where he had dined the previous day. Philippa explained that Sir John was already up and about his business in the

Tower as she set a breakfast of an egg, a small piece of bacon and a piece of bread which was larger than a roll but smaller than a loaf.

On completing his breakfast, Alfred looked out of the window of the Lieutenant's house. A lawn stretched from the house towards what looked like a small church. There was little activity. An occasional yeoman warder walked across the lawn where large black birds were devouring scraps of meat which someone must have thrown out for them. Philippa cleared away the breakfast and came over to see what had caught Alfred's interest. She realised that his attention was directed mainly to the black birds who were squabbling over the remaining pieces of meat.

"They be the Tower ravens," she explained. "People come and go to and from the Tower, but there have always been ravens here. The ravens are never far from the Tower. No, they never leave but I'm afraid that some of the people who come here, leave without their heads." Philippa gave a shudder. "There have been five executions since I've been working here for Sir John. They take place at the far end of the green, just in front of the chapel of St. Peter ad Vincula," she said, pointing to the little church which had caught Alfred's attention earlier. "I hope there won't be any more. I'm so afraid of what might happen to that Princess Elizabeth who came here yesterday."

Philippa sniffed and blew her nose. "You don't have to be bad to be executed. If you have the wrong enemies in court, or dangerous friends outside court, .or the wrong religion, that's all it takes, - Off with your head," she explained. "Do be careful what you say, young man," she added, "and who you speak to, and tell that young lady who came with you yesterday, likewise, that is, if you get the chance. Now she's maid to the Princess Elizabeth, I don't suppose we'll see her roaming round the Tower unless she's with a guard. Oh, it is such a wicked, wicked world."

As Philippa was bemoaning the injustices of the world in general and the dangers facing those incarcerated in the Tower in particular, Sir John Brydges could be seen crossing Tower Green on his way back to his house.

"Ah," he said as he entered the house and saw Alfred up and dressed, "I hope that you slept and breakfasted well. Your new master will be coming here soon. He's currently interrogating one of the prisoners but he must be nearly through by now. Do remember to bow to him when you are introduced, and be very conscientious in your work for him. Indeed, I'm sure that you'll serve him well but take care. Bishop Gardiner is not the man to get on the wrong side of!"

It wasn't long before Bishop Gardiner found his way to Sir John's house. Alfred saw the Bishop making his way across the green in the company of six fully armed men in uniform. Bishop Gardiner himself was dressed very similarly to his guards with a purple cloak over a matching purple tunic, but he was not carrying a sword. The cloaks of Bishop Gardiner and his bodyguard were each embroidered with two coats of arms, the royal coat of arms, (three lions in two of the quarterings and three fleurs-de-lys in the other two), and the arms of the diocese of Winchester, (a pair of keys along one diagonal and a sword across the other).

Alfred bowed as instructed by Sir John on being introduced to Stephen Gardiner, Lord Chancellor of England and Bishop of Winchester. Sir John described Alfred as a lad who'd been recommended by someone whose judgement was invariably sound so that he could absolutely guarantee that Alfred would make an excellent servant.

Alfred paid close attention to Stephen Gardiner and felt rather afraid. The steely grey eyes, each side of his hooked nose, penetrated those upon whom he directed his gaze like needles. The thin mouth never smiled. Purely on the basis of his appearance, Alfred judged the Bishop to be a cruel and cunning man, totally devoid of humour. Appearances can be very deceptive, but in this case, Alfred was not far wrong in his assessment.

"Can you read?" the Bishop asked Alfred curtly.
"Yes, Sir," replied Alfred politely.
The Bishop pulled out a book from under his cloak, opened it at a random page and thrust it at Alfred.

"Read that!" he commanded.

Alfred took the book. The print was not very clear and the text was in Latin but Alfred found that he could read it aloud, even though he couldn't translate what he was reading. After he'd read a couple of sentences, the Bishop snatched back the book.

"You'll do," he said. "You're the first presentable looking lad I've seen in two months who can read properly, but we'll have to get you some smarter clothes."

Alfred looked down at his clothes which he considered to be rather splendid, especially compared with those he wore in his own time in the twenty-first century, and with those he had worn in his last adventure in the thirteenth century.

The Bishop addressed the Lieutenant of the Tower.

"Thank you, Sir John, for finding this lad for me. I'll send him to you tomorrow with the warrant for Sir Thomas Wyatt's execution. I want you to

send me a report of anything the Princess Elizabeth says which throws light on her connections with Sir Thomas Wyatt. Write them down and send them back with the lad tomorrow. Good day, Sir John.
Alfred, come with me."

The Bishop turned abruptly and made his way to the door. Philippa was already standing there to open it for him. The Bishop swept through, not looking to left or right, followed by Alfred. He stopped outside and told his men who were lounging there to pick themselves up smartly and fall in. They arranged themselves into two columns of three each side of the Bishop. As soon as they were in place, the Bishop set off at a smart pace, and the guards kept in step with him as they made their way briskly to the Tower gates with Alfred following behind, almost running to keep up. The Bishop and his bodyguards were not challenged as they reached the gates which they marched through and left the Tower. The yeoman warders recognised the authority of the Lord Chancellor of England and they knew it would be unwise to do anything to inconvenience this haughty gentleman.

Alfred has to run to keep up with
Bishop Gardiner and his bodyguard as
they hasten towards London Bridge

.The Lord Chancellor's party continued in a westerly direction, keeping fairly close to the banks of the Thames. They seemed to make a point of avoiding busy thoroughfares, always taking the quieter street of any alternative roads available when they could no longer proceed by the river. Then, as they once more reached the river's side, Alfred's attention was taken by a bridge across the River, the like of which he'd never seen before. This was London Bridge. It spanned the River in about two dozen arches, supported on stone islands which must have been laboriously built up from the river's bed, leaving only narrow channels for the transit of shipping. The feature which particularly interested Alfred were the houses and shops actually built on the bridge. The Chancellor's men turned left on to the Bridge, and they marched across, Alfred still struggling to maintain the smart pace at which the party moved. Once across London Bridge with its crowded buildings, they entered a part of London which was far less congested than the metropolis which Alfred and Alice had passed through the previous day with Chronavon.

London Bridge c.1555

St. Saviour's, Southwark

This was the Borough of Southwark. Now that they were away from the crowded streets of the City of London on the north bank, the danger of an urban ambush had receded. Such an attack was an ever present hazard for politically unpopular statesmen. In the more open space of Southwark, the pace of the Lord Chancellor's party significantly slackened. Alfred found it easier to keep up and he got his breath back. Soon after crossing the River, they passed a large and very beautiful gothic church. Alfred read on a board outside, 'The Parish Church of St. Saviour'.

In mediaeval parlance, St. = Holy. Thus the dedication of the church would be interpreted as 'Holy Saviour'. When the monasteries were dissolved, this former priory became a parish church. At a later time in history, this church was to be raised to cathedral status and become known as Southwark Cathedral.

Southwark was quite a contrast to the City of London. The city had been busy and commercial. Southwark was laid-back and recreational. There were many ale houses. Food, heated on braziers was being sold and consumed by individuals who loafed about in no particular hurry to do anything. The party passed two buildings of a very strange shape. Alfred realised from their prominently displayed names, 'the Bear Garden' and 'The Globe' that these were famous theatres.

At last they reached the Lord Chancellor's house. Unlike the timber framed houses nearby, Bishop Gardiner's house was built of stone. It was significantly larger than other nearby houses. The small downstairs windows were fitted with robust shutters, and a pair of guards wearing the same livery as the soldiers who had escorted the Lord Chancellor from the Tower stood each side of the door. One of the guards opened the door for Bishop Gardiner to pass through while the six guards who made up the escort went round the outside of the house to the back.

Bishop Gardiner paused before entering to look round to check that Alfred was still with them and beckoned him to enter the house. Alfred followed him down a corridor, up a flight of stairs and into a large room towards the rear of the house.

The GLOBE, ROSE and BEAR BAITING
THEATRES;
As they appeared about the year 1612.
Bear-baiting
Rose
Globe

It was richly panelled in oak. A large desk occupied the centre of the room and wooden chairs were arranged around the walls. A particularly large and well-polished armchair was situated on the far side of the desk on which papers and books were neatly piled.

"This is my office," explained Bishop Gardiner.

He then led Alfred into an adjoining room. The walls were lined with shelves, well stocked with leather bound books. Alfred hardly needed to be told that this was the Bishop's library. Bishop Gardiner explained to Alfred that one of his jobs would be to keep the books tidied and dusted, to study the names of the books and learn where they were placed, and to fetch and return books as and when required by the Bishop. Alfred felt quite daunted by this task. The Bishop then ushered Alfred through a door at the end of the library, across a corridor and into a small room with a single window, furnished with just a chair and a bed. This was where Alfred was to sleep. He then led Alfred down another flight of stairs into a kitchen where a maid was plucking poultry. She was a nice looking girl with dark curly hair and olive brown skin which suggested she may have been of Mediterranean origin.

"Maria, this is Alfred, my new odd job and messenger boy," the Bishop explained. "I want you to see to it that he is well fed at meal times, but first things first. Find him a set of livery which fits and then send him up to my office." With that the Bishop turned and was gone.

Maria put down her half plucked capon and smiled at Alfred.

"He is a funny man," she said shaking her head, and Alfred took that to mean, 'funny-peculiar' rather than 'funny-ha ha'.

Maria washed her hands and led Alfred to a room where a large number of purple cloaks, tabards and tunics of various sizes were hanging.

"I think we'll be able to find something to fit you," she said, rummaging among these garments. The first set she came out with were too small but the next set fitted Alfred perfectly. He was now looked just like a scaled down version of one of the guards who had escorted the Bishop from the Tower that morning.

"We'd better take you back to the study now," said Maria. "It doesn't do to keep his Lordship waiting.

Alfred spent the rest of the day, cataloguing the books in Bishop Gardiner's library. Maria came up and fetched him when food was ready. Needless to say, she approached the library from the passage which led past Alfred's new bedroom and did not attempt to come in via Bishop Gardiner's office.

Alfred turned in that night, full of excited anticipation. What might Bishop Gardiner ask him to do tomorrow? Alfred also found himself giving some thought to how Alice might be faring in the Tower. When would they next meet up to exchange news?

Chapter 6

The room into which Sir John Brydges conducted the Princess Elizabeth, her ladies-in-waiting and Alice was not really the sort of room where one would choose to spend much time, but choice was not an option for Elizabeth and her attendants. It was not that the room was too small. It accommodated a good sized table, several fairly comfortable chairs, wall cupboards, two small dressing tables with badly silvered mirrors and a large couch, well upholstered in a fabric upon which heraldic motifs had been embroidered. The main problem with the room was lack of illumination. There were only three fairly small windows to gather the light. A room of that size would have required three times that area of window space to provide adequate illumination on a bright day, but today was not a bright day. The heavy rain, incessantly falling on the roof, generated a depressing background noise and even the small fire which had been lit in the grate in preparation for the arrival of a royal prisoner, failed to add much cheer to the chamber. The Princess Elizabeth was not impressed.

"What a gloomy place you have prepared for me to spend my last days, Sir John," she sighed in a melancholy voice.

"I apologise for what I know to be far from adequate accommodation for a Princess," said Sir John, "Sadly, this place was built as a castle and not a palace, and the other accommodation I have available is far, far worse than this. Yes, today is indeed gloomy. I'll get some candles brought up to you. Tomorrow promises to be a brighter day and I'll arrange for you to be able to take some exercise on the Tower Green which I find to be a very pleasant place to be this time of the year. I'm sure these are not to be your last days, my lady, for as I said when I greeted you, the Tower of London can provide you with better protection against any who may mean you ill than any other fortress in the land."

Sir John was aware that he was talking at cross purposes to the Princess, but continued to make pleasantries, knowing that Elizabeth would not pursue the gloomy forebodings she had expressed concerning her own future during this discussion.

251

"I will arrange for Philippa, my maid, to show you where all the things you ladies will need during your stay here are kept. Shell be with you presently."

With a bow and a flourish of his hat, Sir John left the company through the door by which they'd just entered. A few minutes later Philippa bustled in. She curtsied and told them that she would soon be back with some food for them but indicated that the immediate priority was for them to get into dry clothes.

"This has been set aside as your bedroom, Your Highness," she said, opening a door which led from the main room. In this side room was a bed and a large wardrobe. Philippa opened the door of the wardrobe to display a number of dresses, similar in style to the one Elizabeth now wore.

"I hope that you will find something to your satisfaction among these, Your Highness," she said. "It's of great concern to us that you won't catch a chill through wearing damp clothes. Sir John will seek out some more clothes if none of these suit."

Philippa bowed and came out of the room, leaving Elizabeth to rummage through the clothes that had been provided for her.

"Your room is this one," Philippa said to the maids which now numbered three since Alice had entered Elizabeth's service.

Philippa opened the door of the other room which led from the main chamber. This room had been prepared with three beds. Philippa opened the doors of two spacious wardrobes and Alice was delighted to discover how thorough Sir John had been in his preparation. There was a good selection of clothes which would fit her as well as larger clothes for the adult maids.

Philippa left and the three of them started to select a dress to change into. During this time, the older maids told Alice that their names were Lady Margaret and Lady Barbara. Alice had great fun looking through the dresses. It was obvious which ones were hers. She had no need to compete with someone her own size when she found the dress she most liked. Lady Margaret and Lady Barbara on the other hand had quite a little argument over a dress they both wanted. In the end, they compromised by their both choosing completely different dresses from the one they both identified as their first choice. Once they had changed they looked very becoming and seemed content with their alternative choices. They'd barely finished making the final adjustments to their new dry clothes when Philippa returned, carrying a tray with food. Elizabeth emerged from her room, looking quite lovely in a blue velvet dress, trimmed with white lace and a matching lace collar. Philippa left and the four of them sat round the table to eat.

Conversation was stilted. The Princess Elizabeth did not seem in the mood for conversation. Alice could only disclose a little about where she was from and what she did, as she knew that a strict condition of being entrusted with this adventure, was that neither she nor Alfred should give any hint that they really came from a time in the future. Alice further knew that this was a future which could only be guaranteed if they successfully completed their mission.

The meal ended. Philippa came to collect the crockery. They talked a little more. They all started to yawn, a sure sign that they were tired. Alice was impressed that Elizabeth insisted that they spent some time in prayer before they turned in. Elizabeth led the prayers which included references to obvious matters of concern like their safety and comfort in these new quarters. Elizabeth also prayed for her half-sister, Queen Mary, and for the safety of the Realm of England. After about half-an-hour, they went to their rooms, changed into the night attire provided for them and went to bed. Alice was blissfully unaware that both the Lady Margaret and the Lady Barbara snored for Alice fell into a deep sleep almost as soon as her head touched the pillow.

The next day Philippa brought up breakfast but again, the conversation was stilted. At the end of the meal, Elizabeth told Alice to collect up the breakfast things on to the tray and leave it by the door and then tidy up the rest of the room. Alice was very happy to do this. She knew that as the youngest maid, she would be expected to perform the most menial tasks.

When she was away from the table, Alice noticed that the conversation between Elizabeth and her maids entered into more animated conversation but they spoke in hushed voices so that Alice wouldn't hear what was said. Alice realised that joining the group as a complete stranger, she wouldn't be trusted as she may have been planted there as a spy, waiting for Elizabeth to say something incriminating. She wondered how ever she could break down this mistrust. .Alice prayed long and hard that she would be accepted as a confidant of the Princess Elizabeth, for she knew that difficulties would arise in fulfilling the task that Chronavon had set if she continued to be mistrusted. Alice felt an outsider to the Princess's group of trusted attendants for several days. It wasn't until a change in the regime at the Tower occurred that a situation arose which enabled Alice to establish herself as being accepted among Elizabeth and her senior maids as one of them. The effect of this incident was for Alice to be seen as a victim of circumstances like themselves, contending against the evil forces ranged against them.

During the early days, Princess Elizabeth's imprisonment was supervised by Sir John Brydges. He allowed Elizabeth and her maids to take exercise as often as they wanted provided that they walked along the battlements, no further than the Beauchamp Tower. He also arranged for the Princess to have most of her meals with him in the Lieutenant's House, the pleasant accommodation to which Alfred and Alice had been introduced when they had first arrived at the Tower with Chronavon. Alice and the Ladies Margaret and Barbara were confined to the Bell Tower for their meals.

It was not until the third day that Alice was in the Tower that she saw Alfred again. Alice was taking an exercise walk with the Princess Elizabeth and her two lady attendants. Alfred was sauntering across Tower Green, looking very smart in the purple livery he now wore. Alice envied the freedom he seemed to be enjoying. The splendour of his attire suggested that he was enjoying a far better lifestyle than herself.

When Alfred reached the Princess's party, Alice stopped to exchange a few words with him.

"What are you doing? Where are you living now?" she asked.

Alfred seemed to know that they wouldn't be allowed long to converse and spoke tersely. Chronavon had warned them that Elizabeth would be guarded in such a way that neither she nor her attendants would be able to communicate freely with the outside world.

"I'm working for Stephen Gardiner, Bishop of Winchester and Lord Chancellor of England. I'm living in his house but I come to the Tower most days. I've left a note for you. It's written in the two letters displaced code. Count twenty five stones across from the tenth step leading up to the Bell Tower where you're staying and then, three stones up. You'll see a sliver of mortar missing between two of the large stones, just large enough to slip in a paper or an envelope. This gap between the stones is sheltered by yew trees. If you get the ladies you are with to be, one in front of you and one behind you, as you pass that point, you should be able to take the letter out without the guards being able to see what you're doing. Leave me a reply if this works all right. I will ...."

Alfred's words were cut short by one of the Yeoman Warders, deputed to keep watch over Elizabeth and her small entourage, shouting, "Move on there!" The warder was standing some twenty yards away on the edge of the green and couldn't have heard what passed between Alfred and Alice. Indeed, he didn't even suspect that a significant conversation was taking place, but he was merely doing his job of ensuring that Elizabeth remained incommunicado.

Alice ran to catch up with Elizabeth and her ladies. She knew what Alfred meat by 'two letters displaced code'. It meant that each letter in the original message would be replaced by a letter which came two letters later in the alphabet. Thus 'a' becomes 'c', 'b' becomes 'd' , 'c' becomes 'e' and so on. Alfred and Alice had had a lot of fun in Hillington, communicating in coded messages and when necessary, it was very easy to arrange to change the code, simply by varying the number of letters of displacement.

As soon as she had caught up, Alice told Elizabeth that the boy she was speaking to was working for Bishop Gardiner, but had been placed there by a friend to make sure that no plots were being hatched against Elizabeth. She explained about the message which had been left concealed in the wall of the Bell Tower. Alice could not tell whether or not Elizabeth believed that a friend had been placed in her enemy's service to protect her from those who might scheme against her. Alice knew that she was still viewed with suspicion. However, as they returned to the Bell Tower and passed behind the yew tree, Lady Margaret walked in front of Alice and Lady Barbara behind. Elizabeth knew that no charge of treason could be levelled against her on the basis of an unsolicited letter that was sent to her or her servants. The treasonable act would be for her to send a letter inciting others to rebellion. Why not see then just what this friend of Alice's had sent? Elizabeth thirsted for news of the outside world.

As they approached the Bell Tower steps, Alice identified the slot between the stones quite easily without having to carefully count the stones from the Bell tower stairs. The corner of a piece of parchment could just be seen protruding out. Alice deftly slid the note from its hiding place and concealed it under her apron without changing her step. By the time they passed beyond the Yew trees, coming back into full view as they reached the base of the Bell Tower steps, the guards around the perimeter of Tower Green, observing the progress of the foursome, would have been aware of nothing unusual taking place. Just the Princess, her two ladies in waiting and a serving girl passing behind a couple of yew trees on an uneventful walk back to the room in the Bell Tower where they were confined.

As soon as they were back in the privacy of their room, they opened up the note that Alfred had left.

Jcnnq Cnkeg, K co yqtmkoi hqt vjg Nqtf Ejcpegnnqt; Pqvjkpi uwurkekqwu vq tgrqtv agv. Oa hktuv lqd ycu vq fgnkxgt c fqewogpv vq vjg Vqygt. K vjkpm kv ycu vjg ycttcpv hqt vjg gzgewvkqp qh Vjqocu Yacvv. K yknn mggr aqw kp vqwej. Cnn vjg dguv, Cnhtgf.

At first glance, it looked like a meaningless jumble of letter, but Alice explained the code and they deciphered the message.

> **Hallo Alice, I am working for the Lord Chancellor. Nothing suspicious to report yet. My first job was to deliver a document to the Tower. I think it was the warrant for the execution of Thomas Wyatt. I will keep you in touch. All the best, Alfred.**

Elizabeth and her ladies-in waiting seemed most impressed and for the first time, Alice felt she was beginning to gain their confidence. Elizabeth showed some distress at the news of Thomas Wyatt's death warrant, although this development was not unexpected, and she started to bewail the fact that it would only be a few more days before it would be her turn to go to the block. Over the past few days, Alice had become acutely aware that the belief that her own execution was impending was a preoccupation which left Elizabeth tense and nervous, and sometimes rather snappy. However, she always apologised when she realised that she had said something unnecessarily unkind to her ladies-in-waiting, and Margaret and Barbara seemed to have an inexhaustible ability to absorb any tetchiness that Elizabeth displayed from time to time. They were very sweet young women and were fully aware of the stress under which Elizabeth was living from day to day.

"Even though it's in code, we must destroy Alfred's letter, and indeed, any other we receive in the future, once we have deciphered the messages," said Alice.

She sensed Elizabeth's approval and growing trust as she gave obviously sound advice.

"We must also compose a reply so that Alfred knows that we have received his message and that it hasn't gone astray and fallen into the wrong hands."

The four of them worked together to compose a simple reply into code.

which translates as :-

The next time they went on exercise, Alice placed the reply to Alfred's letter in the slot in the mortar as deftly as she had retrieved the original.

The day after they had received Alfred's coded note, Sir John Brydges came to their room to inform Elizabeth that the Lord Chancellor wished to have a chat with her.

"Don't use euphemisms with me, Sir John," Elizabeth said to Sir John with an aggression which was uncalled for, but which served to cover Elizabeth's fear of what might be in store for her. "'Stephen Gardiner wants to subject me to an interrogation, not a friendly chat."

Elizabeth was of course right. When she returned after her ordeal, Elizabeth was seething with indignation.

"The wretched man is trying to get me to admit that I was in collusion with Thomas Wyatt and put him up to leading a rebellion. He's trying to put words into my mouth and is postulating theories which are based on a complete pack of lies. However," Elizabeth added with a slight smile of satisfaction, "he couldn't shake me and I caught him out several times contradicting his own statements!"

Elizabeth's imprisonment continued in much the same way over the next few days. She took frequent walks with her ladies round Tower Green and along the battlements as far as she was allowed to go. Alice saw Alfred on several occasions when they were out walking, but he was always in the distance and they could do no more than acknowledge each other with a wave. Further coded notes were exchanged, using the secret makeshift posting box in the slot in the mortar just behind the Yew trees but there was nothing of particular significance concerning the Princess Elizabeth to report. Elizabeth was subjected to further interrogation sessions with Stephen Gardiner, but this Bishop of Winchester couldn't shake her in her perfectly justified claim that she'd no knowledge of Thomas Wyatt's rebellion, that there was no evidence, let alone proof, that she'd been in any way involved and that she'd always shown complete loyalty to her half-sister, Queen Mary.

Early one morning, the four of them were wakened by the sound of muffled drums. They went to the windows to see what this signified and were met with the sad sight of Sir Thomas Wyatt being led from his dungeon in another part of the castle at the start of his last journey to Tower Hill for his execution. The poor man had been so weakened by torture that he could hardly walk but, valiant man that he was, Thomas insisted on moving in his own remaining strength, refusing the arms which were proffered to assist him on his way to the scaffold.

As the execution party disappeared from view and the drum beat faded into the distance, the four ladies sat on the chairs around the room in the state of stunned silence. After a full ten minutes, Elizabeth broke the silence, expressing a wish that someone would just tell her the date which had been fixed for her own execution so that the suspense of living day to day with an unknown future could be lifted. Barbara, Margaret and Alice did their best to comfort her, telling Elizabeth that it was by no means certain that she would be executed and that it was far better to live in hope than despair. Elizabeth took heart at their words.

The following day, Sir John Brydges entered the prison room to bring Elizabeth some very unwelcome news. He was embarrassed and very apologetic. He explained that Stephen Gardiner had brought pressure to bear on the Constable of the Tower, a man by the name of Sir John Gage, to increase the rigour of Elizabeth's imprisonment. She was no longer to be allowed to share her meals with Sir John Brydges, nor would she be allowed to continue to exercise freely around Tower Green and along the battlements as far as the Beauchamp Tower. Sir John Brydges was disconsolate. He was merely the Lieutenant of the Tower. Sir John Gage was Constable of the Tower. Sir John Gage, as the senior officer of the Tower, outranked Sir John Brydges, and the Lieutenant of the Tower had no alternative but to comply with his orders.

Elizabeth was absolutely furious, but on whom could she vent her fury. She realised that Sir John Brydges had to obey those senior to himself The Princess let off steam by expressing her very unfavourable opinion of that detestable man, Stephen Gardiner. However, she graciously thanked Sir John Brydges for his kindness and courtesy to her and regretted the fact that it was unlikely that she would ever be able to repay Sir John Brydges for the wonderful favours he had shown her.

Once Sir John Gage had taken over full responsibility for supervising Elizabeth's imprisonment, further unwelcome restrictions and intrusions on her privacy were imposed. One day, the booming sound of the butt of a halberd striking the door of the prison room three times was followed by the door being flung open as four surly Yeoman Warders burst in. Elizabeth rose from her place to protest but her voice was drowned out by

the strident tones of the Sergeant of the party.
"We have orders to search these rooms for papers relating to the security of the State. Long live Queen Mary."

With that, the Yeoman Warders went through the main room and the adjoining two bedrooms, overturning tables and chairs, knocking over candelabra, and strewing clothes and possessions across the floor. Needless to say, they found nothing of any significance and left after half an hour, leaving the rooms in a shambles. Margaret and Barbara started to weep but Elizabeth scolded them.

"Come on you young ladies, we need to show that Sir John Gage that we are made of sterner stuff than to be intimidated by a gang of his ruffians. Come on, Alice, let's start to tidy up."

Alice set to work with a will and after a few more sobs, the Ladies Margaret and Barbara put their handkerchiefs away and joined in with the tidying up. The unwelcome incursion of the gang of Yeoman Warders might almost have been seen as a blessing in disguise, for even before their intrusion, the room had been getting very untidy. After an hour of quite hard work the room was restored to a state of tidiness and order, and indeed, looked far better than it had before their privacy had been infringed.

The searching of the prison rooms was not an isolated occurrence. During the next week, the rooms were searched again on three more occasions. On the third occasion, Alice noticed one of the Yeoman Warders grab some jewellery which had been left out on one of the dressing tables and stow these items in his pocket. Alice ran forward to where the Warder was standing against the dressing table, his back to the room, fully believing that his body had obstructed everybody's view of the top of the dressing table so that no one could observe what he had done.

"Put those back, you thief!" she screamed.

The warder turned and struck Alice a blow on the face which sent her reeling to the floor. The Sergeant came over to see what was going on.

"He's stolen my ladies' jewellery," cried Alice from the floor.

"Turn out your pockets, Jack," ordered the sergeant.

The warder shamefacedly withdrew three pendants, two bracelets and half a dozen rings from his pocket and placed them back on the dressing table.

"Why, you scurvy knave," shouted the Sergeant, "I'll deal with you severely when we leave this place."

"And I demand to see Sir John Gage, immediately," roared the Princess in indignant fury. "How dare you burst into our rooms and steal our property before our very eyes."

"Search party, fall in," commanded the Sergeant, and the disgraced party beat a hasty retreat out of the room.

When they had gone, Barbara and Margaret helped Alice to her feet and examined Alice's face. A blue bruise showed prominently on the cheek bone where she had been struck by the thieving Yeoman Warder. The side of Alice's face began to swell and they tenderly bathed the injury. The swelling subsided after a week and the bruise disappeared but from that time on, Alice felt fully integrated into the Princesses party as a trusted member. All four now felt able to speak freely together and Alice was made party to some of their secrets. Room searches continued, but less frequently and the Warders were much more circumspect in the way they carried out this duty.

The increased security of confinement, the loss of privileges and the incursion of privacy occasioned by room searches would have been enough to take a less robust person than Elizabeth to the limits of their endurance but something even worse was to follow. One day, Sir John Brydges arrived at the room in the Bell Tower, looking very grave indeed. Knowing full well Elizabeth's sensitivity, he first told her that her life was in no danger, but that she should sit down to prepare herself for a shock. News had just been confirmed that the man she loved, Edward Courtenay, had died in Padua. He had been exiled a short while before Elizabeth had been imprisoned when it was suspected that both he and Elizabeth were involved in the rebellion of Sir Thomas Wyatt. Elizabeth immediately suspected that foul play had been involved in Edward's death but Sir John reassured her that it had been fully investigated and it had been shown beyond all reasonable doubt that Edward had died from natural causes.

Elizabeth retained her composure until Sir John had left the Bell Tower and then broke down in utter grief and dejection.

"I'll never, never meet a man I could love as much as Edward. We'd planned between ourselves to marry and would have announced our engagement had not this wretched rebellion occurred. Who knows, I may escape the predicament in which I now find myself, and perhaps one day, even become queen, but now that Edward is dead, I know that I shall never ever find another man I could love enough to marry."

Barbara, Margaret, Alice all did their best to comfort the young Princess but for a while, she was quite inconsolable and totally despondent. Over the next few days, the lack of fresh air and exercise, the constant anxiety that another room search was going to take place, the shock arising from the devastating news that the man she loved had just died and the constant fear that she herself would be taken to the block, all took their toll on Elizabeth's health. She became quite ill. Sir John Brydges made sure that Sir John Gage, the Constable of the Tower came to see the distressed state and poor health of the Princess. Sir John Gage was quite alarmed at what he found.

While Stephen Gardiner might have been quite happy to see Elizabeth die quietly in captivity, Sir John Gage was a responsible man, and he knew that his responsibility extended to seeing to the well-being of all under his protection in the Tower. Elizabeth was not even in the Tower, facing charges of being involved in rebellion, whatever Stephen Gardiner might suspect. In the eyes of the law, Elizabeth was a completely innocent woman and deserved courteous consideration. Sir John Gage lifted the order, preventing Elizabeth from being able to leave her room. He even extended the area within which Elizabeth was free to roam to the Tower's walled garden. On being allowed to go out into the fresh air and enjoy a stroll, the Princess Elizabeth's health and strength were gradually restored.

Alice was relieved on two counts, first and foremost, that Elizabeth was getting better, but secondly, she was no longer permanently incarcerated with her mistress in the Bell Tower. This had meant that Alice was unable to check on whether or not Alfred was trying to communicate by leaving letters in the secret posting box in the Bell Tower wall. On being able to resume their exercise within the confines of the outer wall of the Tower of London, Alice was able to check the secret posting box on a daily basis. A few coded notes had been left, but nothing of great consequence. One week after the restoration of the right to outdoor exercise, Alice found a letter delivered by Alfred which was very significant.

Chapter 7

Alfred woke as the first rays of the rising sun entered the east facing window of his bedroom and fell warm upon his face. It took him a moment to take stock of where he was. Yes, he was now in the home of his new master, Stephen Gardiner, Bishop of Winchester and Lord Chancellor of England. Alfred washed, put on his new uniform and went down to the kitchen where Maria served his breakfast. He then reported to the Bishop's office to await his orders for the day. Alfred knocked and the Bishop's voice answered, "Come in."

"Ah, there you are," said the Bishop looking up from the papers he was studying. "I want you to take these to Sir John Brydges at the Tower."

He handed a packet of parchments, some of which were in envelopes, to Alfred. The edge of the largest envelope had been inked in black. Alfred wondered to himself if this was the warrant for Sir Thomas Wyatt's execution.

"Put these in the secret pocket of your grey cloak," ordered Bishop Gardiner. "No matter how warm it gets, wear that cloak so that it covers the rest of your clothes, otherwise, you may find yourself in grave danger. Leave here by the back door and check to see that there is no one around, watching you depart. Return to the Tower by the same route that we used to come here yesterday. Keep away from busy streets and hand over these papers personally to Sir John Brydges and no one else. He may give you some papers to bring back to me."

The Bishop paused thoughtfully.

"I may not be in when you return. There'll be nothing of any great moment among the papers from the Tower so just leave them on my desk and go and work in the library. I'm going to see Cardinal Pole this afternoon. Do you know who he is?" asked the Bishop in his usual gruff tone of voice.

"No," answered Alfred shyly shaking his head. He began to wish he had studied the history of England under the Tudors as avidly as his friend Alice had done when this had been the history topic last term at school.

Lambeth Palace

"Cardinal Pole is the new Archbishop of Canterbury. He lives over there," said Bishop Gardiner pointing out of his window to a large building about half a mile away.

"Is that Lambeth Palace?" asked Alfred, glad to have this opportunity to show he was not completely ignorant of church affairs.

"Yes, it is indeed. Cardinal Pole is a very learned man. I'm hoping to see a great revival of the Catholic Church in England under his leadership," said the Bishop. "Now be off with you on your errand."

Alfred carefully followed his instructions. He left by the back door of the Bishop's London house, checked that no one was watching for his departure and made his way back through Southwark, across London Bridge and on to the Tower. The Yeoman Warders standing guard at the Middle Tower made to stop Alfred entering, but Alfred threw back his grey cloak to display his purple livery and the coats of arms embroidered on his inner cloak. The Warders withdrew the halberds they had crossed in Alfred's path and ushered him through. Alfred made his way straight to the Lieutenant's house where he was cordially greeted by Sir John Brydges who asked him the expected questions about his accommodation at Bishop Gardiner's house, how he was settling in to his new job, and how he was getting on with his new boss. Alfred was very positive on all these points. He handed Sir John the papers he'd brought over. Sir John told him that there were some papers for him to take back, but that they wouldn't be ready for an hour or so, and he suggested that in the meantime, Alfred should go out and explore the Tower.

Alfred left his grey cloak in Sir John Brydges' house and wandered out to Tower Green. He guessed that being seen in the Lord Chancellor's livery would be advantageous and was quite right in this assumption. He found that he could roam where he chose without at any time being challenged by a Yeoman Warder. He hoped that he might see Alice but was disappointed on that count. He knew that Alice was in the Bell Tower and he started to give serious thought as to how he might establish communication with her. Alfred realised that if he couldn't communicate with Alice, there was no way he could do anything to protect the Princess Elizabeth, should he discover that someone outside the Tower was posing a threat to her safety. However could he communicate with his friend while she was guarded with the utmost security in a prison with a high profile, political prisoner? Alfred wandered over to the Chapel of St. Peter ad Vincula which he'd seen from the window while he had sat waiting in Sir John Brydges' house the previous day. He went in and spent some time praying over the dilemma that faced him and then came out.

He returned to the Bell Tower which he'd already walked round that morning and discovered the slot in the masonry near the steps leading up to the door of the Bell Tower which he hadn't noticed previously. The slot was sheltered from the view of any standing around Tower Green by two large yew trees and was just the right size to take a few letters or papers which wouldn't be noticed by the casual passer-by. This set Alfred thinking and gave him the idea of using it as a posting box to pass on secret messages.

After a pleasant morning strolling in the sun in the precincts of the Tower of London, Alfred returned to Sir John Brydges' house where the papers for Bishop Gardiner were now ready for him. He stowed them in the secret pocket in his grey cloak and returned to the Bishop's house in Southwark. He spent the rest of the day busying himself in the library.

Alfred returned many times to the Tower over the next couple of weeks or so, sometimes alone, carrying out a delivery, at other times, in the company of Bishop Gardiner and his armed escort. Alfred was not entirely surprised to discover that Bishop Gardiner wore a mail shirt under his outer clothes whenever he ventured out.

"He must have even more enemies than I'd at first realised," thought Alfred to himself.

On the third occasion that he visited the Tower he did see Alice, taking exercise in the company of Elizabeth and her maids and he managed to have that brief conversation which enabled the secret means of communication to be set up. Coded notes were passed between them but it wasn't until two, maybe three, weeks had passed that a really important development occurred.

Alfred was in the kitchen, just finishing the lunch that Maria had prepared for him when he heard one of the Bishop's other servants announce that there was a Reverend Tobias Maltravers to see my Lord Bishop of Winchester. This name was significant. It had been mentioned by Chronavon. Yes, this was the agent of Ahrimanes who would scheme to change the allotted course of history.

Alfred hurriedly finished his last mouthful and quickly made his way to the library where he removed the books which covered the knot hole through which it was possible to see into the Bishop's office. Alfred was in position, looking through the knot hole, just before Tobias Maltravers was ushered into the office.

The Bishop stood to shake Tobias's hand and motioned him to sit opposite him at his desk. The Bishop started the conversation with the usual pleasantries.
"And how is life in Owslebury?" he enquired.

"The church is running wonderfully well," replied Tobias. "Fifty people attend mass every Sunday. That's almost the whole village you know."

Alfred studied Tobias through the knot hole. He reminded Alfred of a weasel. His nose was long and pointed and he furtively looked around as he spoke as if he didn't want his words to be heard by some third party. Little did he know that in the next room, someone could hear everything that was being said.

"And what brings you to see me?" asked the Bishop. "This is some way from your parish."

"I had to come to London to see an aunt and I thought that I would take the opportunity of seeing you while I was up here. I know that affairs of state make it very difficult for you to spend much time in Winchester. I've also heard rumours about your concern over that rebel, Sir Thomas Wyatt and the way that Princess Elizabeth put him up to it. I may be able to help you get to the bottom of the matter."

Tobias knew exactly the thing to say to gain the Bishop's full attention.

"Oh yes, I know, I'm sure that we all know, that the Princess was the schemer behind the rebellion, but we have no proof. We have the letters that Sir Thomas tried to send to the Princess and to Edward Courtenay, the Earl of Devon. Sadly, we can't find the letters that they must have sent to him," explained the Bishop.

"Didn't Sir Thomas tell you that he was acting under their orders when you interrogated him?" asked Tobias.

"No, the stubborn man would say nothing of the sort. In his final speech to the crowd before his head was severed, he declared that Elizabeth and Edward were not involved in any way with the rebellion, that he, Thomas Wyatt, took full responsibility, and that no other royal personage was involved. The final words of condemned man are invariably regarded as having the nature of absolute truth."

Bishop Stephen sounded quite exasperated as he described his failure to extract what he wanted to believe was the true state of affairs.

"Did you put him on the rack or use thumb screws? Did you dip his feet in boiling oil?"

Tobias Maltravers seemed to delight in recalling the mediaeval tortures used to 'persuade' prisoners to make a confession.

"We used all the usual means."

"Did you gouge out his eyes," asked Tobias with ghoulish anticipation of a positive answer.

"That doesn't work," answered the Bishop, "Once a prisoner has been mutilated to that extent, he has no other wish but to die and no more information can be extracted."

The Bishop spoke as speaking from his own experience of interrogating prisoners. Alfred became acutely aware of how careful he and Alice would have to be in carrying out actions which might displease the Bishop and which could be traced back to them!

"How careful has the search of Sir Thomas Wyatt's property been?" asked Tobias. "There surely must be a letter from the Princess Elizabeth, but perhaps one that Sir Thomas didn't have time to read because he was so busy with the rebellion. This is where I might be able to be of some help. I'm very good at looking for things and finding them."

Tobias rubbed the side of his nose with his forefinger and nodded in a knowing sort of way.

"You're very welcome to have a warrant to search through Sir Thomas's house if you really think you can come up with something."

"Oh, I'm sure I can, I'm sure I can," repeated Tobias, "but I'll need some things to help me in my search."

"If l can make it available to you, you shall have it," replied the Bishop.

"In order for me to recognise a letter from the Princess, it would be most helpful if I had a specimen of her handwriting," requested Tobias.

"You can certainly have that," replied the Bishop. "Come into the library. I have a couple of letters from the Princess among those which I've stored in my box of state correspondence."

Alfred now realised that he was in immediate danger. While being found in the library would arouse no suspicion in the Bishop's mind in view of the fact that caring for the library was part of Alfred's job, the Bishop might become anxious if he knew that the conversation that had just taken place had been overheard. What should Alfred do? He had only a split second to make up his mind. Should he leave the library by the other door before the Bishop and Tobias came in? But he needed to hear the rest of the conversation.

Alfred offered up a quick arrow prayer. "God, what do I do now?"

A bold plan came to mind. As quick as lightning, Alfred replaced the books on the shelf in front of the knot hole and dashed to the window. The office and the library were on the first floor of the Bishop's house. A sturdy Wisteria covered most of the wall outside the library. Alfred climbed out of the window and down the Wisteria until he was below the level of the window sill. He clung on to the creeper as hard as he could.

The Bishop and Tobias entered the library just after Alfred's head had disappeared from view. Although Alfred could no longer see what was happening, he could hear all he needed to, to know what was going on. The Bishop walked over to the shelves where state papers were stored and found the letter which would provide Tobias with a specimen of Elizabeth's handwriting.

"There you are," said the Bishop, "The Princess wrote that letter to the Queen last year."

"It would also be very useful if you could let me have a specimen of Elizabeth's seal. I wouldn't want to open a sealed letter myself, but if the only writing available for me to identify the sender is on the envelope, ability to recognise the seal would be a great advantage."

"I can do better than that. I can let you have a seal just like that used by the Princess. Being Lord Chancellor of England has its advantages at times like this. I've no problem in getting hold of seals."

"I'd also like some parchment and envelopes," asked Tobias. "I'm only a poor priest and such items come very expensive to the likes of me."

"No problem in that either," said the Bishop. "Come back into my office and I'll see what I can find."

Alfred heard the library door click shut and climbed from his precarious position clinging on to the creeper, back into the library. He made his way once again to the shelf where he could remove books to look through the knot hole into the Bishop's office. By the time Alfred was in position, the Bishop and Tobias were back, sitting round the desk.

"It must be clear to the Bishop as it is to me," thought Alfred, "that this Maltravers fellow is going off to forge a letter which will incriminate the Princess, He knows that this is what the Bishop needs to get the Princess executed. This Bishop is pretending to go along with the pretence that Tobias is merely going to Sir Thomas's house to look for a letter from the Princess Elizabeth."

Alfred began to get a true measure of the sort of man Bishop Gardiner was.

"If you find a sealed letter," the Bishop was saying, "Don't open it. It will look far more convincing if I take it to the Queen and get her to open it herself."

"What a devious man is this Bishop," thought Alfred to himself.

"Are there any other matters you wish to raise with me?" continued the Bishop.

"It's only concerning my little parish," continued Tobias. "I told you how well mass was attended at Owslebury, but the same is not true at my neighbouring parishes. The priest at Morestead is too old to be effective and those at Hensting and Upham are just too lazy. If I could take over those parishes and join them to Owslebury, the church in that part of your diocese would really begin to thrive."

"Your stipend would considerably increase too," said the Bishop wryly.

"Oh, I hadn't thought of that," lied Tobias. "Money isn't important to me. As you may know, when I first became a priest, my dearest wish was to become a residentiary canon at Winchester Cathedral.

"A residentiary canon has food and housing provided and very little else," explained the Bishop.

"Ah, yes," replied Tobias, "but unlike the canons

at other cathedrals, the clerical staff at Winchester Cathedral enjoy the not inconsiderable benefit of hearing you preach from time to time."

Again, Tobias was lying. The last thing he wanted was a virtually unpaid job at the Cathedral but he thought it worth flattering the Bishop. This was a sure means of ingratiating himself with one whom he expected would bestow favours on a poor priest like himself.

Bishop Gardiner was worldly enough to recognise obsequiousness.

"Well, we'll see what can be done about your parish, but first, set about trying to find any letters that the Princess Elizabeth might have sent to that rebel, Sir Thomas Wyatt. Come here the same time tomorrow and I'll have the warrant to search the house and a seal, just like the Princess Elizabeth's, ready for you."

Tobias stood, bowed to the Bishop and left the room. Alfred immediately replaced the books which concealed his means of viewing the Bishop's office from the library, and returned to his bedroom to compose a coded letter to Alice.

It was with some excitement that Alice returned with the Princess Elizabeth and the ladies in waiting from their exercise walk, having picked up from the secret posting box, a longer coded note than usual, a blank sheet of parchment and an unused envelope. The excitement increased when Alice realised that the easily decoded word which Alfred had written in large letters at the head of the note indicated that the message called for immediate attention.

WTIGPV

Cnkeg,

C ugtxcpv qh Dkujqr Ictfkpgt ku cttcpikpi *vq* ikxg jko c hqthgf ngwvgt kp cp gpxgnqrg, ugcngf ykvj vjg Rtkpeguu Gnkbcdgvj'u ugcn, yjkej yknn crrgct *vq* dg c ngwvgt htqo vjg Rtkpeguu vq Ukt Vjqocu Yacw, gpeqwtcikpi jko *vq* ngcf c tgdgnnkqp *vq* rwv jgt qp vjg vjtqpg. Vjg Dkujqr ku iqkpi *vq* encko vjcv vjg ngwvgt jcu lwuv dggp hqwpf kp Vjqocu Yacw'u jqwtg yjkej Vjqocu fkf pqv jcxg vkog *vq* qrgp *qt* jcf pqv

293

tgegkxgf dghqsg ngcxkpi jku jqwug *vq* ngcf
vjg tgdgnnkqp. Vjg Dkujqr ku iqkpi *vq* ikxg
vjku ugcngf ngwgt rgtuqpcnna *vq* Swggp
Octa.

Cum vjg Rtkpeguu *vq* ytkvg cpqvjgt ngwgt,
cfftguugf vq Ukt Vjqocu Yacw, ugcngf cpf
fcvgf dghqtg vjg tgdgnnkqp, yjkej
eqpvckpu qpna ocvgtkcn yjkej ujg yqgnf
dg rngcugf hqt Swggp Octa *vq* tgcf. Ngcxg
vjg ngwgt kp vjg rquvkpi *dqz* cu uqqp cu
aqw ctg cdng. K yknn vta *vq* gzejcpig vjku
ngwgt ykvj vjg qpg ytkwgp vq kpetkokocvg
vjg Rtkpeguu, dghqtg vjg Ckujqr vcmgu
kv vq vjg Swggp.

K jcxg nghv cp gpxgnqrg cpf c rctejogpv
htqo vjg Dkujqr'u qhhkeg cu vjgug yknn dg
vjg ucog cu vjg qpgu wugf vq ocmg vjg
hqtigta.

Iqqf nwem,

Cnhtgf.

Alice and the Ladies Margaret and Barbara set
to work and soon had the letter deciphered.

URGENT

Alice,

**A servant of Bishop Gardiner is arranging
to give him a forged letter in an envelope,
sealed with the Princess Elizabeth's seal,
which will appear to be a letter from the
Princess to Sir Thomas Wyatt, encouraging
him to lead a rebellion to put her on the
throne. The Bishop is going to claim that
the letter has just been found in Thomas
Wyatt's house which Thomas did not have
time to open or had not received before
leaving his house to lead the rebellion. The
Bishop is going to give this sealed letter
personally to Queen Mary.**

**Ask the Princess to write another letter,
addressed to Sir Thomas Wyatt, sealed and
dated before the rebellion, which contains
only material which she would be pleased
for Queen Mary to read. Leave the letter in**

295

They showed the letter to the Princess Elizabeth whose eyes blazed with fury as she took in its contents.

"Is there no end to the evil this man will do, no depths to which he will not stoop to accomplish his purposes? Come, give the parchment and a quill," Elizabeth ordered in a shrill voice, "and I will put the matter right."

Then the anger seemed to drain from Elizabeth and a smile crossed her face.

"I would love to see Gardiner's face when my sister opens the letter that I shall write." Then a note of anxiety crept into her voice.

"Is there any doubt that your friend really will be able to exchange the letters in such a way that it will be my letter and not the forgery which reaches the Queen?" she enquired of Alice.

"Alfred is the most resourceful and competent fellow I know," she replied with great confidence. "If anyone can carry this off, Alfred can."

Elizabeth seemed reassured and started to write, dating the letter well before the rebellion.

20th November 1553

My dear Sir Thomas,

It has come to my attention that you are not pleased that my sister Mary has ascended to the throne. This is unbecoming of a knight of your chivalrous reputation. For the sake of the love you bore my mother, please serve my

newly crowned sister, faithfully and loyally, for England could not have a more just and virtuous lady to rule over our great realm.

I have no great wish to be queen myself and my dearest prayer is that Mary should marry and have many children to secure the succession of our royal house. It would only be in the most regrettable circumstances of my beloved sister dying without issue that I would reluctantly consent to wear the crown myself.

However, that situation is unlikely to arise and I urge all honourable English men, whether they be lord or commoner, knight or burger, to put their hearts and swords at the service of our most beloved Queen.

Long live Queen Mary,

Her most loyal and obedient subject,

Elizabeth.

After signing the letter with her characteristic flourish, Elizabeth passed it across to Alice and her Ladies-in-waiting who read the letter with approval.

"That should convince your sister that you are no traitor," said the Lady Barbara reassuringly.

"Shall we pray that it will indeed reach the Queen," suggested Alice.

"An excellent suggestion, young maid," said the Princess. "We mustn't forget that ultimately, these affairs are in the hand of God and we are but His servants, sent here to fulfil His purposes."

Alice felt inwardly that these wise words particularly applied to herself and Albert who'd been sent with the express purpose of thwarting Ahrimanes' designs to change the ordained course of history.

The four ladies prayed together for about three quarters of an hour. At the end of the prayer time, the Princess gave the orders which would enable the next phase of the plan to be put into effect.

"Fetch me a candle and some wax. Give me the envelope." she commanded. Elizabeth addressed the envelope in a clear hand,

Sir Thomas Wyatt

She folded the parchment, put it into the envelope, melted some sealing wax on the flap of the envelope and pressed her signet ring into the wax, leaving a clear imprint of the letter 'E'.

Elizabeth was now impatient for the letter to be placed where Alfred could pick it up at the earliest opportunity.

"Margaret, tell the guards that I am feeling faint and need some more fresh air."

Margaret called to the guard outside and they heard the key turn and the massive bolt being drawn back. The door opened and the ladies left their prison room once again for a stroll round Tower Green. As they passed behind the yew trees, Alice took the letter from under her tunic and neatly placed it in the gap between the stones in the Bell Tower wall for Alfred to pick up, next time he came that way.

The following day, Alfred came alone to the Tower on another of Bishop Gardiner's errands. He was relieved to find the letter addressed to Sir Thomas Wyatt in place. He placed the envelope in the secret pocket of his grey cloak and made his way back to Bishop Gardiner's house.

Alfred now began to feel very worried. All had gone to plan so far, but a very difficult task lay ahead. However was he going to switch letters? Suppose Tobias returned to the house when he was out on an errand so that he wouldn't be able to observe where the incriminating latter was put. Suppose the letter was put in some place which was quite inaccessible to himself. Suppose Bishop Gardiner took it into his head to take it immediately to Queen Mary. These were all things over which Alfred had no control. Alfred did what he always did when confronted with circumstances which he could not control and which could seriously affect the outcome of a venture on which he was engaged. Alfred went to his room and prayed.

During that day, as he worked in the library, Alfred kept a keen ear open to detect the arrival at the Bishop's house of the Reverend Tobias Maltravers. The Bishop had several visitors that day and Alfred began to despair that Tobias would never come, but late in the afternoon, he heard Tobias's ingratiating voice, speaking to the Bishop in his office. Alfred immediately made his way to the point where he could observe what was going on in the Bishop's office.

"Well done," said the Bishop as he received the letter from Tobias. "Did you have difficulty in finding it?" he asked, as if he really thought that Tobias had made a thorough search of Sir Thomas's house. He was told the lie he expected to be told.

"Oh yes, indeed," replied Tobias, "I searched high and low for them but finally found some letters under a chair in the hall. They must have been dropped by whatever person delivered them to the house and never reached Sir Thomas. I recognised

Elizabeth's letter from her hand writing of which you kindly gave me a specimen, and of course, also by the seal."

"How careless of someone to drop such important letters," said the Bishop, "How strange they were not found earlier for you are not the first person to have searched the house."

Tobias shrugged.

"Oh, not really," he said, "I'm a very thorough person. There's very little which escapes my notice."

Tobias looked straight towards the panelling from which Alfred was peering through the knot hole. For a dreadful moment, Alfred felt a sudden pang of panic. He felt that Tobias could see the knot hole and knew that he was there, but it was a false alarm. Tobias soon looked away and carried on his conversation with the Bishop.

"I'll take this to the Queen, tomorrow," the Bishop informed Tobias. "Meanwhile, I'll need to put it somewhere safe."

The Bishop opened the second drawer down of his desk, put the letter in and firmly closed the drawer. Alfred's heart sank as the Bishop took a bunch of keys from his pocket and locked the drawer.

"When should I come to see you again?" Tobias asked the Bishop. "As I indicated to you during our last meeting, I have ideas on how my ministry might be developed beyond the narrow confines of my small and humble parish."

"Come and see me tomorrow," said the Bishop, "after I have seen the Queen."

The Bishop stood and Tobias followed suit.

"I'll see you out," said the Bishop with a gesture to the door.

The Bishop led Tobias to the door and they both went out of the office. Alfred rushed to his bed room where he had hidden the letter the Princess Elizabeth had written the previous day. He dashed back with it, through the library and into the Bishop's office. He tried the drawer where he had seen the Bishop put Tobias's letter. As Alfred already knew, the drawer was locked. What was he to do? Picking locks in double quick time was not a skill that Alfred had acquired. He offered up a quick arrow prayer.

"Lord, help me now or all will be lost."

Alfred looked down at the set of drawers again. He tried the top drawer. It slid open. This drawer was not locked. Alfred took the drawer right out of the desk, and wonderful, he could see down into the locked second drawer, that is, the drawer immediately beneath the top drawer. This contained the letter that Tobias had just brought in to the Bishop. Alfred removed the letter, replacing it with the one the Princess Elizabeth had written. Alfred then replaced the top drawer and hastened out of the office, back to his bedroom. He hid Tobias's letter in the cupboard where it would remain until the next occasion that he returned to the Tower. Alfred didn't realise how close the timing had been. He had in fact moved from the Bishop's office into the library, a split second before the Bishop returned after having seen Tobias off the premises.

The following day, Alfred returned to the Tower on another errand and placed Tobias's letter in the slot in the masonry which had become such a useful posting box. This was picked up by Alice when she went with the Princess and her ladies-in-waiting on their exercise walk. Once back in the privacy of their prison room, they examined the letter. The Princess's attention was first drawn to the seal. She compared the letter 'E' with her signet ring.

"They're not quite the same," she said. "Look, there's a slight difference in the E on my signet ring and it's definitely larger."

On receipt of such a letter, it would be very unlikely for anyone to have noticed these subtle differences between the original seal and its copy, before the seal was broken to take the letter out.

Elizabeth commented that the writing on the envelope was tolerably like her own handwriting. She withdrew the letter and started to read. Alice noticed her become tense and a look of almost panic crossed the Princess's face.

"Whoever had the audacity to present such a contentious document as if it came from my hand?!" she angrily exclaimed. "If this letter fell into the wrong hands, it would be my death sentence!"

She passed the letter across for the others to read.

27th November 1553

My dear Sir Thomas Wyatt,

As this country now knows to its cost, my illegitimate half-sister has become Queen of England. I call upon all valiant men at arms in our land to rise up against this tyrant, Mary, so that I, the only surviving legitimate heir of King Henry VIII, may take my rightful place upon the throne, to rule this realm with all the wisdom and benevolence that my poor demented half-sister is incapable of bringing to this noble task,

The one who hopes soon to be your crowned and anointed Queen,

Elizabeth.

The letter was returned to Elizabeth who placed it on the table in front of her.

Just then, the door burst open, and four Yeoman Warders barged in to carry out one of their randomly timed searches of the rooms which the Princess Elizabeth occupied with her maids. They'd never found anything incriminating, but today, there was in front of the Princess, this forged document which would send her to the block if it came into the wrong hands. Alice looked across to where Elizabeth was sitting. With great presence of mind, she'd slid the letter under the table cloth as the warders came in, but it was only a matter of time before the warders would discover this incriminating document. Finding this sort of thing was the very purpose of these random raids. A diversion was needed. In their usual disorderly way, the warders had emptied drawers, scattering their contents on the floor, turned over tables and moved the candelabra around. One of these was now uncomfortably near a curtain to one of the windows. Unnoticed by the warders, Alice slid the candelabra another couple of inches towards the curtain, and in no time this was ablaze. The necessary diversion was created.

Alice slides the candelabra towards the curtains to start a fire which will divert the attention of the Yeoman Warders searching Princess Elizabeth's room

"Fire! fire!" shouted the warders to the guards outside and started rushing around. "Water! Water!"

Buckets of water were quickly brought through the door and in no time the fire was quenched. Then the search was resumed. They threw the clothes out of the wardrobes. They tore off the table cloth and unceremoniously chucked it on the floor. Alice was relieved to see that there was no sign of the letter. They ripped off the bed clothes. This was all part of their clumsy attempt to make the search look as thorough as possible. They found nothing. They left the room, empty handed as usual.

"You showed great presence of mind in creating that diversion," said the Princess to Alice. "It gave me the opportunity to hide the letter where they could not search," and Elizabeth withdrew the letter from under her bodice. "We must now destroy this piece of writing of evil intent for once and for all. Bring me a pair of scissors."

Elizabeth started to cut the document into small pieces and Alice helped Margaret and Barbara burn them in the candle flames.

Chapter 9

It was with some satisfaction that Stephen Gardiner prepared himself to enter the Queen's presence. It was not a formal court occasion. There'd been no trumpet fanfare followed by a herald announcing the entry of the Lord Chancellor of England and Bishop of Winchester. A servant had quietly come in to tell the junior lady-in-waiting that the Lord Chancellor wished an audience. Queen Mary was in one of her private rooms in Hampton Court Palace with two of her ladies-in-waiting. The message was passed up to the Queen via the senior lady-in-waiting. Stephen Gardiner was always welcome to visit the Queen on an informal basis. She regarded him as her trusted first minister who had shared the persecution she felt that she and her mother, Katherine of Aragon, had experienced when the Reformation had swept England during the reign of her father. On hearing that Stephen Gardiner waited without, she'd put down the sewing which she found a pleasant and therapeutic diversion from the continued round of official functions and seeing to matters of state.

"Shew him in," she commanded.

The Bishop entered, bowed to his Queen and sat on the seat which the Queen gestured with the much practised sweep of her hand.

"What brings you down the River this spring morning, Lord Chancellor," she asked.

"One of my servants has carried out a very thorough search of Thomas Wyatt's house," explained the Bishop. "He found a letter which I recognised to be in Elizabeth's hand. The seal confirmed that it is she who sent the letter. The seal is unbroken and it's clear that Thomas, for whatever reason, never opened the letter. Even as Lord Chancellor, I hesitate to break the seal on a piece of royal correspondence which may contain matters of great sensitivity relating to yourself"

"Do you have the letter with you?"

"To show you the letter was the very reason for my visit this morning, Your Majesty," said the Bishop, withdrawing the letter from his inner pocket and handing it to the Queen.

Queen Mary broke the seal, took out the parchment and perused it.

"I have treated my half-sister very harshly, and very unjustly," the Queen said on assimilating the contents of the letter. "It was on the basis of your advice that I had her confined to the Tower but I realise now that that was quite unnecessary. Arrange to have her released from the Tower."

She handed the Bishop Elizabeth's letter. If any had suspected that Stephen Gardiner was aware of the nature of the contents of the letter before he had handed it to the Queen, they would have realised on observing him now that what he read in that letter came as a complete shock to him. The shock gave place to anger as first his neck and then his face turned red, and then became almost purple, but he had to retain his composure in the presence of the Queen.

"What was that fool, Tobias Maltravers, playing at?" the Bishop mentally asked himself.

"My Lord Bishop, are you all right?" asked the Queen, observing the unnatural colour of his countenance.

With admirable self-control, the Bishop regained his composure. He swallowed hard.

"Just a touch of quinsy, it's nothing, it's nothing. If I release the Lady Elizabeth, to where should she be sent?" enquired the Bishop, turning his attention back to the immediate needs of running the state. The Queen thought for moment.

"Sir Henry Bedingfield has a very pleasant house and estate at Woodstock," she answered. "Sir Henry was very kind to my mother during those difficult final years of her life. Arrange for Elizabeth to go to Woodstock. Sir Henry will look after Elizabeth well. She'll be happy there. Are there any other matters which need to be brought to my attention?"

"Not just at this moment," said the Bishop somewhat faintly.

The Bishop took his leave of the Queen and returned to his house in Southwark. He prepared the papers authorising the release of Princess Elizabeth from the Tower and her transfer to

Woodstock. He gave these to Alfred to deliver to Sir John Brydges. Later that afternoon, the Reverend Tobias Maltravers paid the prearranged visit to his diocesan Bishop.

"Have you considered my suggestion concerning the livings of my parish at Owslebury and the neighbouring benefices," he asked the Bishop, expecting a favourable reply.

"I have considered your future career as a cleric very carefully indeed," replied the Bishop. There was a menacing tone in his voice. "There's a vacancy among the residentiary canons at Winchester Cathedral. I'm arranging for you to be transferred there. After all, this was your heartfelt wish as a young priest, wasn't it? From time to time, I'll be preaching at the Cathedral and you'll have the benefit of listening to my sermons. Good day Mr. Maltravers."

"B B But that is not. ...."

"Good day Mr. Maltravers. That will be all."

The Bishop rang a hand bell and a maid arrived to show this devious priest to the door before he could make any protestations concerning the tum his career was about to take.

Alfred arrived at Sir John Brydges house in the Tower, totally unaware that the papers he was bearing were documents giving authority for the Princess Elizabeth to be released from the Tower. He was surprised when shown into Sir John's drawing room to see that Chronavon was also there. Sir John seemed in a particularly benevolent mood. He received the papers from Alfred and opened them out on his desk. It was almost as if he already knew their contents. He looked up from the papers.

"The Princess is to be released. I think that we should invite the ladies in, don't you Chronavon?" Sir John beamed as he spoke.

"An excellent suggestion," replied Chronavon.

Sir John went out to summon a senior Yeoman Warder to release the Princess and invite Elizabeth and her attendants to his house. While he was out,

Chronavon told Alfred how pleased and proud he had been at the way in which he and Alice had carried out their duties. Alfred didn't have time to let Chronavon know how much he'd enjoyed this adventure before Sir John returned to his room, to be followed a few moments later by the Princess Elizabeth, the Ladies Margaret and Barbara, and Alice.

Sir John directed the Princess to sit in the largest chair in the room, a huge, button-backed armchair, upholstered in maroon coloured leather. Having taken her place, the rest of the company sat at the other chairs around the room.

"I am pleased to announce," began Sir John, "that this young man has just brought me papers signed by the Lord Chancellor of England. They state that it is her Majesty, Queen Mary's, pleasure that the Princess Elizabeth should leave the Tower to stay at the home of Sir Henry Bedingfield at Woodstock in the county of Oxfordshire. There she is to be shown every courtesy and consideration".

Sir John Brydges announces to Elizabeth,
her maids and Alfred and Alice the good
news that has come from Queen Mary.

318

Delighted smiles illuminated the faces of Elizabeth and her maids.

"I think that this calls for a little celebration," continued Sir John and he called in Philippa to pour a glass of sherry for all present.

"And are my ladies-in-waiting to accompany me?" asked Elizabeth.

"Yes, of course," said Sir John. "Orders have been given that comfortable quarters are to be provided at Woodstock for my Ladies Margaret and Barbara."

"And what about Alice?" asked Elizabeth.

"No, she is not to accompany you. A higher authority requires her to be elsewhere."

A cry of disappointment went up from the Ladies Margaret and Barbara. Alice had found a secure place in the affections of all those with whom she'd shared the Bell Tower accommodation over the past few weeks. Margaret, Barbara and Elizabeth all came over to embrace Alice. The ladies-in-waiting were shedding tears of genuine sadness at being parted from one who had come to mean so much to them in so short a time.

"I believe that I owe more to you and to this young man than I can ever imagine or shall ever know." said the Princess. "If it ever falls to my power to bestow power or rank, you are both people whom I should wish to honour."

Elizabeth's attention then fell upon Chronavon whom she had barely noticed before in all the excitement of receiving the news of her release.

"And who is this?" she asked Sir John. She surveyed Chronavon's monk's habit. "He's obviously a holy man."

"He is indeed a most holy man, my lady," replied Sir John. "This is my good friend, my very good friend, Chronavon. Just as you believe that Alice and Alfred have helped you more than you can ever know, so Chronavon has helped me, and indeed all of us here, in ways we shall never know in this life. Chronavon wishes now to enter the

Chapel of St. Peter ad Vincula on the other side of the Green to spend some time in prayer with Alfred and Alice.

Alfred and Alice, along with Chronavon, took their leave of the company and made their way across Tower Green which had become so familiar to them over the past weeks. They entered the chapel. Here they knelt in silence for a while, thinking back on the adventure of the past few weeks, and how something had always happened to rectify dangerous situations when things appeared to be in danger of going badly wrong.

"My Lord, we thank You for your protection over us during the past days," prayed Chronavon, now speaking aloud. "We thank You that Alfred and Alice remained faithful in the task that was set them. We thank You that Elizabeth has now been released, and history is able to follow its preordained course. Thank You, thank You Lord, Amen"

The three of them stood up.

"You'd better change back into your own-time clothes," said Chronavon, pointing to an oak chest by the chapel wall which looked very much like the one where they had deposited their clothes in St. Paul's Cathedral Chapter House when they first entered this time.

Sure enough, when they opened the chest, there were the clothes they had left, neatly folded, along with the Tudor style garments they hadn't selected when they had first changed to fit in with the period scene. Alfred and Alice put their own clothes back on, folded the clothes they had just been wearing and returned these to the chest. The three of them returned to the door of the chapel and went out, but the sight which greeted their eyes was not Tower Green but the interior of the vestry of St. Giles' Church, Hillington.

"Thank you both, once again," said Chronavon. "If Ahrirnanes tries any more tricks, this may not be the last time I see you."

With that, Chronavon went out of the vestry and

closed the door behind him. Alfred and Alice rushed to the door in order to say a proper goodbye, but when they opened it, no person could be seen in the church. Chronavon was not there. The church was quite, quite empty,

They waited for a moment, myriad thoughts spinning in their minds.

"Come on," said Alfred, "let's finish making up these bunches of flowers. I bet there are lots and lots of things we'll want to tell each other about. Wasn't it marvellous being in Tudor England!"

Alfred and Alice started to share the stories of their experiences in the different roles they had played in ensuring that Princess Elizabeth was not unjustly executed. They'd so much to say that they were still talking with great excitement, long after the last bouquet had been made up.

Bishop Gardiner never did find out why Alfred didn't return from his errand to the Tower. He assumed that Alfred had been careless in concealing his livery under the grey cloak and had been assassinated by some enemy of the Bishop who had recognised him as one of his servants from the uniform.

"Pity to have lost the boy," thought the Bishop to himself. "He was a capable worker. Still, I've lost boys that way before and I expect it will happen again."

Chapter 10

Let us remind ourselves of the way that the history of England unfolded after the release of the Princess Elizabeth from the Tower of London.

Elizabeth's stay in the home of Sir Henry Bedingfield was not entirely to Elizabeth's liking. Although infinitely better than the Tower, where the spectre of sudden execution ever loomed, Elizabeth was still regarded as a dangerous rival to the Queen for the throne and her liberty was restricted. After a time however, the situation became more relaxed and Elizabeth was allowed to return to her own house in Hatfield.

Sir John Brydges, Lieutenant of the Tower during Elizabeth's imprisonment there, was created Lord Chandos of Sudeley.

Queen Mary married King Philip of Spain, but she had no children and died in 1558. Stephen Gardiner predeceased her in 1555. He is buried in Winchester Cathedral where a chantry chapel stands over his tomb. By one of the great coincidences of history, the Archbishop of Canterbury, Cardinal Reginald Pole, died on the very same day as Queen Mary.

On the death of Mary Tudor, Elizabeth was proclaimed queen and enjoyed the most glorious reign in English history. She adhered to the protestant faith, but wisely allowed England to follow the middle way by which both Catholics and Protestants were free to worship according to their conscience without any fear of persecution. Elizabeth was prudent in her dealings and was an inspiration to her people, rousing her troops with a stirring speech at Tilbury when threatened by invasion from Spain. However, the English fleet defeated King Philip's Armada, avoiding the need to repel a Spanish invasion with a land battle.

As there was a vacancy in the diocese of Canterbury when she came to the throne, Elizabeth was able to appoint a protestant, her former tutor, Dr. Parker, to become the new Archbishop

Elizabeth surrounded herself at court with handsome men, Sir Christopher Hatton, Robert Dudley, Earl of Leicester and Robert Devereux,

Earl of Essex, to name but three of the better known courtiers. Although showing obvious affection for these great nobles, she never married. Many attempts were made to arrange marriages with great continental nobles. She even had a proposal from none other than King Philip of Spain, but she remained resolutely single. Perhaps no one was ever able to replace her first love, Edward Courtenay, who had died in exile.

It was of great concern to many in authority in England that the Queen did not marry to produce an heir. The next in line of succession was Henry VII's great granddaughter, Mary, Queen of Scots, but she plotted to dethrone Elizabeth and was beheaded. When Elizabeth died in 1603 after a reign of forty-five years, she was succeeded by Mary Queen of Scots' son, James, the first king of the Stewart dynasty. The tomb of Queen Elizabeth stands among many other royal tombs in Westminster Abbey.

Although little of the London of Elizabeth's day still exists, most was burned along with the Old St. Paul's Cathedral in the Great Fire of London, the Tower of London still remains intact. The

Lieutenant's House, the White Tower within which is the Chapel of St. John, the Bell Tower, where Elizabeth was imprisoned, Traitors Gate beneath St. Thomas's Tower, Tower Green, the site of several executions, and the Chapel of St. Peter-ad-Vincula which stands beyond the Green, are still there to this day, much as Queen Elizabeth would have known them during her reign.

Family Tree of descendants of Henry VII showing Elizabeth I's near relatives

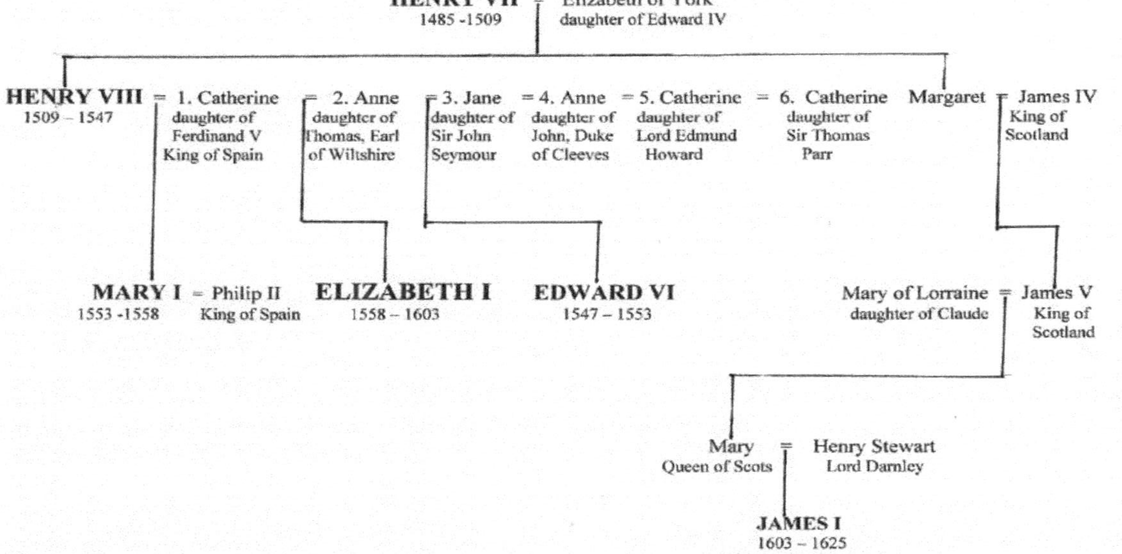

329

Prince Charles

Can Alfred and Alice secure the Succession of Charles II?

Oliver Cromwell

Colonel Carstairs

Chapter 1

Alfred and Alice were in the vestry of St. Giles Church, Hillington, on a day of the week which would normally have found them at school. However, it was mid-October and this was their half term. Both Alfred and Alice had a great love of horse riding and they had a number of rides over the Cotswold Hills planned for this half term break from school. They couldn't enjoy themselves this way every day of the holiday. On Wednesday, Alfred's mother had arranged for them to go to Cheltenham to buy some winter clothes for Alfred to replace the ones he had grown out of in March and on Thursday, Alice's mother was taking her to Gloucester to choose curtains and wall paper for her bedroom which had not been decorated for seven years. Alice' s dad, Mr. Campbell, had finally managed, under considerable pressure from Mrs. Campbell, to find a slot in his busy life which he could set aside to get down to this overdue task of decorating. Choice of paint was no problem as Mr. Campbell's hardware shop was well stocked with one-coat gloss paints for the woodwork and non-drip brilliant white matt paint for the ceiling.

However, Mrs. Campbell was not satisfied with the range of wall papers available in the shop and hence, the trip to Gloucester. Mr. Campbell had not been pleased about this. He was sensitive to the fact that he couldn't compete with the do-it-yourself hyper-markets in Gloucester and Cheltenham, but he could just about make a living in a village where many of the inhabitants didn't have cars to take them to the cities, and in any case, preferred to do their shopping in the familiar local store.

Why then were Alice and Alfred in this dismal church vestry on this first day of their half term holiday and not out riding on the hills and enjoying the fine Autumn weather outside? The Indian summer had lasted right through September and the days were still warm and sunny, even now in mid-October. The russet reds and browns of the Autumn leaves lent the Cotswold countryside a beauty which wasn't even rivalled by the Spring when the early flowers bloomed in all their freshness and glory to announce that Winter's gloom was past. Alice and Alfred were in the vestry because the previous day had been celebrated as Harvest Festival at St. Giles' Church. The vestry was full of bags and baskets of apples and tomatoes, lettuce and cucumber, pears and plums, contributed by the farming folk, as well as tins and packets provided by those who did not work on the land and who had followed the Vicar's suggestion that they should contribute non-perishable foodstuffs at the Harvest Thanksgiving service.

Alice and Alfred had been assigned the task of organising the distribution of harvest produce. Alice and Alfred had a list of names of elderly and infirm people in the parish, many of whom lived in sheltered housing but some who lived independently in cottages on the edge of Hillington. Alice and Alfred knew all these old people well and were sorting appropriate items into boxes to supplement the meagre larders on which these senior citizens subsisted.

As they busied themselves, they heard the vestry door creak open. Alfred and Alice tingled with excitement. They knew that the vestry door only creaked when a very special friend was entering, and sure enough, Chronavon, the mysterious person who dressed in a monk's habit, came into the room where the young people were working. "How great to see you again, Chronavon!" exclaimed Alfred.

"Wonderful! Wonderful! Chronavon," whooped Alice at the same moment. "Have you come with another adventure?"

"That depends on whether or not you are again prepared to take the risks that are involved," said Chronavon solemnly. "You know that if things go seriously wrong when you're carrying out the tasks I set, it will spell disaster. That disaster will affect not only yourselves, but everybody who will live in the time which follows the period of history in which the task sees you placed."

Alfred and Alice's excitement subsided.

"We've always taken your tasks seriously," said Alfred. "I know that because we've been successful twice, we could too easily assume that we'll always be successful. We can see that you're not going to lightly launch us on a new venture. That really does bring home to us the fact that there's a real chance of failure if we become blase. It's been so thrilling to be involved in the making of history that I, we both, would absolutely love to help out yet again, that is, if you think you can trust us."

Alice nodded in assent as Alfred spoke.

"Yes, of course I can trust you," Chronavon replied. "The way you've just spoken shows a responsibility, far beyond your years. Indeed, that is why you were both chosen in the first place. Come with me then and I'll set the scene for this next task."

The door creaked as Chronavon pulled it open again, and Alice and Alfred entered, not into the old familiar Parish Church of St. Giles, but into a new place in a different time.

<u>**Chapter 2**</u>

As had been the case with their previous adventures, Alfred and Alice found that they had entered what appeared to be the Chapter House of a Cathedral. In common with most mediaeval chapter houses, the building in which they now stood was octagonal, and yet, so constructed with the angles of the octagon softened, that it appeared almost round. The windows were clearly gothic, and yet, Alfred felt that the rounded wall decorations, the vault and the unfluted pillar at the centre came from an earlier era. They were characteristically Norman in style. Alfred and Alice stood silently, first looking around themselves to absorb the ambience of the place which they'd just entered, and then focused on Chronavon to discover where and when they now were. They'd both noticed a large chest at one side of the Chapter House and guessed that this would contain the clothes for this new adventure.

Chronavon paused before speaking to allow the young people to begin to become acclimatised once again to being in a new place and a new era. At last he spoke.

"You are now in the year, 1651. You are standing in the Chapter House of Worcester Cathedral. Can you think back to your history lessons to suggest what is now happening in England?"

Alfred spoke first, glad of an opportunity to show that he knew some dates in history. On previous occasions, Alice had always shown herself up as the more knowledgeable of the two of them when it came to dates.

"A date I seem to remember very well is 1649." said Alfred. "That's when Charles I was beheaded. That must mean that Oliver Cromwell now rules England."

"Excellent," said Chronavon, "and what about Worcester? Why might I have brought you here?"

"I know that one of the battles of the civil war was fought at Worcester," said Alice, "but that must have been a few years earlier. Didn't all the fighting stop, once King Charles I had been captured by the Roundheads?"

"Although King Charles was captured," explained Chronavon, "his eldest son, Charles, escaped and fought a number of other battles against Cromwell's men, some in Scotland, and one final battle here in Worcester."

"Another date I find easy to remember is 1660," said Alfred. "That year, Charles was invited back to England to become King Charles II."

"That's the point of my bringing you here," said Chronavon. "That hasn't yet happened. Charles is not yet King of England. Ahrimanes is again misusing the power he was given to travel backwards and forwards in time. He's attempting to do that utterly forbidden thing of changing something which has already happened, so that the whole course of history will be different from what my Lord has ordained. Ahrirnanes has arranged for one of his servants to make sure that Prince Charles is killed before he becomes King of England.

I call him Prince Charles, although he has already been proclaimed King in Scotland. However, he won't be truly King until he has been proclaimed King in England. Ahrimanes has identified a roundhead colonel, Adonijah Bartholomew Carstairss, one who will be his agent in preventing Prince Charles, coming to the throne of England. This colonel has made it his mission to have Prince Charles executed as was his father. Your task is to keep Prince Charles safe from the clutches of Colonel Carstairs until he has been able to leave England.

Prince Charles will have to wait in exile until the time that he'll be invited back as King by the English people. They'll become sick of the repression associated with the Puritanism which will characterise the rule of Oliver Cromwell. I think you'll find that this task will give you lots of opportunity for horse riding. This and others of your talents will be called upon if you're to succeed, but don't forget, use of the power of prayer is of utmost importance. Although you'll not see me, I won't be far away and will be able to come and help you if you become exposed to excessively great danger.

However, if you keep your wits about you, you probably won't need my direct help. You didn't in your last two adventures, did you?

Now, to the plan ahead. First of all, you'll be staying at the home of a Mr. and Mrs. Penderell. They're great Royalists and are also, friends of mine. I've told them that you're coming and I know that they'll give you lots of help and advice. It's while you are at the home of Mr. and Mrs. Penderell, that you'll first meet Prince Charles who's also one of their friends. He'll come to stay with them on the eve of the battle of Worcester. I can't anticipate in advance how things will turn out for you, but if you cooperate with those you discover to be genuine friends of Prince Charles, you'll have the best chance of getting Prince Charles safely across the English Channel where he'll be able to bide his time until his hour comes.

Before we go to meet Mr. and Mrs. Penderell, you need to get yourselves changed into clothing in keeping with the period. I think you'll find something suitable in there."

Chronavon pointed to the box by the Chapter House wall. Alice and Alfred opened the box and found several sets of clothes which fitted them. They were both slightly disappointed because, although clean and smart, they were drab grey in colour and at first glance, they looked rather uninteresting. When Alfred had realised that they were in the period of the Stewart dynasty, he had been hoping to wear a dashing Cavalier outfit but there was nothing like that in the chest. Chronavon realised what he was thinking.

"The things in there are the sort of clothes that the Puritans wear," explained Chronavon. "If you wear those clothes, you'll arouse much less suspicion among any Roundheads you may meet than if you come dressed like the young son or daughter of an aristocrat or landed English gentleman. You'll find it much easier to serve Prince Charles in his efforts to keep out of the clutches of Colonel Carstairs, dressed like a Roundhead rather than a Cavalier!"

Chronavon shows Alfred and Alice the box
in the Chapter House of Worcester Cathedral
which contains the clothes they'll wear
to fit in with the time of Prince Charles

Alice and Alfred at last found clothes they liked which fitted. Although both were dressed mainly in grey, they made a handsome couple in their Puritan garb, Alfred in grey jacket, breeches, black buckle shoes and a black steeple hat, Alice in a well-fitting grey dress, trimmed in white, white apron and matching mob cap. Chronavon surveyed them in their seventeenth century clothes and nodded approvingly.

"Let's first spend a little time in the Cathedral before I take you to meet your hosts for your first few nights here at least," said Chronavon, "but I rather think this adventure is going to involve you both in a lot of travelling around England. You won't remain in Worcester for long. Follow me. Don't be too shocked by the state of the Cathedral."

They followed Chronavon out of the Chapter House and entered the cloisters, surrounding the usual square quadrangle on the south side of the Cathedral. This is known as the cloister garth. The lawn of a cloister garth is usually properly tended and well mown but the garth at Worcester was in a sorry state. The grass was almost waist high and obviously had not been cut for a season. There were puddles too in the cloister walk where rain had leaked through holes in the roof. Chronavon led them into the Cathedral through a door at the end of the cloister walk.

Alice and Alfred were amazed at the sight which met their eyes. They'd expected to see at least a few people in the Cathedral but there wasn't a single person in view. It was quite deserted. The thing which chiefly shocked Alice and Alfred was the state of dereliction of the place. Broken furniture lay around the floor, many of the lower windows in the aisles were broken and here and there, remains of smashed statues could be seen. The young people looked upwards. The lofty vault and clerestorey windows were intact, and the beauty of the Cathedral could still be appreciated. The absence of people gave the place a quiet peace.

"Cromwell has turned the Dean and the Canons out of their houses in the Close," explained Chronavon, "so there are no staff left to look after the building and conduct services. Most of the damage you can see around you was carried out by Cromwell's soldiers. I won't say nothing is sacred to them but they seem to think that there's something wrong in worshipping God in any church which is different from the very simple buildings in which they worship themselves. At least, we won't have to look for a side chapel to find somewhere quiet to pray in this Cathedral."

Chronavon turned to the right and led them to the choir stalls arranged each side of a tomb which Chronavon told them marked the burial place of King John. They knelt in the choir stalls and after a short time of silence, Chronavon led them in prayer.

"Lord God," he prayed, "as we see the terrible state into which your house has been allowed to decay, we become acutely aware that all is not well in the state of England. Sadly Lord, we know that some of the problems have arisen because devout and sincere men have been over zealous in the service they have sought to give you. We pray that in due course, the monarchy may be restored, and with it, enlightenment in the way this country is governed. To this end, we pray that Alice and Alfred here may be able to help Prince Charles to fulfil his destiny. Keep him safe from those that would do him harm and use the problems he now experiences to bring him the wisdom he'll need when he becomes King. Protect Alice and Alfred so that when their task has been fulfilled, they may safely return to their own time. Amen"

The three of them remained kneeling for at least another five minutes. Anxious thoughts passed through the minds of Alice and Alfred as they anticipated the difficulties they might face in these troubled times, but these anxious thoughts became resolved into calm confidence as they made their petitions to God for all the courage, peace of mind and wisdom they would need to fulfil their mission.

Chronavon stood up. Alice and Alfred got to their feet and followed Chronavon as he made his way to the west door of the Cathedral. They stepped through the door which was not locked but just swinging on its hinges in the wind. Once outside, Alice and Alfred looked around to get their bearings. Beneath them, the lovely River Severn flowed gently on its way towards the Bristol Channel. On the opposite banks, cows grazed in the water meadows. Beyond the River, the Malvern Hills were silhouetted on the skyline as they stretched southwards towards Tewkesbury. A short way upstream, a single bridge spanned the river.

Chronavon led them to the bustling town centre behind the Cathedral where children played in the cobbled streets and shoppers wandered through the stalls, occasionally stopping to barter if an item caught their eye.

"We are now on our way to the home of Richard and Dorothea Penderell," explained Chronavon as he continued to lead Alice and Alfred through the city. After they had walked no more than a couple of hundred yards, Chronavon stopped, declaring, "Here we are!"

They had reached a lovely timbered building with four prominent gables, the gable to the right being larger than the other three. The windows were large and the house gave the impression of being amply proportioned and spacious inside. A lady sitting at a downstairs window had seen them approach and she immediately came out to meet them. This was Dorothea Penderell, a pleasant, plump woman with curly hair and dimpled cheeks.

"How lovely to see you again, Chronavon," she said as she hugged him. She stepped back. "And this must be Alice and Alfred whom you told me about. Welcome to Worcester," she beamed as she looked at the young people. "Chronavon thinks a lot of you two and he says that you could be of great help to us. We're trying to carry on as normal here but we think something big is going to happen. Prince Charles is on his way here with an army. Cromwell is not far away either. There is bound to be a battle and who can say what the outcome will be. We're all very nervous. Chronavon has told us that you're two very resourceful young people whom it will good to have around whatever tomorrow might bring.

Come inside and meet Mr. Penderell."

"Richard," she called as they entered the door, "Chronavon is here with his young friends."

A tall and distinguished looking man stepped out from the back of the house and warmly shook Chronavon's hand.

"This is Alfred, and this is Alice," said Chronavon as he introduced the two young people to Mr. Penderell.

"Very pleased to meet you both," said Mr. Penderell. "Chronavon seems to think that you'll be useful to have around when things hot up, and we're expecting big things to happen very soon now. There are two armies converging on Worcester. A battle could take place any day now. I've had news that Prince Charles will ask if he may lodge here when he arrives and of course he's welcome. I expect he'll bring a couple of officers with him to stay the night. It's lucky we have a big house. We heard that you were coming so we've prepared rooms for you both as well. Mrs. Penderell will show you where you'll be sleeping. Then we can all have something to eat.

Will you stay for a bite, Chronavon?"

Mr. Penderell looked quizzically at Chronavon whom he obviously knew quite well. It was as if he expected a negative answer.

"I'm sorry, Richard," he said, "I'm fasting but I will have a drink with you if one is available."

"I've never seen you eat, Chronavon," said Mr. Penderell. "You seem to be on a permanent fast. However, you always look strong and healthy enough. Do come and have a drink though. What is your favourite tipple, beer? or I have a very fine port that may be to your taste?"

Chronavon went into the dining room with Richard Penderell while Dorothea Penderell took the young people upstairs to show them their rooms. They came down to the dining room to find Chronavon and Mr. Penderell in deep conversation. Richard Penderell was looking very grave. A meal had been set and they all sat round the dining table. Chronavon sat at the place where no plate of food had been placed, but brought his large glass of port with him.

"I hope the Prince can win," said Mr. Penderell as he sat down to eat, "but I don't give him much chance. He's got no more than a rag tag army, mainly Scotsmen including just a few Highlanders. He's picked up a few irregulars from the north and his gentry friends make up his cavalry but that's nothing to the sort of army that Cromwell and Ireton will bring against him."

"Charles main problem is not the size of his army but the discipline of his troops. That's where the Roundheads have the edge. If their infantry are scattered, say by a cavalry charge, they quickly regroup and are no less formidable than before. After the King's cavalry have had a successful charge, they ride around, congratulating themselves and do nothing more for the rest of the day. I saw this very thing happen at Edgehill. Prince Rupert successfully charged Cromwell's lines and scattered his troops. Had Rupert regrouped his cavalry and pressed home his advantage, the day would have been the King's but that was the last time we saw Prince Rupert's cavalry in action that day. In half an hour,

Cromwell's men had reformed and there was no decisive victory in that battle. "

Mr. Penderell monopolised most of the conversation that meal time. He pontificated on the battle tactics which had led to Charles I's defeats at Marston Moor and Naseby. He bemoaned the fact that if things went wrong for Prince Charles when he next faced Cromwell, Worcester would once again be swarming with Roundheads, stealing from the market stalls, desecrating churches and vandalising the Cathedral. He expressed his hopes that the day would soon come when the monarchy was restored and things returned to what Mr. Penderell regarded as normal.

Chronavon sat impassively as one who'd heard it all before while Mrs. Penderell fidgeted, anxious that the young people weren't being bored by Mr. Penderell's monologues. She need not have worried. Alice and Alfred were absolutely fascinated by all they were hearing and Mr. Penderell was obviously enjoying having an attentive audience.

At the end of the meal, Chronavon announced that he must now go to attend to other important matters. Dorothea Penderell tried to persuade him to stay on for a few days.

"It would be so reassuring to have you around at times like this," she said "when our world looks like being turned right upside down. You always seem so calm, so resourceful, so knowledgeable."

Mrs. Penderell's pleadings were to no avail. Chronavon thanked her profusely for her hospitality but insisted that he had obligations he had to fulfil. He wished them all good bye, and in the case of Alice and Alfred, he wished them every success in dealing with emergencies which were likely to come up in the next few days, whichever way the forthcoming battle might go.

<u>**Chapter 3**</u>

After Chronavon had left, Mrs. Penderell suggested that Alfred and Alice should go out and explore Worcester while she cleared away. Alfred and Alice spent an enjoyable hour, wandering around this very pleasant city. They crossed the river by the bridge to get a view of the Cathedral from the opposite bank of the Severn. In spite of the damage which they knew had been done on the inside, the Cathedral looked magnificent from the west bank of the river. They swore that there were surely, few more wonderful sights in England than this majestic Cathedral, towering above the City at its riverside location.

Worcester Cathedral

They became aware of the distant sound of bagpipes and drums which gradually increased in volume.

"That must be one of the armies," whispered Alice in excitement.
"It'll be Prince Charles' army," said Alfred. "Mr. Penderell was saying that he had recruited most of his troops from Scotland."

They decided it would be prudent to return to the home of the Penderells. When they got there, they found that Mrs. Penderell was outside with a group of neighbours. The place was really buzzing with excitement. The Prince was setting up his camp just outside the City. Some of Mrs. Penderell's neighbours knew that they would be billeting officers from the army that night. They were very envious of Mrs. Penderell when they found that the Prince himself was going to stay at her house.

The group dispersed and Alice and Alfred went into the house with Mrs. Penderell. She went to sit by the window where they had first seen her when they had approached the house earlier that day with Chronavon. Mrs. Penderell was obviously looking out for the Prince. After about half an hour, she excitedly jumped up and rushed out of the door to meet a handsome young man and his companion. Alice and Alfred correctly guessed that this was Prince Charles. Mrs. Penderell returned to the house with her guests. She didn't have to call Mr. Penderell from the back of the house. He was already waiting in the hall to greet the Prince. He was every bit the typical Cavalier with his long curly black hair, well-tailored frock coat and leather riding boots. A sword hung from his waist and he wore a lace cravat.

"Welcome to our humble home, Your Majesty," said Mr. Penderell by way of greeting as he bowed and took the hand offered to him.

"Don't call me your majesty yet," said the Prince. "I may have been proclaimed King in Scotland, but until I sort out this matter tomorrow, I'm not yet officially King here. Come tomorrow, it will be quite a different story. My troops are in fine spirits and we are raring to go. Mr. Penderell, may I introduce to you my adjutant, Captain Anthony Careless, careless by name but not by nature. I don't know what I would do without him. He organises everything to the last detail."

Mr. Penderell and Captain Careless shook each other's hand.

"And who have we here," said the Prince as he saw Alice and Alfred standing by Mrs. Penderell. "A Puritan lad and maid by the appearance of things."

"This is Alfred and the young lady is called Alice," said Richard Penderell by way of introduction. "They have been sent here by an old and trusted friend. He assures me that they are both very intelligent and very resourceful and will be able to be of great service to us after the battle. It was my friend who suggested that they should dress in Puritan clothes. It will be much easier for them wander among the Roundheads and listen to what they are saying dressed like that than if they were dressed in velvet with ruffs and had sleeves finished in lace."

Alfred and Alice are introduced to Prince Charles

360

"That sounds like a very wise precaution," said the Prince. "How would you like to work in my service?" he asked Alfred.

"We should be most honoured, sir," said Alfred politely.

"And you, young maid," said the Prince turning to Alice, "What do you think of Cromwell?"

Apart from the damage she had seen in the Cathedral, Alice had a reasonably good knowledge from her school history of the things that Cromwell had done to make himself unpopular.

"I think he's a most disgraceful man," said Alice with some vehemence. "He executed your Father. His men have desecrated churches all over the country. The Cathedral here has been left a right shambles. He's massacred the people of Drogheda and Wexford for no particularly good reason, and he professes to practice a brand of Christianity which is superior to that observed in the Church of England of which your Father was Head."

The Prince was in1pressed both by what Alice said, and also, the way she said it.

"Well said, well said, young lady" said the Prince patting Alice's shoulder. "If ever that man comes to trial for his sins, I want him to come up before a judge like you. What a pity that ladies cannot be judges. I would otherwise make you my Lord Chief Justice, - no, I couldn't do that, you would have to be my Lady Chief Justice."

Everyone laughed at the Prince's attempt at a joke.

Mrs. Penderell asked for leave to depart and off she went to prepare the evening meal. Mr. Penderell showed the Prince and the Captain to the comfortable armchairs by the fireplace. Everybody sat down and the banter continued. Alfred and Alice didn't have to contribute much to the conversation for the Prince and Captain Careless had more than enough to say, Captain Careless speaking in the same easy relaxed manner as the Prince. When Mrs. Penderell announced that supper was ready, they followed her into the dining room where she had prepared a sumptuous spread. After this meal, they all turned in. The beds which had been provided for Alice and Alfred were really comfortable and they were both soon fast asleep.

<u>Chapter 4</u>

Next morning, Alice and Alfred woke, got dressed and came down stairs to find Mr. and Mrs. Penderell talking together and looking very worried. They looked up when they saw Alice and Alfred and told them that some breakfast had been laid for them in the dining room.

'The Prince and Captain Careless left at the crack of dawn to join their army," Richard Penderell informed them, "but in spite of the Prince's confidence, I'm far from sure of the outcome. I went to the top of the Cathedral Tower earlier this morning and I could see Cromwell's army approaching in the distance. It is a larger army than the Prince's and is made up of well trained and well-disciplined veterans of the Civil War. It will be a miracle if the Prince can win the victory."

Just then, the distant rumble of gunfire was heard. Hostilities had started.

"I'm going back to the Cathedral Tower to see if I can assess how the battle is going," said Richard Penderell and immediately left the room.

The Battle of Worcester

Alice and Alfred completed their breakfast without speaking, the ominous sound of gunfire punctuating their thoughts. Dorothea Penderell cleared away. About an hour later, Richard Penderell returned in an agitated state.

Things are going badly for the Prince," he reported. "Large sections of his army are already deserting, and Cromwell's Ironsides seem to have split his main force in half"

The Ironsides was a name originally given to the elite cavalry, trained by Oliver Cromwell himself, but later, it came to be a name used to refer to all of Cromwell's soldiers.

"What'll the Prince do if he loses," asked Dorothea Penderell, "Will he come back here to Worcester?"

"He may think of doing this," replied her husband "but that's the last thing he should do. If Cromwell wins, Worcester will be swarming with Roundhead troops within the hour. The Prince won't find an effective hiding place in the City. He'll be hunted down and then he could end up on the block as did his father. The best thing for him to do would be to hide in the countryside beyond Worcester."

Richard Penderell paused for thought.

"There's a fairly dense wood just beyond White Ladies," he said at last, "He could hide in there and he would be very difficult to find."

"If he rides there, what'll he do with his horse when he gets there?" enquired Dorothea Penderell who was of a very practical frame of mind. "He may be able to hide himself but he won't be able to hide his horse. If the Roundheads see a stray horse near the wood, it will be a give-away that someone important will have taken refuge there after the battle. If they are sure the Prince is hiding there, they'll cut every tree down in the wood if necessary until they find him."

Dorothea had made a good point. Richard Penderell sunk once more into thought. He looked up at Alice and Alfred.

"Chronavon told me that you two would be a valuable resource to help out if an emergency arose." he said. "Can you both ride horses?"

Alice and Alfred nodded.

"Would you go to Boscobel Wood and wait on the outskirts? I'll go to meet the Prince, should he have to flee the battle field and direct him to the Wood. I'll tell him that you will be waiting to collect his horse. Bring the horse back to Worcester, following the Stratford Road. I'll be waiting near the road at a safe distance from Worcester to meet you. I know a farm where we can take the horse and keep it well out of the way of Cromwell's men. Let's look at a map so that you'll know the lie of the land and where the key places are situated."

Richard Penderell got a map out from a drawer in the side board and they spent the next ten minutes planning their routes and strategy.
"There's no time to lose," said Richard Penderell. "The wood is a good five miles from here. All the horses in the City have been commandeered for

the battle so you'll have to walk. However, if you set off right away, even though on foot, you'll be there before the Prince arrives. The battle is not lost yet. There is quite a bit of fighting still to be done.

It would save time when you get there if one of you seeks a good hiding place for the Prince while the other keeps watch for his arrival, waiting outside the wood. As soon as he's safely concealed, make your way straight back towards Worcester where I will be keeping watch for you as you approach the City. The Prince has a strong horse and he'll be able to carry you both."

The young people made to leave right away but Dorothea Penderell insisted that they should take some food, enough both for themselves and for the Prince.

"If the battle goes against him as you fear it might," she said, "the Prince will be famished. It will be no good saving him from Cromwell if he dies of starvation in the meantime."

Alice and Alfred set off at a smart pace along the Stratford Road. The sounds of the battle receded as they distanced themselves from the City. After an hour and a half of brisk walking, they came to a hamlet they identified as White Ladies and there, sure enough, was a sizeable wood beyond the hamlet and well off the main road. Alice took up her position on the outskirts of the wood while Alfred went into the wood to find a suitable place for the Prince to hide.

Twenty minutes later Alfred came back and told Alice that there were any number of oaks which wouldn't be too difficult to climb. They hadn't yet lost their leaves, so there'd be plenty of foliage to conceal the Prince, once he'd climbed above ten feet or so. They then settled down to wait. An hour went by. They ate some of the food Mrs. Penderell had provided. Another hour started to slip by and Alice and Alfred began to wonder if the Prince would ever come.

Perhaps the Prince had won the battle, or had other plans for his escape been made, or, horror of horrors, had he been captured by the Roundheads. Then, quite unexpectedly, not one but two horsemen came into view, riding fast across the fields and so avoiding the villages and hamlets between Worcester and Boscobel Wood.

Alfred and Alice stood up and waved. The horsemen saw them and veered, steering their horses to where the young people were waiting. They dismounted. It was the Prince and his equerry, Captain Careless.

"The battle went badly," said the Prince. "I think that Cromwell's men aren't far behind. Mr. Penderell told me that I would find you both here. Well done."

He was breathless from his ride, desperately disappointed and, the young people felt, close to tears.

"I've identified some trees where you can hide up." Alfred informed them. "No one will be able to find you once you are above the lower branches."

"And Mrs. Penderell has provided some food for you," said Alice, handing a bag to Captain Careless.

They tethered the horses and Alfred led them into the wood, pointing out two sturdy oaks which stood adjacent to each other, surrounded by thick undergrowth. Other trees nearby would assist in concealing anyone up those oaks.

"Well done again, and thank you both," said the Prince. "Get the horses away from this wood as soon as you can. I've already discarded the horse armour and saddle cloths, so there's nothing that'll immediately enable them to be identified as horses involved in the battle."

Without more ado, the Prince and Captain Careless climbed the trees and were soon out of sight. Alfred and Alice rearranged the undergrowth so that it was not obvious that it had recently been disturbed and made their way back to the horses. Alice was wearing her long Puritan skirt, so she readjusted the saddle, moving one of the stirrups across the horse so that she could ride side-saddle. They made their way as planned along the Stratford Road towards Worcester. On their route, they met a troop of Cromwell's soldiers, making fairly slow progress on tired horses, carrying soldiers weighed down with heavy cuirasses and helmets.

"Have you seen a lone horseman headed this way?" their captain asked Alfred and Alice.

"No," they truthfully replied and continued on their way.

Prince Charles and Captain Careless climb
into the oak tree that Alfred has identified
as a tree which will provide good cover.

The tower of Worcester Cathedral came into view and a little way further along the road, a horseman who had been waiting, concealed in a thicket, rode down to the road to meet them. It was Richard Penderell. He looked reassured when he saw the horses they were riding but he asked them anxiously,

"Did the Prince arrive safely?"

"Yes," they told him, "He and Captain Careless are now safely concealed in a thick oak."

They continued on their way back to Worcester. The dusk was fast drawing in. Richard left the road, just before Worcester and they rode to the farm where Richard had arranged for the horses to be stabled for the night. They walked the last half mile to Worcester. They found the city, full of raucous soldiers, laughing, joking with each other, drinking, and shouting. These were Cromwell's men in high spirits after the day's victory.

They reached the Penderells' house and found the place in a mess. Mrs. Penderell came out, looking quite upset.

"Cromwell's men have been through the house," she explained. "Their officer was called Colonel

Carstairs. He was most unpleasant. He said he had good reason to believe that the Prince, the Charley Brat he called him, was hiding in this house. As you can see, they have turned everything upside down in their search. I think some of the chairs have been broken. This Colonel was most annoyed when nothing could be found and he went away swearing that when he found him, he would beat the Charley Brat and have him hung, drawn and quartered."

Alice and Alfred remembered that during Chronavon's briefing of the previous day, Colonel Carstairs had been identified as Ahrimanes' agent in his plan to prevent Prince Charles succeeding to the English throne.

Alice and Alfred set to in helping Richard Penderell straighten out the house. Two chairs had been broken but Richard Penderell didn't anticipate any problem in gluing the broken parts together. The house was soon looking as tidy as ever. Everybody was now very tired, and Richard and Dorothea Penderell looked depressed and dispirited. Dorothea rustled up some supper. They said very little to each other. Richard suggested that they went to bed to sleep on the day's events and the problems that had been created. They could discuss what might be the best course of action to follow in the morning.
They all turned in.

Chapter 5

The following morning, Richard and Dorothea Penderell, Alice and Alfred settled down for a discussion after breakfast to plan the next stage in the Prince's escape. Alfred and Alice had both slept well but the noise created by Cromwell's soldiers in the streets had kept Richard and Dorothea awake for most of the night. They looked tired and were clearly preoccupied with the problem of getting the Prince to safety.

"They'd probably be safe in the woods for another night," started Richard, "but they obviously can't stay there for ever. All the towns for twenty miles around Worcester will be thronging with Roundhead soldiers. There'll be patrols out on the roads, so these will be impassable."

"Captain Careless said that he had a friend who used to live in a small cottage, only fifteen or so miles from Worcester but well away from any village or town. Perhaps they could hide up there." ventured Dorothea.

"Yes, that's an idea I'm coming to," continued Richard. "The problem is, Captain Careless hasn't been in touch with this friend for over ten years. He knows he is loyal to the Royalist cause but there's no guarantee that when we get the Prince to this cottage, it will still be in the possession of Captain Careless's friend."

"What's this friend's name and where is the cottage?" asked Alfred. "One of us could go and investigate if the land is clear and report back."

There was a moment of silence while they considered this option.

"Yes," said Richard at last, "I think that might be a good idea. The cottage lies between Eckington and Great Comberton in the lee of a knoll called Bredon Hill. It's nothing much. I gather that Captain Careless's friend is quite a poor man. That's all to the good if we're looking for a safe place for the Prince to hide. His name is John Ploughman. That's what he actually does. His father and grandfather before him were all ploughmen. It looks like a family whose trade has remained with their surname ever since surnames were invented. Let me get the map out again. I think I can locate the cottage fairly closely. It's the only cottage for miles around in that area. If you are anywhere between Eckington and Great Comberton, and see a cottage, that'll be it."

They spread the map over the table and began to examine it. They were now beginning to look at an area not too far from the Cotswolds which Alfred and Alice knew well, but the pattern of roads was significantly different from twenty-first century England.

"Yes, I think I can find the cottage all right." said Alfred.

"We must keep the Prince informed," said Richard, "and work out with him a safe way of getting to the cottage."

"And get some food to them both," said Dorothea, practical as ever.

"Yes, of course," added Richard.

"I know exactly where the Prince is hiding," said Alice. "I could take them food and keep them up to date with plans."

"Yes," continued Richard, "we must think this through carefully. A short way from Boscobel Wood is a farmhouse. It's quite a prominent building, red brick, thatched roof, duck pond in the yard."

"Yes, we passed it on our way to the wood yesterday," Alice said. Alfred nodded to indicate that he too recognised the farm.

"That farm is owned by a friend of mine, Arthur Moncrief. Don't take your horse into the wood or tether it nearby, Alice. That could arouse suspicion should any of Cromwell's men be passing by. Introduce yourself to Arthur, tell him that you are a friend of mine and that you've business in White Ladies. Ask if you can tether your horse at the farm and after seeing to your business, return to wait for a friend. He'll say yes. He's a most obliging fellow. Don't tell him anything about the Prince. The fewer the people who know his whereabouts, the better. Go to the wood and make contact with the Prince. Tell him that you'll return later when you've made contact with Alfred who'll let you know if Anthony Careless's friend is still in his cottage and ready to receive the Prince. Then return to the farm and wait for Alfred.

Alfred, when you've found out whether or not the Prince can find refuge with John Ploughman, make your way to Arthur Moncrief s farm and rendezvous with Alice. Depending on the outcome of your search for John Ploughman, the Prince may need you to stay with him to assist him further on his escape. If so, you'll not return here and we'll understand why if we don't see you again. On the other hand, if the plan turns out to be impracticable, come back here and we'll work out a new strategy."

They all agreed that Richard had thought things through well. There was no time for delay, so they hugged Dorothea goodbye and made their way with Richard to the farm outside Worcester where the horses had been left for the night. Richard

wished them both goodbye and good luck as they
left him, Alice heading east to Boscobel Wood
and Alfred, south to find John Ploughman's
cottage.

Alice found the farm as directed and knocked at
the door. It was opened by a stout ruddy faced
man in a check shirt and trousers tied at the knees
with string. He had a kindly face and Alice felt
quite confident in introducing herself as someone
whom his friend, Mr. Penderell, had
recommended her to visit. This man was indeed
Arthur Moncrief and he showed Alice to a stable
where she could feed and rest her horse. Arthur
was aware of the outcome of the battle at
Worcester. He told Alice that Cromwell's soldiers
had been there earlier that day and turned the
place upside down, searching for Royalists, and
particularly for the 'Charley Brat', the name their
officer had used to refer to Prince Charles. Alice
guessed that the officer was in all probability,
Colonel Carstairs.

Alice made her way to Boscobel Wood with her
bag of food and found the trees where the Prince

and Captain Careless were hiding. The wood appeared to be deserted but the undergrowth was heavily trampled.

"It's Alice," she called up softly. "I have brought you some food from Mrs. Penderell."

A face peered down through the branches. It was the Prince. A moment later, Captain Careless's face appeared in the other tree.

"Thank you very much," said the Prince, reaching down to relieve Alice of her bag. "We're absolutely famished. Cromwell's men have already been through the wood looking for us. What's the news in Worcester?"

Alice explained the strategy that had been worked out that morning with Richard and Dorothea Penderell. Just then, voices could be heard approaching and the sound of cracking twigs breaking under the feet of heavy men coming towards them.

"Quick, up here," said the Prince in a whisper, and reached down a hand to help Alice up. She deftly clambered into the tree and they climbed up a few more branches until they were completely concealed from below by the branches and foliage. They sat in silence, holding their breath, unnecessarily fearful that this might be heard above the rustle of the leaves as the breeze, wafting through the branches, gently shook the foliage, now rapidly losing its green hue with the onset of autumn.

After a few more minutes, the voices became quite clear. "We thoroughly searched the wood this morning, sir."

"Well, search it again. Two men were seen riding towards here yesterday, and no one has seen two men riding away from here. That means they're still here. You lazy layabouts have just not searched thoroughly enough."

"There's not an inch of undergrowth we haven't searched. We can't climb every tree in the place. If they were hiding up the trees there would have been tell-tale signs in the undergrowth round the trees. There wasn't, and now that everything has been flattened we won't be able to identify any tree that has been climbed from the state of the ground round them."

"You are just making excuses for being inefficient. If l lay my hands on Charley Brat, he'll wish he'd never been born."

"Another thing, sir, if two horses were seen riding into the woods, and no horses were seen riding out, then the horses must still be in the wood. Well, they aren't and horses can't climb trees."

"Don't you dare talk to your senior officer in that insolent tone, Sergeant. Give it another hour and if nothing shows up, we'll have to move on, but somehow, I feel it in my bones. Charley Brat is in this wood somewhere."

The voices of Colonel Carstairs, for it was none other than he who instinctively knew that Prince Charles was nearby, and his sergeant faded as they moved beyond the trees concealing the royal fugitive. They could hear the voices and the grumbling of the men who followed them, repeating their morning search and beating down the undergrowth even further. They banged the trunk of the tree where the Prince and Alice sat holding their breath. Alice prayed silently that they would soon move on without climbing the tree. A few leaves fluttered down, but the foliage cover remained adequate to keep them hidden from the view of those at ground level. These voices too soon faded from earshot.

After about half an hour, Prince Charles suggested that it would be safe for Alice to return to the farm to await the arrival of Alfred with his news. Alice climbed to ground level and looked around her. It was with some relief that she couldn't see or hear a Roundhead soldier anywhere. She made her way back to the farm where Arthur Moncrief provided Alice with a meal, and they chatted away about the war, about horses, about Arthur Moncrief's family who had all moved away to their own farms, and about his wife who had died two years earlier, just before the execution of Charles I. Alice often cast anxious glances out of the window hoping that Alfred would soon return.

When they had separated from Mr. Penderell, Alice proceeding to Boscobel Wood, Alfred made his way to where he expected to find John Ploughman's cottage. He rode over the fields rather than by the lanes and roads to avoid detachments of Roundhead soldiers. Dressed as a Puritan lad, he wouldn't have been in personal danger, but there was always the chance that some soldier might exceed his authority and commandeer his horse for the army.

After just over an hour's hard riding, Alfred located the cottage. It was just as Richard Penderell had said, in the middle of nowhere. There were no other houses in sight and there wasn't even a road or a lane passing nearby. A small hill rose behind the cottage.

"An ideal place for the Prince to hide up," thought Alfred to himself

He tethered the horse to a rail outside the cottage and knocked on the door.

It was answered by a tall lean man, his face brown and weather beaten, indicating that here was a man who spent much of his time in the healthy open air of the countryside. He wore a collarless shirt, unbuttoned at the neck, and his cuff-less sleeves flapped round his wrists.

"I believe that you are a friend of Anthony Careless," said Alfred by way of introduction.

"I am indeed," replied the man, "but I haven't had word of him these ten or eleven years. He joined the army, and the war has made it very difficult to keep in touch. Do you have news of him? Is he still alive? I hope he hasn't been wounded in the fighting. He did me a lot of favours many years ago. I would like to see him again."

Alfred then explained the situation. John Ploughman hadn't heard about the battle of Worcester but was well aware that the Civil War was not going well for the Royalists.

"Yes, it would be an honour to give the Captain and his royal master shelter during these difficult times. I shall look forward to meeting Anthony again."

Alfred rode back to Arthur Moncrief s farm. It was with some relief that Alice saw him ride up to the door. Alice introduced Alfred and they asked Arthur if they could leave his horse at the farm while they completed unfinished business in White Ladies. Arthur was obviously puzzled as to whatever was going on but he was an obliging chap. He didn't pry into their business and readily agreed to stable the horse for a while.

Alfred and Alice made their way to the wood. No sign of Roundhead soldiers. They located the trees which concealed the Prince and Captain Careless. They brought the fugitives up to date with the situation and said that they would bring the horses to the wood to enable the Prince and the Captain to get to John Ploughman's cottage as quickly as possible. Prince Charles and his equerry held a brief discussion between themselves and Alfred and Alice could follow the thread of the argument they were making. Two men on horseback so near to Worcester would be very conspicuous and news would soon get back to the Roundheads. After all, unbeknown to themselves, someone had seen them ride to the wood the previous day. They suggested that Alice and Alfred should ride back to John Ploughman to announce that the Prince and the Captain were on their way and wait for them there. The Prince and the Captain would wait until dusk and then make their way under cover of semi-darkness to the cottage. Anthony Careless knew how to find it, even in relatively dark conditions. There would at least be a half-moon that night. Two men without horses could hide so much more easily in the event of a potentially dangerous situation threatening, than horsemen who would need to conceal their animals as well as themselves - not an easy task.

Alice and Alfred went back to Arthur Moncrief's farm to collect their horses. They thanked him kindly for his hospitality and then made their way to John Ploughman's cottage. It was getting quite dark by the time they arrived. Alfred introduced Alice, and John made them most welcome. John led them to a nearby barn where they stabled the horses. John then put some food out for Alfred and Alice which they consumed with relish. It was now quite dark. The Prince and the Captain hadn't yet arrived but they weren't expected until the middle of the night. Alfred and Alice were now very tired and pleased to settle down into the beds John had made up for them. They were soon fast asleep.

<u>**Chapter 6**</u>

Alfred and Alice woke as the sun streamed into the windows of the two upstairs rooms in the cottage which John Ploughman had prepared as bedrooms for the young people. They came down to find that John was already eating his breakfast. He stopped eating as soon as he saw Alfred and Alice, drew two chairs up to the table for them and started to prepare some food for them.

"Please finish your own breakfast before getting us anything." pleaded Alice.

"Have the Prince and the Captain arrived?" asked Alfred, raising the question which was foremost in their minds.

Alice and Alfred looked round the room in which they now stood, but could see no sign to indicate that the fugitives had made it to the cottage.

"Yes, indeed they have," answered John, stirring porridge in a cauldron being heated over a wood fire. "That's a relief to you, isn't it? They got here at about three in the morning, completely

390

exhausted. They didn't get much sleep, sitting up in a tree for a couple of days and they really need to make up sleep. They didn't think it safe to sleep in the house as there are still soldiers, somewhere out there, looking for them. They decided to sleep in the hay loft where the horses are stabled. Reckon they'll sleep on till midday or longer. Hasn't been a sign of a soldier anywhere near here I'm glad to say."

John placed a couple of bowls of steaming porridge before the young people.

"Have any more plans been made for the Prince's escape?" asked Alice.

"The Prince and Anthony were too tired to do much talking," John replied, "but I gather the Prince wants to make for Bristol where he thinks he can get a ship which will take him to the continent. I've been thinking. He won't get to Bristol without a lot of help and the right help won't be easy to find. There are too many who would betray the Prince for whatever paltry reward is being offered. However, there is someone I know who would help. That's Colonel Lane. He's too old to serve in the army now, but he was a faithful soldier in the armies of both King James and King Charles. He lives at a place called Winstone which lies between Cirencester and Gloucester. It wouldn't be safe for the Prince to try to get there unless he was expected. If Colonel Lane knew that the Prince was coming, he would be able to arrange cover for him in advance. This would avoid the Prince having to take the risk of being recognised. Otherwise, he would have to go into places where there are people, in order to make contact with Colonel Lane. But how can we get in touch with Colonel Lane?"

"We could go ahead and make contact," volunteered Alfred.

"Ah, but could you find the place?" queried John Ploughman, "1 don't have any maps."

Now although neither Alfred nor Alice were familiar with the Worcestershire countryside where they were now staying, they did know

Gloucestershire. This was the county where they had spent many afternoons riding round the Cotswold Hills.

They had even ridden through Winstone. Alfred and Alice were confident that if they rode southwards, even allowing for the fact that in three hundred and fifty years, there would have been enormous changes in the environment, they could find Winstone. John's face lightened when they told him that they could make it.

"When you locate Colonel Lane, it would be useful if you could provide something which will prove to him that you are bona fides messengers," said John. "These are dangerous times, and people are wary about being tricked into incriminating themselves."

John pondered on what he could use to identify the young people to Colonel Lane as reliable messengers. The Prince or Captain Careless would doubtless have a recognisable trinket that they could show but John was unwilling to wake them while they were still making up their sleep deficit. Then John remembered an item which would suffice very well.

"I will give you the most valuable thing I have in the cottage. It is a Bible which Colonel Lane gave to me as a boy when my father used to plough his fields. I am not a good reader and so I find it difficult to understand as I try to read this Bible but I still value it very much. If you show it to Colonel Lane, he will recognise it. He's written my name in the front. Please bring it back to me. It's a gift I have always treasured, but I'm glad to make it available in the service of the Prince."

John Ploughman went to a room at the back of the cottage and emerged a few minutes later with a small, leather bound Bible, and showed them Colonel Lane's inscription in the front. He handed it to Alice for safe keeping.

"The sooner you depart, the sooner we'll get the Prince to safety," said John. "There's no point in waiting for the Prince and Anthony to wake up. That'll only delay things. I'll make up a bag of food for the journey. I reckon it'll take you most of the day to get there. With any luck, you could be back by tomorrow evening."

After John Ploughman had put a couple of loaves, a cheddar cheese and some apples in a bag for them, they went out to saddle the horses. Alice and Alfred set off, riding south. It was a beautiful day. The sun shone and the trees, now clothed in autumn hues, rustled in the westerly breeze which freshened the air. The horses left a clear trail in the dew laden grass, but there was no one who would want to follow them. Cromwell's soldiers had no idea how the Prince's escape was being planned. After the tension of the last few days, Alfred and Alice could just relax and enjoy the ride.

"I wish we knew the names of our horses," said Alice.

"Life's been so busy that that's one of the things we just haven't thought about asking," replied Alfred.

"It's the first thing I'm going to ask the Prince when next I see him," said Alice.

They kept away from the roads as much as possible, but every now and then, made their way to road intersections to read the sign posts and get their bearings. They were relieved not to encounter any of Cromwell's soldiers during the day. By mid-afternoon, they knew that they were somewhere between Gloucester and Cirencester, but there was no familiar landmark which would help them in their quest for Winstone, neither was there anyone they could ask. The countryside seemed to be completely deserted.

They rode for another .hour with no clear idea of where they should direct themselves to find Winstone and began to feel a bit panicky. They began to realise that the confidence which they had expressed to John Ploughman, of being able to find Winstone quite easily, might have been misplaced. What should they do? They remembered the advice that Chronavon had given them on all their missions. They dismounted, tethered the horses to the low branches of a nearby tree and spent some time in prayer. Their panic drained and they felt much calmer after they had remounted. They carried on across the field until they reached a lane. Two men, who could have been shepherds as they had a couple of dogs with them, were talking together. These were the first people Alfred and Alice had seen for two hours.

"Do you know if we are far from Winstone?" enquired Alfred.

"Next village back there," said one of the men pointing down the lane.

"Thank you."

They reached the village and found it to be quite bustling, compared to the relative solitude they'd experienced during the day's ride. There were still no soldiers to be seen. They made enquiries and found Colonel Lane's house on the edge of the village. They knocked at the door which was answered by a cheerful looking maid with dimpled cheeks and hair done in long ringlets. She looked surprised to see what appeared to be two young Puritans requesting to see the Colonel. He evidently didn't often have that sort of visitor.

The maid showed them into the front room and after a few minutes, a distinguished gentleman dressed in an elegant blue coat, matching breeches and white cravat entered the room. This was Colonel Lane. He too looked surprised to see the young callers.

Once the door was shut, Alfred and Alice explained their errand, Alice producing John Ploughman's Bible to authenticate their identity. The Colonel took the Bible, flicked through the pages and spent a moment or two looking at the inscription on the fly leaf he'd entered so many years earlier. He appeared to be experiencing great emotion, but remained self-controlled.

"The Roundheads know that the Prince is travelling with Captain Careless," said the Colonel. "There's a notice at the end of the village which gives a fairly good description of them both, and offering a thousand pound reward for evidence which leads to the arrest of the Prince."

(One thousand pounds in those days would be the equivalent of several million pounds today.)

"It wouldn't be safe for the Prince to stay here for long. As a former officer in the Royalist army, I know that some sort of surveillance is kept on me. The soldiers don't come round every day, but they've been here twice since the battle of Worcester. Until I saw John Ploughman's Bible, I must admit that I thought that you were a couple of Puritans who had been sent round by the army to trick me into doing something which would get me into trouble.

Now, my daughter-in-law, Jane, is very resourceful. She lives a few villages away. I suggest that we arrange for the Prince to make his way here to meet up with myself and Jane. It would be risky for the Prince to come up to the front door of the house, but I have a barn a hundred yards behind the house which can be approached by crossing the field at the back of the barn.

This would be the safest way for the Prince to get into the barn. We can then plan together to work out a way for the Prince to evade the army and catch a boat in Bristol which is bound for the continent. However, it's too late to do anything today. Rest up here for the night, and then tomorrow, we will set about discussing the details."

After spending a comfortable night in the Colonel's house, and enjoying a good breakfast, it was decided that Alice should proceed to the village where Jane Lane lived, and brief her on the mission, while Alfred should return to John Ploughman's cottage and arrange for the Prince and Captain Careless to make their way to the Colonel's barn.

Alfred, with John Ploughman's Bible safely in his pocket, set out to return to the cottage in the lee of Bredon Hill where the Prince and Captain Careless were hiding up. As Alfred left the village, he saw the notice advertising the thousand pound reward for information leading to the capture of the Prince. It was signed, Colonel A. B. Carstairs.

When Alfred reached the cottage, later that evening, he found the Prince and the Captain looking very different from the dashing Cavaliers they must have been at the beginning of the Battle of Worcester. They had now adopted disguises. Their Cavalier locks had been cut off, their faces darkened and they were wearing peasant style clothes. These had been supplied by John Ploughman who was highly delighted to have the Prince's elegant clothes in exchange.

Alfred told them about the reward notice and this caused some concern. After a short discussion, the Prince and Captain Careless decided that it would be wise to separate, as bounty hunters would initially be looking out for two men travelling together. Captain Careless would make for London while the Prince's objective would be to reach Bristol.

The next day, Prince Charles, looking every bit a peasant and travelling on foot to remain inconspicuous, followed Alfred, riding some way ahead along the cross country route to Winstone that Alfred and Alice had used to reach the village, two days earlier. As before, they met few people along the way, and the

Prince commended Alfred for finding such a deserted route. Alfred did not acknowledge that this was more by luck than judgement because he firmly believed that this had been very much an answer to the prayers that he and Alice had made before they had first set out from John Ploughman's cottage to find Colonel Lane's house. Progress was slower than when Alfred and Alice had ridden the route because the Prince was cautiously following Alfred on foot. Alfred and the Prince slept rough one night under a hedge and arrived at the outskirts of Winstone, late the following afternoon.

The Prince made his way to Colonel Lane's barn across the fields as advised, thus avoiding the bustling village centre of Winstone, while Alfred rode to the house. In the privacy of Colonel Lane's drawing room, he announced to the Colonel, to Alice and to Jane Lane, who had been there since the previous evening, that the Prince had arrived safely. That evening found the Prince, Colonel Lane, his daughter-in-law, Jane, together with Alfred and Alice in the barn behind Colonel Lane's house, planning the next stage of the escape.

Alice's earnest desire to know more about the horses was resolved. The Prince told them that the horses they had been riding were in fact brothers called Amsterdam and Stockholm.

<u>Chapter 7</u>

Jane was a smart, attractive young woman with a slightly brusque and officious manner which many men might have found off-putting. She was very shrewd and certainly had a good grasp of the situation now facing them. One of the reasons that Prince Charles had identified Bristol as a port from which to organise his departure to the Continent .lay in the fact that during the civil War, Bristol had been a staunchly loyalist city. However, Jane warned him that Bristol was now heavily garrisoned with Roundhead troops and that you needed a pass to enter the city. She had such a pass which would allow her and a servant to go into Bristol. She also had a friend, Lord Wilmot, who had been able to obtain such a pass.

This Lord Wilmot was already known to Prince Charles who regarded him to be a splendid fellow. Jane considered that there could be advantages in having this Lord Wilmot ride with them. As an obvious aristocrat, he would attract some hostility from the soldiers, although they would have no reason to detain him. If the Prince, dressed in servant's attire, were to ride with them as Jane's manservant, covered by her pass, the attention of the soldiers would tend to be directed away from Charles and focus on Lord Wilmot.

"Will we need passes to get into Bristol?" asked Alice.

"No," Jane replied, "It will be assumed that you're either my children, or children in my care. Mothers will normally be expected to take their children with them when travelling around, even on business. Your presence will again help in diverting attention away from Prince Charles."

Jane then looked at Alfred and Alice's clothing. She had already recognised the advantages of their wearing Puritan clothes when travelling through Roundhead country, but these clothes had been worn for several days and were now very grubby, especially Alfred's. This was not surprising. Alfred had slept the previous night under a hedge.

"It will look suspicious if you are seen riding in the company of a gentle lady as her children, grubbily turned out. I'll need to get you some fresh clothes for tomorrow when we start our journey," said the sagacious Jane.

Jane now turned her attention to Prince Charles.

"The servant covered by my pass is called William Jackson." Jane told the Prince. "You'll need to assume his identity. If we also claim that you are suffering from some infectious disease and our purpose of visiting Bristol is to seek out a cure, people will tend to keep their distance. We'll need to travel at the normal rate people move around here, otherwise we'll look conspicuous by hurrying and hence, attract attention. That means moving at a leisurely pace. The journey will therefore take over two days, requiring that we organise overnight stays, once or even twice. Your pretended illness will then have another advantage. It will give us a pretext for having you stay in a room which is isolated from any visitors except ourselves who will need to visit you to bring you your food. This isolation will also reduce the chance of your being recognised by anyone who might know you, for

even your supposed friends could be tempted by
the reward on offer."

Lord Wilmot, Jane Lane, Alfred and Alice, and
Prince Charles, disguised as a servant, ride
towards Bristol.

The capable Jane seemed to have thought of everything. It was decided that they should all meet up, midmorning the next day to start this journey. Jane then left for her home.

Jane arrived the following morning, accompanied by Lord Wilmot. She'd brought Puritan clothes for Alfred and Alice, very similar to the ones they were now wearing but clean and well pressed. For the Prince, she'd brought a set of clothes bearing the prominent monogram, W.J, standing for William Jackson, the name under which the Prince would travel.

They changed into their new clothes, thanked Colonel Lane for his hospitality and set off at a leisurely pace, Lord Wilmot riding ahead, Jane Lane with Alfred and Alice a little way behind, and Prince Charles, alias William Jackson, a short way further behind them. Alfred and Alice rode Amsterdam and Stockholm, the Prince riding quite an unpretentious pony who responded to the name, Sallylass. It was Jane's suggestion that being mounted on the smallest horse in the party would contribute to the Prince's disguise as a servant. Most of the other travellers they passed on the rode gave a courteous salutation but continued on their way without showing any undue interest in the party. One garrulous couple stopped for a chat and complained that Bristol was not currently a decent place to stay in while it was full of Cromwell's soldiers. Jane warned them not to speak to her servant following just behind in view of his infection for which they were going to seek a cure.

The party made Wotton-under-Edge by late afternoon and Lord Wilmot set about finding an inn which had a private room where an infectious member of the party could be isolated during their stay. The first hostelry tried, a typical coaching inn called the White Hart, provided ideal accommodation. The Prince (William Jackson) went off to his private room, an attic on the very top floor of the inn, pretending to be afflicted with uncontrollable shivering. Separate but adjoining rooms were made available for the rest of the party. They all spent a very jolly time here. Lord Wilmot was quite a wit, and Alfred and Alice soon became accustomed to what passed for humour in the age where they were now sharing this adventure. They went down to the dining room for their meals, and Alice was given the responsibility of taking a tray of food up to William Jackson in the attic to avoid any of the inn staff being exposed to the risk of infection.

The following morning, Lord Wilmot paid the innkeeper and they set off again. All seemed to be going well with Jane's plan. The following afternoon, they reached Pucklechurch, just outside Bristol. There, they found another suitable inn, the Golden Lion, where they planned to stay until they could find a way of securing a safe passage to France for the Prince. They would need to carefully investigate not only the destinations but owners of ships docked at Bristol. It was now that problems started to occur.

As they had been told en route, Bristol and the villages around the city were swarming with Roundhead soldiers. Lord Wilmot was wary about the Prince coming out into the open in this city, but that was going to be necessary. The Prince would have to pass through the city on his way to the docks to board a ship. Notices, informing all and sundry of the magnificent reward available to anyone providing information which enabled the Prince to be apprehended were prominently on display around Pucklechurch.

As they had arrived at the inn, Alice had noticed a man dressed in attire which marked him out as a clergyman, sitting on a bench opposite the Golden Lion. He seemed to take unusual interest in the party but then moved off, once they had arranged their accommodation and taken the horses round the back for stabling. The following day, she saw this person, in the inn and talking to the staff. She alerted Alfred to the fact that there might be danger afoot and pointed the cleric out to Alfred.

The man left the hotel and Alfred and Alice thought that they may have been unnecessarily alarmed, but their mental alarm bells rang again when Jane found Alfred and Alice to tell them that the proprietor had just been speaking to her. It seemed that a priest who was also a doctor had noticed a sick man arrive at the Golden Lion the previous day, and told the proprietor that he would return soon with medicines.

As Jane Lane spoke, the priest entered the inn again, carrying his doctor's bag. He spoke to a porter who pointed to a flight of stairs which they knew would lead to the landing from which there was another flight of stairs, straight to the room where the Prince was feigning illness. The priest started to go up the stairs. Plans had to be made in case this was an emergency. Jane went to find Lord Wilmot to alert him to the need to be ready to settle with the innkeeper and leave the place at short notice if necessary. Alfred was to watch out for what the man did when he left the inn. Alice was to follow the man upstairs and try to listen in on their conversation.

Alice made her way up to the room where the Prince was resting up. She put her ear to the door. She could hear a conversation taking place, but she couldn't hear what was said. The conversation stopped and Alice stepped into the shadow cast by a wardrobe on that dark landing. The door opened and the priest came out. He

412

made his way downstairs, unaware that Alice was hiding a short way along the corridor. Alice went into the Prince's room which had purposely been kept dark with the curtains drawn. The Prince was under the sheets on the far side of the bed, trying to keep as far in the shade as possible. Alice enquired about the Prince's visitor.

"That was Father Doubleton," the Prince explained. "He used to be my chaplain, many years ago, and yes, he's also a doctor. He brought me some medicine, foul tasting stuff. Although I recognised him, I can't be sure whether he recognised me. I didn't disclose my identity to him, even though he used to be my chaplain. I rather think he knew who I was but he never said anything."

Alice told the Prince that plans were being made which would enable them to make a quick departure if necessary, and that Alfred was keeping an eye on where this priest went on leaving the inn.

Alfred waited in the lobby of the inn, waiting to see if this priest would soon come downstairs.

Alfred didn't have long to wait. He made after the man as he left the inn, keeping a safe distance so that it wasn't obvious that he was being trailed. The man (Father Doubleton) made his way to the edge of Pucklechurch where a dozen or so tents pitched in neat rows indicated that an army contingent was encamped here. Father Doubleton approached two soldiers, sitting on a bench, placed at the entrance of the first tent in the encampment. Alfred was near enough to hear the priest speak.

"Is your senior officer here?" he enquired. I have urgent news for him."

"Colonel Carstairs is in Bristol," he was told. "He should return within the hour."

"Then I'll wait for him," said the priest.

"Please yourself," said the soldier, and motioned the priest to sit on the bench they occupied. The bench was large enough to accommodate a dozen soldiers. Thus, the priest was able to sit down at the far end of the bench, so avoiding the soldiers feeling that they were being crowded, or that he was trying to listen in to their conversation.

It was obvious to Alfred that the Priest was going to betray the Prince in order to receive the reward. He hurried back to the hotel. Lord Wilmot, Jane Lane and Alice were waiting. Alfred reported where the man had gone and what he'd said to the soldiers. Lord Wilmot went to find the landlord. Alice ran up the stairs to tell the Prince to get ready to leave. Alfred went round to the stables to get the horses saddled. Ten minutes later, they had all gathered round in the stable, ready to move off.

"I have informed the innkeeper that Jane Lane's servant is much worse and that she's returning with him to her home in Edgeworth," explained Lord Wilmot. "I've also told him that I am going with you young people to find accommodation in the middle of Bristol."

They then all bid a fond farewell to Jane who rode alone, northwards, back along the road on which they had entered Pucklechurch the previous day. Lord Wilmot, the Prince, Alfred and Alice set off, not for the middle of Bristol as the innkeeper had been led to believe, but south towards Dorset and Hampshire. Lord Wilmot declared to the Prince that he stood a much better chance of getting a ship to France from the south coast than from Bristol.

Two days later, Colonel Carstairs reached Edgeworth with a small posse of soldiers. He sought out Jane and demanded to see her servant, William Jackson.

"Of course," said Jane, "he has been very ill but is now, almost fully recovered."

She presented the real William Jackson to the Colonel. Colonel Carstairs knew what Prince Charles looked like and he could see that this William Jackson was a completely different man: Colonel Carstairs returned to his camp at Pucklechurch, just outside Bristol, a very angry and bad tempered man. Every step of the way, back to his camp, Colonel Carstairs was breathing dire threats against Father Doubleton, should that apology for a priest and doctor ever cross his path again.

Chapter 8

On leaving Pucklechurch, the Prince, Lord Wilmot, Alfred and Alice spent several days travelling across the southern part of England, making for a channel port where they might find a ship which would take the Prince to France. Their journey took them through Somerset and on to Bridport on the Dorset coast. They had some hope of finding a boat at Bridport but they had no contacts who lived there whom they could trust to identify a reliable captain and then carry out the negotiations involved in planning the passage. With notices all over the town advertising the £1,000 reward for information leading to the apprehension of Charles Stewart, they dared not risk confiding in a stranger.

As the foursome considered carefully what options were viable, they began to despair whether a way for the Prince to leave England could ever be found. Alice suggested that they should spend some time in prayer. Prince Charles agreed that this was an excellent idea. After a prayer time lasting about half an hour, they continued to discuss possibilities. The Prince suddenly thought of a contact who might be able to help, but he lived some way away. This was a Captain Nicholas Tattersall of Brighton. Charles had sailed along the south coast with Nicholas as a young lad when the Royal family had spent some days as guests in Arundel Castle.

"Brighton must be over a hundred miles away from here," rued the Prince. "Can we possibly make it before someone discovers just who we are?"

Lord Wilmot was full of optimism.

"If you were going to get caught, they would have captured you within a couple of days of the battle at Worcester. Worcester is now fairly old news. People are no longer looking at everybody they meet, thinking, 'Could this be Charles Stewart?' It's nearly two weeks since you started your escape. The Roundheads can no longer concentrate their search. As far as they're concerned, you could be anywhere in the country, if not already safe overseas. We'll carry on and in less than a week we'll be in Brighton!"

They all felt encouraged by these confident words. So, they continued eastwards, crossing the New Forest and the Hampshire Downs, then through Houghton Forest, up to Amberley and by the High Downs path to Steyning. Alfred and Alice really enjoyed the company of Lord Wilmot and the Prince. Lord Wilmot was a very jovial man, always making jokes and so absolutely positive about the outcome of this venture. The Prince was always good humoured and easy going, even though he was now going through a very stressful time. Alfred and Alice really took to him.

They travelled on routes which kept them away from large centres of population. Alice and Alfred rode those really lovely horses, Amsterdam and Stockholm, while Prince Charles continued on Sallylass. It was considered that less attention would be directed towards the Prince if his garb and mount marked him out as no more than a lowly servant. Occasionally they would see small troops of Roundhead soldiers coming towards them.

"The worst thing we can do when Ironsides approach us, is to change course and move in the opposite direction," advised Lord Wilmot. "This will only attract their attention and suggest that we have something to hide. If we just ride past them when we meet, there will be nothing to arouse their suspicions and they'll take no notice of us. After all, the rank and file of Cromwell's army have no idea what Prince Charles looks like close up."

This indeed turned out to be the case. Occasionally, the more ill-bred amongst the soldiers would make derisory comments about Lord Wilmot. This was largely because he would insist on dressing himself in the style of a Cavalier. Lord Wilmot's clothes and flowing, long hair didn't meet with the approval of the Roundhead soldiery. On the other hand, they seemed to accept Prince Charles in servant's garb, and the young people, dressed as Puritans, as people who belonged to the same section of society as themselves.

Whenever the foursome found a deserted cottage or barn during the latter part of the day, they would make that their headquarters for the night. There were also several occasions when they stayed at wayside inns. At Lord Wilmot's suggestion, they used different names at each inn where they put up. On these occasions, Alfred and Alice enjoyed choosing names which were linked by double alliteration as were their real names. 'Joseph and Joan', 'Peter and Penelope', ' Martin and Martha' were pairs of names they used. They were perhaps being too clever, too inventive for their own good.

Meanwhile, Colonel Adonijah Carstairs in his headquarters at Bristol was still at work on the task of locating the Prince. Computerised information processing was not available of course, but he had amassed vast amounts of data on people travelling through the country. This had been collected by soldiers, interrogating inn keepers and making enquiries of local inhabitants about any strangers who had been seen in the location. Colonel Carstairs painstakingly sifted through all his data. Most of it led up blind alleys. The swarthy, six foot man with long curly black hair who was wearing a frock coat, believed to be characteristic of Charles Stewart's mode of attire, turned out to be a farmer paying a courtesy visit to his brother in Derbyshire. The two Cavaliers seen walking through the Forest of Dean turned out to be just that, two Cavaliers (with no royal connection) walking through the Forest of Dean. The tall furtive man, who had been seen running up an alley to avoid coming face to face with a party walking towards him from the other end of the street, turned out to be a man, heavily in debt, trying to avoid his creditors. Very few sightings of the Prince were reported about which the informants sounded absolutely positive. These sightings were checked out with special care but invariably turned out to be negative.

Father Doubleton's sighting at Pucklechurch was one such very positive report which had been followed up. It had ended with Carstairs and a posse of soldiers arriving at Jane Lane's house, only to discover that the person they had been directed to apprehend was just William Jackson and not the Prince.

One had to admire the tenacity with which the Colonel carried out his research. He never allowed himself to become discouraged. Every lead, no matter how apparently insignificant, was investigated and once checked, was recorded and systematically filed. As Adonijah Carstairs looked through his data again and again, he discerned a repeating pattern, almost concealed among the vastness of the mass of data accumulated.

There were several records of a Cavalier, his servant, a lad and a girl, staying at inns in the southern part of England. The lad and the girl were dressed as Puritans. Colonel Carstairs considered that young people dressed like this seemed strange companions for a Cavalier. Information given by the various innkeepers ascribed different names to these four people, and as a result, the information had been filed in separate places in Carstairs' system. The similarity between these groups of four people could so easily have remained overlooked among the overwhelming mass of data being sifted. Only one as assiduous as Colonel Carstairs would have ever spotted this pattern. He looked at the names again and noticed another pattern. The boy and the girl's name always shared the same pair of first letters. Colonel Carstairs realised that these groups of four people were not different people but the same people, changing their names, each time they put up somewhere. Why should they be doing this? He looked again at the names. The servant had once booked in as William Jackson. Wasn't this the name of a lady's servant who had been positively identified as Charles Stewart by a priest when staying right under his nose at Pucklechurch? But this William Jackson had been checked out and was not Charles Stewart.

Colonel Carstairs went to his filing system and looked up 'William Jackson'. He was the servant of a Miss Jane Lane and had been staying at the Golden Lion. On the same date, a Cavalier and a lad and girl, dressed as Puritans, had been staying there. The innkeeper had reported that the Cavalier and the young people were moving on to stay in Bristol, but there was no record of a threesome, matching this description at any inn in Bristol.

The Colonel looked again at the records of the four people who were staying at inns in the south of the country, and changing their names each time they moved to a new hostel. The dates showed very dearly that they were moving from west to east, from Bridport towards Brighton. The Colonel put down his papers and smiled to himself. This was Charley Brat, travelling in the company of a Cavalier and two youngsters. He hadn't left the country yet, nor would he. Adonijah Carstairs started to make arrangements to go down to the Brighton area with some of his best soldiers. Armed with the knowledge he now had, he would soon be able to find Charles Stewart.

Chapter 9

The inn at Steyning was particularly comfortable. They were right on the edge of Brighton. Perhaps they would be able to make contact with Captain Nicholas Tattersall as soon as the next day. The spirits of the four of them were now very high. They were confident that a successful outcome was just round the comer. Evening was drawing in and they started to get ready to tum in for the night. Alfred went downstairs to get a drink and was relaxing in the bar area when four Ironsides came in and ordered drinks for themselves. They'd just marched down from Bristol and had been stood down for the night. They were obviously very tired after the last three days hard marching and were now resting up before starting a new phase of duty on the following day.

Over the past couple of weeks, the Prince, Lord Wilmot and Alfred and Alice had encountered so many Roundhead soldiers who had paid no attention to the group that they no longer felt nervous when soldiers were nearby. Alfred sat and listened to the conversation of these soldiers. They were evidently veterans of the complete civil war and were sharing reminiscences of battles fought. They all seemed in agreement that the Battle of Worcester was the hardest battle that Cromwell had fought in the whole of the war. They were full of praise for the conspicuous bravery with which Charles Stewart had led his army. Scots soldiers captured in the battle had indicated that Lord Leslie had failed to bring the reserves into action when commanded to do so. The Ironsides acknowledged that the outcome of the battle could have been different had the reserves been deployed, but then pride in their own army took over the conversation.

Anyone listening in as Alfred was, would have been left with the impression that the calibre of the men, their discipline and the generalship of Cromwell and Ireton made the model army quite invincible.

Alfred already held Prince Charles in great esteem. This esteem grew as he listened to the account of the Battle of Worcester from the standpoint of the Prince's opponents.

The conversation then took on a new turn. Alfred's blood froze as he heard that the men's Colonel, Adonijah Carstairs, knew that Charles Stewart was in the Brighton area. The men also knew that he was disguised as a servant and travelling in the company of a Cavalier and two young Puritans. The next day, they were going to search out every inn between Bognor and Seaford. There was no chance that Charles Stewart could escape. They joked as they speculated on whether the first soldier to positively identify Charles Stewart would receive the thousand pound reward.

The soldiers then started to grumble that they were going to have to return to their tents for the night when they would have been much better off, billeted in one of these inns. They deserved to be treated better than they were, in view of the amount of marching they had done over the past three days.

Cromwell's soldiers in the inn at Steyning talk
about how they will capture Prince Charles,
unaware that the boy (Alfred) sitting not
far away and listening to their conversation
is helping Prince Charles to escape!

Alfred left the bar area, trying to look completely casual. He made his way up to the rooms where they had expected to spend the night. He reported what he had just heard. The sense of elation they had experienced earlier that day was now replaced by gloom and despair.

"We need to spend a bit of time in prayer," advised Alice.

Although they felt that they needed to make plans immediately, perhaps rush out of the inn where they felt trapped, they recognised that Alice had given good advice and they disciplined themselves to pray quietly for quarter of an hour. They then started to appraise their situation in a fairly calm manner.

"From what Alfred has told us," Lord Wilmot started, "they're not going to start searching for us until tomorrow. That gives us tonight to reorganise and plan. From tomorrow, we obviously won't be able to stay here, or in any other inn in the area. Also, as they know the make-up of our party, I would be a liability if I remained with you. It would be a good idea if I separate from you and serve the group by seeking out this Captain Tattersall whom you knew when you stayed at Arundel as a child. I must then organise a way of passing messages between the Captain and you, Prince Charles, which will not attract the attention of Cromwell's men. Alfred and Alice's Puritan clothes will have to be discarded. We can buy them something different. Shortage of money has not been a problem for us and there are plenty of clothes shops in the Brighton area."

"You're quite right, Wilmot," said the Prince. "We can stay here and get whatever sleep we can before first light. If we're seen leaving now in the middle of the night, suspicion will immediately be roused and in any case, floundering around in the dark in an area with which we are unfamiliar, could land us in even more difficulty. However, we dare not still be here at sunrise. Get some sleep everyone and we'll depart, just before dawn."

They went to the different rooms they had arranged to rent for the night and turned in but none of them could sleep properly. They were all apprehensive of what the morrow might bring. Sometime before six o'clock, the Prince came round and told them to get ready to leave. Lord Wilmot went down and settled with the landlord. Innkeepers are invariably up very early to get their establishments ready before their guests need breakfast. Lord Wilmot told the innkeeper that they were leaving early in the hope that they might make the outskirts of London before nightfall. He hoped that this false trail might put the soldiers off the scent when they came looking for the Prince the following day. They then collected their horses and rode towards the coast.

The sun had risen by the time they reached the sea but there were no people around at that early hour. They were on the edge of a village outside Brighton called Portslade. A dilapidated cottage stood nearby, well outside the village. The door was open and several windows were broken.

"We could use this as a temporary headquarters and hiding place," suggested Lord Wilmot. "It's not very safe with Cromwell's soldiers knowing that we're in this area and carrying out a search but it's the best we can do. With any luck, we'll be out of here before many hours are up. I suggest that you hide in there, Your Majesty, while I proceed to Brighton and seek out Captain Tattersall at the address you have given me. I'll take Alfred and

Alice with me to buy some different clothes. As soon as possible, one of these young people will return to you to let you know how things are proceeding."

"God speed," said the Prince. "Take my horse and set it to graze in some field. A riderless horse hanging round outside a ruined cottage would be sure to attract the attention of Roundhead search parties."

Without more ado, the Prince went into the cottage. Lord Wilmot set off with Alfred and Alice, leading Sallylass behind them. They let her loose in a field, half a mile further on, and proceeded to Brighton. People were up and around now. Lord Wilmot left Alfred looking after the horses while he went off with Alice to get different clothes. Normally, Alice would have really enjoyed trying on the different clothes of this period, available in the shop they found in a side street, but time was of the essence. The first dress she tried fitted her. This would have to do. At least, it was an improvement on the drab Puritan dress which they were now able to discard. Lord Wilmot paid the shopkeeper and they went back to the main street.

They met up with Alfred and rode further into town. They came to a cluster of shops. Lord Wilmot pointed out a shop where Alfred could buy himself some clothes and gave him some money. He said that he would make his way to Captain Tattersall's house with Alice and that he would send Alice back to this point with news of any plans being made. Lord Wilmot said that he'd not stay with them once Alice had left Captain Tattersall's house, in view of their knowledge of the intelligence now in the possession of Colonel Carstairs. Two young people in the company of a Cavalier would attract the attention of Carstairs' soldiers, even though they were no longer dressed as Puritans.

Alfred tethered his horse outside the shop and went in to choose some clothes for himself. He had a bit more time than Alice for this, but the general urgency of the current situation left Alfred feeling he would have to take the first set of clothes which fitted adequately. He soon found a green velvet jacket, matching breeches, white hose, black buckled shoes and an elegant hat. These were the sort of clothes he had expected to be available when they had first opened the clothes box in Worcester Cathedral Chapter House the day that Chronavon had visited them. That seemed like a very long time ago now. Alfred paid the shopkeeper and went outside to wait for Alice. He didn't have to wait long. Alice rode up before ten minutes had passed. He could tell from her face that she was impressed with his new clothes. Indeed, he was also impressed with the transformation the new clothes had effected in Alice.

'We're to go and fetch the Prince and bring him to an inn in the middle of Brighton called 'The Greyhound'. I've been told how to find that inn," said Alice. "Captain Tattersall will meet the Prince in an upper room there. At the moment, he's getting his crew together and sending them to make ready his ship, harboured at Shoreham."

They rode back along the front to Portslade. They collected Sallylass from the field where she had been grazing and continued to the dilapidated cottage. Alice waited outside with the horses while Alfred went inside to find the Prince. A few moments later, they emerged and rode back to Brighton where Alice guided them to the Greyhound Inn. There were several groups of soldiers around now, and Alfred and Alice were aware that much more attention was being paid to the three of them as they rode by than on previous occasions when they had passed soldiers.

Captain Tattersall was waiting at the door of the inn, and went inside with the Prince as soon as he had dismounted. Alfred and Alice remained outside with the horses, ready to make a quick getaway. After they had been waiting there for a few minutes, they were conscious that a man standing opposite the Greyhound Inn was paying them quite a bit of attention. Now that the news was out that the Prince was somewhere in Brighton, this man was probably aware that he had just seen Charles Stewart enter the Inn but Alfred and Alice couldn't be sure. They hit on a plan which might deceive the man into thinking that the Prince was still within the inn, even when he had departed. Alice dismounted and went into the inn. Meanwhile, Alfred rode off at a leisurely pace down the street, leading Stockholm and Sallylass.

Alice had been in the Inn for no more than two minutes when the Prince and Captain Tattersall came down the stairs from the upper room where they had been meeting. The Prince had changed into a completely new set of clothes and looked every bit a Prince. What a marvellous disguise in a town full of soldiers who didn't know what the Prince looked like and who were searching for someone disguised as a servant.

"I think the Inn is being watched from the front," Alice whispered to the Prince. "We can leave by the back door and walk down the street behind the houses and the shops. Alfred will be waiting for us at the other end of the street with the horses."

They went out of the back door as Alice had suggested. Captain Tattersall went to the stable where his horse was waiting and they made their way to the end of the street, out of sight of the man watching the Inn from the front. There, they met up with Alfred leading the horses. The Prince pointed out that a combination of two men and two young people would be a grouping that the soldiers might be looking out for in view of what Alfred had overheard the previous evening. It was decided that Captain Tattersall should ride ahead with Alfred and make their way to Shoreham where the Captain's boat was moored. The Prince would follow with Alice, about a hundred yards behind, Alice changing her mount to Sallylass and the Prince riding Stockholm. They would proceed at a slow, unhurried pace. The strategy worked. Several groups of soldiers were hanging around inns in Brighton. They paid scant attention to the pairs of riders going by. There was no reason why they should. Just a couple of horsemen among many others on horseback, riding up and down the streets of Brighton.

An hour later, they reached Shoreham. Captain Tattersall's ship was anchored just off shore, her sails ready to be unfurled. A longboat and crew of four were on the beach, ready and waiting to convey the Captain and the Prince to the ship. They rode down the beach to the longboat and dismounted. They looked back towards the shore. A lone horseman sat just in front of a church. He doffed his Cavalier hat which he waved to the beach party. The Prince waved back. He had been well served by Lord Wilmot. The Prince embraced Alice and Alfred.

"I may be departing as a defeated Prince, but one day I will return as King. Come to me then, and I'll see you richly rewarded. "

The Prince embraced them once again. They were aware that there were tears in his eyes. He climbed into the longboat where Captain Tattersall was waiting. Two of the crew pushed the boat into the deeper water, jumped into the boat and grabbed the unmanned oars. The longboat was rowed to the waiting ship and when all were aboard, the anchor weighed, the sails unfurled and the freshening wind set them bulging as the ship set sail for France.

Alfred and Alice watch Prince Charles board
the boat which will take him to Captain
Tattersall's ship moored off-shore.

When the ship was far out to sea, Alfred and Alice gathered the horses' reigns and led them up the beach, making for the point where they had seen Lord Wilmot wave. It was with a start that they looked up and saw waiting for them outside the church, not Lord Wilmot, but Chronavon.

"Well done again, young people," Chronavon said as he greeted them. "Let's now go into the church."

"What shall we do with the horses?" asked Alice.

"Leave them there," said Chronavon. "Lord Wilmot will be along shortly to see to them."

They entered the church. It was quiet and peaceful. Two candles had been lit and were burning on the altar. Chronavon went to the front pew and knelt. Alfred and Alice joined him. After kneeling for several minutes in silence, Chronavon gave thanks for all that Alfred and Alice had achieved over the past few weeks. He gave thanks that history would run its appointed course and that Prince Charles, already crowned King of Scotland, would one day be able to return to his realm as King of England too. They remained in silent prayer for a little longer and then, Chronavon directed their attention to an oak chest by the wall.

"In there," he told them as if they didn't already know, "you will find the clothes you wear in the twenty-first century."

Alfred and Alice changed in silence from the seventeenth century clothes they had only first worn earlier that day in Brighton and stowed them back in the chest.

"Thank you once again for the faithful way you've fulfilled this task," he said to them as he led them back to the church door.

They walked through the door, but instead of the sight of the waves breaking on the beach at Shoreham, they were in the vestry of Hillington Parish Church.

"It looks as if you have a few more baskets of harvest produce still to sort," said Chronavon as he went back through the door. It creaked as it closed behind him. Alfred and Alice didn't rush to open it again to say farewell, for they knew that on the other side of that door was the empty church of St. Giles. If Chronavon was there, he wouldn't now be visible to them.

Alfred and Alice continued sorting the harvest produce in silence. Were they sad this adventure had ended? Perhaps, but they had a sense of peace and satisfaction at knowing the job had been well done and they'd achieved something very important. This was an adventure they would remember and talk about together for years to come. Something of which Alfred and Alice would have been quite unaware, was an event taking place in Brighton as they were saying their goodbyes to the Prince on Shoreham beach. Colonel Adonijah Bartholomew Carstairs was leading a troop of twenty ironsides down a Brighton street towards an inn where he had good reason to believe he would find Charles Stewart. He had a look of smug satisfaction on his face. A man opposite the Greyhound Inn pointed to the door of the Inn as the Colonel and his men approached. The troop came to a halt outside the door of the Inn. Colonel Carstairs and two soldiers entered the Inn and mounted the stairs to the upper room. Carstairs kicked the door open. He didn't see what he expected. The room was empty. A few old clothes had been strewn across the table. On one of these garments, the letters, W. J. were clearly embroidered, but where was the one who had recently lived under the alias of William Jackson?

Chapter 10

Prince Charles arrived safely in France where he received an enthusiastic welcome, but with no substantial wealth, he was soon forgotten and spent nearly ten difficult years in exile. He travelled round the continent, taking up residence in various countries, finally settling in Breda.

Meanwhile, England was not passing through a happy phase of its history. Under its Lord Protector, Oliver Cromwell, England was known as 'The Commonwealth'. The Commonwealth was characterised by a dour intolerance of anything which might be described as fun. When Oliver Cromwell died and was succeeded by his son, Richard, things became even worse as Richard had neither the ability nor the will to govern the country and adequately fulfil the role of Lord Protector. The most influential figure in the land was General George Monck. He managed to persuade an ineffective parliament which was known with derision as the 'Rump' to dissolve itself and a new free parliament was elected. This was royalist in character. Working in conjunction with a statesman called Edward Hyde, Lord Chancellor of England, a document was drawn up in consultation with Charles, known as the Declaration of Breda. In this, Charles undertook to provide impartial and enlightened rule in England. Charles promised that he would pardon all those who opposed the royal family in the Civil War with the exception of those who were actually responsible for the execution of his father. These are often referred to as 'regicides'. Freedom of conscience in worship was also promised. A very important statement from Charles indicated that his return to become King would be entirely dependent on the good will of his countrymen and that no foreign power would be called upon to assist him to regain the throne.

After so many years of misrule, parliament was delighted to invite Charles back to England as King. The whole nation erupted into a state of celebration. Charles landed at Dover where he was met by General Monck and the Mayor who presented the King with a beautifully bound Bible. Charles declared that he would treasure the Bible above all things in the world. He then made a triumphal march to London via Canterbury and Rochester. He was warmly welcomed along the route by cheering and flag waving crowds, and entered London on his thirtieth birthday to experience the greatest rejoicing the capital had ever known.

Charles was true to his word and the austere years of the Commonwealth were replaced by a free and creative age. Charles' reign was characterised by tolerance and forgiveness. He didn't even pursue with any vigour those responsible for his father's execution. Freedom of worship enabled the Anglican Church to restore the beauty and indeed, gaiety of worship which characterised services before the repressive years of the Commonwealth. The arts, including music, poetry and drama which had not been encouraged by the Puritans, were now able to flourish. People participated in sporting activities with enthusiasm and the development of science was promoted with the foundation of the Royal Society. This numbered among its fellowship such great names as Sir Isaac Newton, Robert Boyle, Edmund Halley, Robert Hooke and Sir Christopher Wren, the latter being responsible for the rebuilding of St-,.Paul's Cathedral to replace the one which was destroyed earlier in Charles' reign by the Great Fire of London.

An enthusiastic eulogy by one of his subjects concluded,

'King Charles is the pattern of patience and piety, the most righteous and just of Kings, the most knowing and experienced of Princes, the holiest and the best of men, the severest punisher of vice and the strictest rewarder of virtue, the constant preserver in religion and the truest lover of his subjects. '

Charles was not without weaknesses, and one cannot turn a blind eye to his moral laxity. King Charles had numerous mistresses and illegitimate children. However, his accession to the throne marked a marvellous turning point in English history and King Charles deserves to be remembered by the nation with great affection.

At his death, Charles was buried in Westminster Abbey and thus shares the same final resting place as the other monarchs who featured in this trilogy, Edward I and Elizabeth I.

Worcester Cathedral still stands majestic above the Severn, looking from the outside much as it did at the time of the Commonwealth. It makes a wonderful back cloth to the first match a touring team of test cricketers play when they come to England. The interior has now been fully restored, but if one looks carefully, the scars inflicted by Cromwell's soldiers may still be seen in places.

Above the main door of one of the public buildings in Worcester is an effigy of Cromwell's head, nailed by his ears to the lintel. This bears testimony to the unpopularity of the Lord Protector, still being expressed by the citizens of this pleasant county town.

Family Tree of descendants of James I showing Charles II's near relations

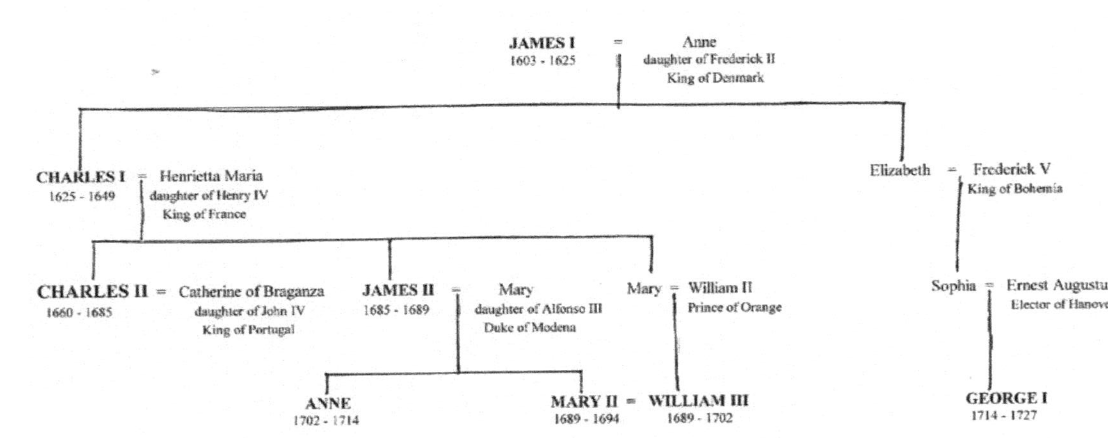

453

Bibliography

Barons and Kings
by Estelle Ross
publ. George G. Harrap
1912

King Henry III and the Lord
Edward
by F. M. Powicke
pub Oxford
(Clarendon Press)l 1947

The Virgin Queen
by Chrisdtopher Hibbert
publ Viking 1990

Tudor England
by Ada Russell
publ. George G. Harrap
1912

The Struggle with the Crown
by E. M. Wilmot-Buxton
publ. George G. Harrap

1912

The Life and Times of Charles II
by Chritopher Falkus
Weidenfeld & Nicholson

1972

St. Thomas Cantilupe,
Bishop of Hereford,
editor M. Jancey
Hereford, 1982

The Royal Line of Succession
by P. W. Montague Smith
Pitkin Pictorials Ltd. 1963

Old St. Paul's Cathedral
by G. H. Cook
Phoenix House 1955

Worcester Cathedral
by the Very Revd. R.P.L.
Milburn
Pitkin Pictorials Ltd. 1969

Herefore Cathedral
by the Very Revd.
H.R.Burrowes
Pitkin Pictorials Ltd. 1971